# "Plenty of outlanders have scars like that."

"Yeah, but this one is unique. Sec chief Robards thinks this Ryan may be the same outlander who chilled Baron DeMann's brother a few years ago in a gaudy house in Spearpoint."

Baron Schini suddenly appeared more interested in DeMann's outlanders. If their leader was the one who chilled the baron's brother, then he was also the one who chilled her son in the very same gaudy house firefight.

"And if this is the outlander who killed the baron's brother, what does that candy-ass Robards plan to do about it?"

"Why, chill the scum and his friends on behalf of Baron DeMann, of course."

The woman shook her head.

"You disapprove?"

"Not at all," the baron said. "It's just that if this one-eyed outlander is the same one who killed the baron's brother, then he's also the one who chilled my son, Luca. And if that's the case, I damn well intend to be there to watch the bastard die."

**Other titles in the Deathlands saga:**

Neutron Solstice
Crater Lake
Homeward Bound
Pony Soldiers
Dectra Chain
Ice and Fire
Red Equinox
Northstar Rising
Time Nomads
Latitude Zero
Seedling
Dark Carnival
Chill Factor
Moon Fate
Fury's Pilgrims
Shockscape
Deep Empire
Cold Asylum
Twilight Children
Rider, Reaper
Road Wars
Trader Redux
Genesis Echo
Shadowfall
Ground Zero
Emerald Fire
Bloodlines
Crossways
Keepers of the Sun
Circle Thrice
Eclipse at Noon
Stoneface
Bitter Fruit
Skydark
Demons of Eden
The Mars Arena
Watersleep
Nightmare Passage
Freedom Lost
Way of the Wolf
Dark Emblem
Crucible of Time
Starfall
Encounter:
Collector's Edition
Gemini Rising
Gaia's Demise
Dark Reckoning
Shadow World
Pandora's Redoubt
Rat King
Zero City
Savage Armada
Judas Strike
Shadow Fortress
Sunchild
Breakthrough
Salvation Road
Amazon Gate
Destiny's Truth
Skydark Spawn
Damnation Road Show
Devil Riders
Bloodfire
Hellbenders
Separation
Death Hunt
Shaking Earth

JAMES AXLER

# DEATH LANDS®

## Black Harvest

TORONTO • NEW YORK • LONDON
AMSTERDAM • PARIS • SYDNEY • HAMBURG
STOCKHOLM • ATHENS • TOKYO • MILAN
MADRID • WARSAW • BUDAPEST • AUCKLAND

For Evan Hollander, fellow warrior

First edition March 2005

ISBN 0-373-62579-0

BLACK HARVEST



**Printed in U.S.A.**

Is it sin
To rush into the secret house of death,
Ere death dare come to us?

—William Shakespeare,
*Antony and Cleopatra*

# THE DEATHLANDS SAGA

This world is their legacy, a world born in the violent nuclear spasm of 2001 that was the bitter outcome of a struggle for global dominance.

There is no real escape from this shockscape where life always hangs in the balance, vulnerable to newly demonic nature, barbarism, lawlessness.

But they are the warrior survivalists, and they endure—in the way of the lion, the hawk and the tiger, true to nature's heart despite its ruination.

**Ryan Cawdor:** The privileged son of an East Coast baron. Acquainted with betrayal from a tender age, he is a master of the hard realities.

**Krysty Wroth:** Harmony ville's own Titian-haired beauty, a woman with the strength of tempered steel. Her premonitions and Gaia powers have been fostered by her Mother Sonja.

**J. B. Dix, the Armorer:** Weapons master and Ryan's close ally, he, too, honed his skills traversing the Deathlands with the legendary Trader.

**Doctor Theophilus Tanner:** Torn from his family and a gentler life in 1896, Doc has been thrown into a future he couldn't have imagined.

**Dr. Mildred Wyeth:** Her father was killed by the Ku Klux Klan, but her fate is not much lighter. Restored from predark cryogenic suspension, she brings twentieth-century healing skills to a nightmare.

**Jak Lauren:** A true child of the wastelands, reared on adversity, loss and danger, the albino teenager is a fierce fighter and loyal friend.

**Dean Cawdor:** Ryan's young son by Sharona accepts the only world he knows, and yet he is the seedling bearing the promise of tomorrow.

In a world where all was lost, they are humanity's last hope....

# Chapter One

Ryan Cawdor let out a gasp and cracked open his eye.

"Everything all right, lover?" Krysty Wroth, Ryan's titian-haired lover looked concerned.

Memories of a jump nightmare swirled around his head.

Even though the jump had been tough on him, Ryan was in top physical condition, and his ability to recover from the mat-trans jumps was better than most in his small band of travelers. He'd experienced a bad jump dream, nothing more than that.

"Been better, but I'm okay," he said. "You?"

"I've been worse," Krysty answered.

Ryan believed that to be true. Her gorgeous mane of bright red hair, which usually lay flat against her head and shoulders after a jump, was full and thick, and cascaded over her shoulders like a waterfall.

She gestured to her right with a nod. "Doc didn't do so well, though."

Ryan looked at Dr. Theophilus Algernon Tanner, a tall and skinny man dressed in an old and worn frock coat. To the casual observer, he appeared to be in his sixties, but it could be argued that the man was actually hundreds of years old. Ryan knelt next to Doc and put a hand on the man's shoulder. "You with us, Doc?"

"'Is this a dagger I see before me—'" Doc muttered.

"Can you hear me, Doc?"

"'—the handle toward my hand?'"

J. B. Dix, the group's armorer and weapons expert, removed his spectacles and rubbed his head. "What's Doc talking about now?"

"It's Shakespeare," Dr. Mildred Wyeth replied. "*Macbeth.*"

"Sounds...interesting," Krysty commented.

"Sounds crazy," Jak Lauren said.

The teenaged albino usually fared the worst of all the members in the group after a jump, but this time he looked as if he came through unscathed.

It was Doc who'd had the hardest ride.

He'd be out of it for a while, his thoughts rambling and erratic, but he'd be all right in time.

Ryan shook one of the old man's shoulders. "Are you all right?"

"What?" Doc said, shaking his head as if the brain inside were shrouded in cobwebs.

When he saw the one-eyed man standing over him, Doc gave Ryan an angry scowl. "I say, my dear Ryan, if you'd like my attention I suggest you use the nomenclature provided for me upon my birth, meaning you can call me Theophilus, or Theo, if you like, or you can simply use the more vernacular terms Doc or Doc Tanner. There is no need to wrench my shoulder from my body!"

Ryan grinned. "I'll take that as a yes."

Doc massaged his aching shoulder.

"Where this place?" Jak asked, turning slowly to study the walls.

Ryan looked around the chamber as well, but didn't recognize the purple-blue tint of the armaglass walls. The colors were similar to several chambers they'd been in before, but none had had this exact pattern or shading.

"Only one way to find out for sure," Ryan said. "Triple red."

He put his left hand on the handle that would open the door to the chamber.

For a moment the inside of the chamber was filled with the sound of the friends' blasters being unholstered and cocked.

Then, silence.

Ryan turned the handle and pushed against the door. Slowly, the door swung open.

And then it stopped with a loud creak.

At the same time, the stench of death wafted into the chamber, causing several of the friends to cough.

"Is it blocked?" J.B. asked.

"Can't tell," Ryan answered.

He pushed against the door and felt resistance. He stopped a moment, reset his feet and tried it again. This time, with the help of J.B. and Jak, he was able to force open the door.

Mildred, Krysty and Doc's blasters swept across the open doorway, but found no one outside the chamber waiting for them.

Ryan and the others pushed the door all the way

open. It came to an abrupt stop with a grinding halt, metal against metal, and it was obvious to them why the door had been so hard to open. The steel had been bashed and scarred on the outside and several of the hinges were gone, either torn away from the door or just smashed beyond recognition.

"Blasterfire?" Jak asked, putting the tip of his index finger into a large pit in the outside of the door.

"Yeah, and mebbe some grens," J.B. added. "Recent, too."

"And all other manner of weaponry as well," Doc offered.

There'd been a firefight in the redoubt, that much was obvious. There were blaster marks on the walls, and entire sections of floor and walls that had been scarred by blasters and who knew what else.

"Thought redoubts nukeproof," Jak stated.

J.B. turned toward the albino teenager. "They are, but that's when the nukes go off on the outside. From the looks of this damage, there were bombs or grens going off in here."

"Then how come the chamber wasn't damaged?" Mildred asked.

Ryan tried to close the door to the chamber, but it wouldn't swing back. He left the door where it was, hanging open at a strange angle. "Inside wasn't damaged. Outside was blasted to hell."

"So it held together just long enough," Mildred continued, "to receive one last band of jumpers."

J.B. nodded again. "Looks like it."

They inspected the outside of the chamber more closely for several moments.

"Ryan, over here," Krysty called from a corner of the control room.

As Ryan made his way over to her, he became aware of the stench of rotting flesh.

"Bodies," Krysty said. "Lots of them."

There were at least a dozen bodies strewed across the floor near the wall. They'd been cut down by blaster-fire and had died where they'd fallen. There were skeletons at the bottom of the mess, but some of the corpses on top didn't look that far gone.

Krysty suddenly raised her hand.

The rest of the friends went silent.

"Someone's coming," Krysty announced, her hair tightly wound around her head and neck as an added indication of the danger.

Ryan signaled the rest of them to scatter and find cover, and then he waited in silence for the sound of footsteps. At last he could hear them, softly padding feet approaching their position at a modest rate, seemingly walking without purpose.

And then he saw her as she rounded the corner to the room surrounding the chamber. Or perhaps more correctly, saw *it*.

*It* was a young, pale-skinned girl. Her hair was a dusty black and her body was covered in fresh red scars and bleeding sores. She wore only a pair of shorts, and the tiny buds of her breasts told Ryan she was younger than twelve.

Ryan stepped forward, and the rest of the friends followed, stepping out of the shadows. "Hello," he said.

She didn't answer. Instead she just looked at him and smiled. "You got bang?" she said.

Ryan wasn't sure what the right answer was, so he said nothing.

"Want bang."

Ryan shook his head, then looked to the rest of the friends for an answer.

Mildred stepped forward. "Are you all right, girl? Is someone you know hurt?" Mildred looked confused. "What's bang?"

"Gimme bang," she said, turning to Mildred.

"I'm sorry, child, but I haven't got any... And from the sounds of it, I don't think I want any, either."

"Gimme bang!" she demanded, louder this time.

"What's wrong with you?"

The girl didn't answer. Instead she ran toward Mildred and leaped into the air, a knife glinting in her hand.

But as the girl soared through the air, there was a sharp crack of a blaster and half of her head vanished in a spray of blood-red mist.

Mildred wiped a bit of the child's blood and brain matter from her face. "Damn! Thanks, Jak."

"Yes, well done, Master Lauren. Quick, decisive and an expert shot," Doc said. "As always."

"What did she want?" Krysty asked.

"Bang, whatever that is," Mildred answered. "I don't think she was hurting." She knelt over the body and examined it. "Most of these scars have been healed over for weeks. The fresh ones look like she'd been picking at them."

"Mebbe was crazy," Jak said.

Mildred ignored the comment. "Well, whatever bang is, she wanted it pretty bad."

"Think it's a drug?" Ryan suggested.

"That would be a good guess." Mildred got up from beside the body. "Can't be sure, though."

"Well, whatever it is, it's a good bet that there are other people in the redoubt," J.B. stated.

Ryan nodded. "Triple red, people."

The chatter going on behind Ryan died down, and his companions followed him through the redoubt in silence.

As they moved up and down stairs, along corridors and through holes blasted in the walls, they could find nothing of value left inside the redoubt and no evidence of anyone else living inside it. Most items left behind had been destroyed, or had otherwise been rendered useless. Two sections of the redoubt that had been cleaned out were the medical lab and the kitchen. Everything inside those rooms had been carted away, with pipes and wires neatly cut from the walls rather than torn out in a hurry. Somebody was making use of the equipment, and likely using it for more than making meals and treating the sick.

They continued searching the redoubt for anything of value, and as they turned the corner at the end of a long corridor, Ryan saw a light in the distance.

It was a dimly reflected light, and had to be checked out.

"Jak," Ryan said.

The albino teen moved to the front of the line and came up by Ryan's side.

"See where that leads," Ryan commanded.

Without a word, Jak headed down the corridor toward the light. The others had their blasters trained on the end of the hallway, covering him just in case.

They watched the teen's body get smaller and smaller until all that could be seen was his stark white hair growing brighter the closer he got to the light source. And then, all of a sudden it was gone as he turned the corner into the light. Minutes later he reemerged, and when he neared, it was obvious that he had some good news.

"Outside," he said, gesturing down the hall.

"People?" Ryan asked.

Jak shook his head. "No."

"What's out there, then?"

"Sky. Rolling fields. River."

"Anything else?"

"What more want?"

Ryan and the others walked toward the light and exited the redoubt to a hot, sunny day, the sky tinged by a slight purple hue with streaks of green and orange throughout. The surrounding fields were barren, or else overgrown by weeds, but they seemed to roll with the irregular undulation of foothills, suggesting they might be somewhere in the Midwest.

Jak tapped Ryan on the shoulder and pointed to the south. "River, near trees."

Ryan took out his marine telescope from a pocket in his coat, extended it to its full length and brought the lens up to his eye.

After making several adjustments to focus, he said, "About an hour away on foot. We can make camp there, mebbe catch something to eat in the river."

"Sounds like a plan," J.B. said.

And then, without another word, the friends were off, heading south in single file to cover their tracks in the earth, Ryan leading the way, J.B. bringing up the rear.

They didn't know what to expect.

But together, they were ready for anything.

# Chapter Two

When they got to the river's edge, Mildred did a quick rudimentary test of the water to see if it might make them sick. "It's pretty clean," she said, holding up a test tube of the clear liquid.

Ryan nodded. "Let's make camp, then. Krysty, Doc and Mildred set up a perimeter. Jak, you and J.B. see if you can catch us something to eat."

In silence, the friends split up and took their positions.

Meanwhile, Ryan gathered a few dried branches and set them in a pile for a fire. He'd light it later, depending on how lucky J.B. and Jak were in the river. If not, they'd have to eat the last of their rations and hope to find something else to eat in the morning.

His stomach growled and churned at the thought of it.

"Help!"

It was a woman's voice coming from somewhere downriver.

"J.B.?" Ryan called.

"Heard it. 'Bout a hundred yards south."

"Let's move."

Almost as one, the friends picked up and headed south through the trees, always sticking close to the river's edge. Ryan could barely see the others through the brush, but he instinctively knew that Jak and J.B. were to his right, spaced about ten yards apart, while his left was flanked by Doc, Mildred and Krysty, with one of them, maybe two, hanging back slightly to cover their rear.

Another scream came from up ahead.

It was a woman's voice, but a different woman than before.

Jak, the best tracker in the group, stopped and signaled to J.B. and Ryan to do the same. Ryan sent the message along to the others and together the friends slowly closed in around a large clearing by the river.

Two women, naked. They were either swimming or just spending some time alone together by the water. One was young, tall and blond, her body lean, taut and muscular. The other was older and a bit shorter, with long dark hair that was streaked with gray. Her flesh sagged a bit, her belly distended slightly, but she was more mature and full figured than old and fat.

The two women were surrounded by four muties similar to the ones the friends had seen in the redoubt. They were dirty and scraggly, their bodies covered by the same sores the girl in the redoubt had.

"Bang," one of the men said.

Another one lunged forward at the women, then stepped back in fear. "Gimme bang."

"More crazies?" Krysty said under her breath.

"There are stranger things in the Deathlands," Ryan answered evenly.

"Want jack."

"Need smash."

"What are they saying?" Krysty asked.

Ryan shook his head. "I'm not sure, but it sounded like jack…"

"And smash."

"What happened to bang?" J.B. asked.

"We don't have any to give you," said the taller of the two women. "Check our clothes, and you'll see it's the truth."

Two of the muties riffled through a small pile of clothes on the riverbank, then threw them to the ground in disgust when it was obvious that it was just the women's clothes and no more. "Nothing."

"There has to be something there, check the pockets again."

"There's nothing, I tell you!"

"What about blasters!" the leader demanded.

The two men began to search the ground around the clothes, then check under a pile of neatly stacked rocks. In no time, each was lifting what looked like decent-quality remade blasters. "Whoo-eee! Look what I found!"

All four of the muties were laughing now.

"These we can trade for bang!"

"You can have them," the older woman said. "Just leave us alone."

The leader stepped forward. "We'll be taking them all right, but before we go, we'll be wanting something else from the two of you…" He leered as he approached the smaller woman. One of the others put a remade in his free hand and he pointed it at the younger woman as the other mutie neared.

She trembled in fear and wanted to run away, but there was no place for her to go. They were surrounded.

"Should we do something?" Krysty asked.

"Not our fight," Ryan answered.

"Yeah, but I don't like the odds."

After a moment's silence, Ryan said, "Me neither." He carefully leveled his SIG-Sauer at the leader, who was now gesturing to the others to help him.

"Hold her down so I can give her a—"

The man never finished his sentence. His last words died in his throat as a thundering round from Doc's huge LeMat blaster took out the man's neck and a large chunk of his shoulder.

The mutie holding one of the blasters turned and squeezed off a single round before he was cut down by blasterfire from Mildred Wyeth's Czech-built ZKR 551. The onetime Olympic target shooter caught the vile man with a perfectly aimed round that hit him between the eyes and slightly above the eyebrows.

With two of their fellows down, the survivors looked scared and confused. They turned to run, but were torn apart by blasterfire from the rest of the friends. Jak's powerful Colt Python struck one of them in the shoulder, sending him tumbling heels over head into the river. And the last mutie fell to a round from Ryan's SIG-Sauer that caught him in the back of the neck. Although it was impossible to know if it was a round from Ryan's blaster or Krysty's Smith & Wesson .38 that actually took the sorry man's life, one thing was for certain—he was chilled and on the last train west before he hit the ground.

In the moments after the volley of blasterfire, all that could be heard were the muted sobs of the two women, who had gone from nearly being raped and killed, to being rescued by a band of outlanders, all in a matter of seconds.

"Anybody hurt?" Ryan called out.

At first no one answered, and then, "Yes."

Ryan looked at each of the friends, searching for the wounded one.

"It's Jak," Mildred said. "Caught him in the shoulder."

Ryan ran to where Mildred was kneeling down beside the white-headed teenager. Even though Ryan could see Jak had suffered a wound in the shoulder that was leaking blood and causing him pain, he deferred to the doctor for a better assessment. "How bad?"

"Bad enough," Jak answered.

Ryan waited to hear from Mildred.

"Bullet went through the shoulder and tore up the flesh pretty good. Can't be sure if there's any damage to the bones unless I get a proper look. I can close the wound easy enough, but there's always a chance the flesh could turn."

Ryan nodded.

"Be fine," Jak said, grimacing in pain as Mildred began giving the wound a field dressing. "Not worry."

Ryan turned toward the two women and saw Doc stepping into the clearing. "It is okay," he said. "You two are going to be all right."

The older of the two women picked up her clothes and covered herself in modesty.

"Ah, excuse me, my good woman, I did not mean to offend," Doc said, turning away slightly. "By all means take a moment to cover yourself if you wish."

The older woman nodded, then hurriedly slipped into her clothes, a pair of loose-fitting pants and long-sleeved sweater with repair patches on the elbows and a picture of a mouse stitched into the fabric over the breast.

The younger woman got dressed more slowly, watching Ryan and the others warily as they slowly moved into the clearing. "Who are you people?" she asked.

"Just passersby," Ryan said, joining Doc and the two women. "Who are you?"

The older woman put a hand on her chest, then gestured to the younger one. "My name is Eleander, and this is my daughter Moira."

"Strange you'd be out here with just the clothes on your back and a couple of remade blasters."

"We were on our way—" Moira began, but she stopped abruptly when her mother put a firm hand on her shoulder.

"We were out for a swim," Eleander said, smiling. "It was such a beautiful day that we thought it would be nice to come out to the river and enjoy the good weather."

"Alone?" Ryan questioned.

"With marauders around?" Krysty asked.

"Foolish of us, I know, but life is hard in the ville and sometimes it's worth the risk just to get away and enjoy life…even if it's just for a little while."

Ryan suddenly became aware of some movement in the trees behind them.

The friends turned in time to see three sec men standing at the edge of the clearing. They had large-caliber longblasters and a few handblasters. All of their weapons were trained on the friends.

"Put down your blasters," the man in the middle of the three said, obviously the leader of the small group of sec men. He stood under six feet tall and was bald on top with a ring of long black hair circling the back of his head. He had a thick black mustache that framed his mouth and hung down a few inches from the bottom of his chin. He wore a khaki-colored T-shirt that exposed his thin but muscular arms.

"Sorry, friend," Ryan said, not even considering putting away his weapon. "There are seven of us, and we're all good with blasters."

"Oh, I don't doubt that," the short man said matter-of-factly.

"No matter how fast your men can get rounds off," Ryan continued, feeling he was still in a strong bargaining position, "we'll chill two of you before you get one of us. That's a promise."

There was silence for several moments as the wind swept through the trees. Behind them, a large mutie fish jumped somewhere in the river.

"Impressive, outlander, but if me and my men aren't back to the ville in thirty minutes, a team of twenty-four sec men will be out looking for us. They'll be shooting first and asking no questions."

"Won't stop us from chillin' you *now,*" Ryan said.

The man with the long black hair paused, as if reassessing the situation, and realizing Ryan and the friends weren't about to be intimidated. "Who are you?"

"They saved us," Eleander offered. "Moira and I came out for a swim when we were attacked by a gang. These people chilled them all."

Again the man was silent, as if considering what Eleander had said. Finally he looked at her and scowled. "You know you're not allowed out of the ville unescorted."

"We know, but it's such a nice day, and the water is so clean and blue that we didn't want to wait to get permission."

The short man looked at Moira suspiciously.

"It's true," she said. "I made my mother take me for a swim. We were planning on coming back before any one even knew we were gone. Sorry to trouble you."

After another long pause, the short man said, "Then we'll escort you back to the ville."

He turned to look at Ryan. "And you're welcome to join us. The baron will be pleased that you not only chilled four troublesome muties, but saved two of our ville's fairer citizens from a fate worse than death." He smiled in a way that wasn't exactly friendly. "I assure you the baron rewards such favors handsomely."

Ryan didn't move.

J.B. came up behind him. "Think it's a trick?"

"Can't say," Ryan said out of the corner of his mouth. "If there's a ville near here, it'd be better to be a friend of the baron than an enemy, seeing as we're so low on supplies."

"I believe Master Cawdor is right," Doc commented. "Refusing such a gracious invitation would likely anger the baron, or at the very least arouse his suspicions about us."

Ryan raised his head to address the short man. "We keep our blasters."

"Of course. The baron will want to reward you for your actions, not punish you."

Mildred stepped forward. "How about some help for Jak?"

Ryan nodded. "We've got one wounded."

"We have medicine that will help him," the sec leader said.

"What kind of medicine?" Mildred asked suspiciously.

"What kind?" Ryan asked.

"Something called penicillin."

Ryan arched a brow in disbelief.

"That's a good one," Mildred said. "But I have to wonder—"

"We accept," Ryan said.

"Excellent," the short man stated.

The weapons of the two sec men behind him were slowly lowered and put away.

Ryan and the friends put away their blasters as well and began walking toward the woods where the sec men had been standing. At first J.B. and Mildred tried to give Jak a hand, but the proud teen was determined to make it on his own.

"How far away is the ville?" Ryan asked Eleander.

"A few klicks."

"You walked all this way just for a swim?" Krysty asked.

"It's the nicest spot on the river," Moira offered.

"For an ambush by muties," J.B. interjected.

Krysty and J.B. were right, Ryan thought. It was an awful long way to go for a swim, especially with muties roaming around. Conditions in the ville had to be horrible.

As they walked, Ryan watched Doc move up beside Eleander.

"Excuse me, ma'am," he said, patting away some of the dust and straightening the lapels of his worn frock coat.

"My name's Eleander," she said.

"Yes, of course, Eleander," Doc stammered. "My name is Theo...Theophilus Algernon Tanner. But everyone calls me Doc, or Doc Tanner."

"Doc," she said inquisitively.

"I was just wondering, and excuse me if I am being far too bold to suggest this, but if we are to be guests of the baron tonight, then perhaps I might have the pleasure of talking with you at some length..."

"Talking? About what?" Eleander asked.

"Oh, about all manner of things, from the dawn of man to the setting of the sun."

"I'd like to, but I'm not sure I'll be allowed."

"But I assure you, I mean you no harm, and I have no ulterior motive than to spend a bit of time with a woman who—and I say this with only the best of intentions—is closer to my own age than my usual company."

"If the baron allows it, then yes."

"By the Three Kennedys!" Doc said, barely able to contain himself. He bowed slightly. "Thank you for giving me something to look forward to."

Eleander just shrugged.

The younger woman smiled at the older one, and shook her head.

Krysty came up beside Ryan. "Are you thinking what I'm thinking, lover?"

"That Doc is attracted to Eleander."

"Well, besides that."

Ryan thought for a moment. "That something's not right here?"

"You got it."

"Any ideas?" Ryan asked. Krysty could be prescient at times and often got a bad feeling just before things were about to go wrong.

"So far nothing solid, but I'll let you know."

They neared the group of waiting sec men and as they did, Ryan was better able to gauge the size of the sec leader. He was about a foot shorter than Ryan, but was probably close to Ryan in actual body weight. He was armed with a 9 mm Heckler & Koch MP-5 machine blaster. It was a small, elegant weapon that was an excellent blaster for close-in fighting, but was far less effective out in the open. He probably used it a lot inside the ville rather than in the surrounding country. However, it wasn't the man's choice of blaster that impressed

Ryan, but its condition. It was pristine, as if it had just been taken out of the box. It was possible that the blaster had once been part of the cache stored in the redoubt they'd just exited, but even so, it would have shown some signs of wear by now.

"You noticed it, too?" J.B. asked, his voice barely a whisper.

"Nice condition," Ryan nodded.

"Ammo looks good, too. Not new but good quality reload stuff."

"Mebbe the baron's a big-time trader," J.B. suggested.

"Trading what?" Ryan wondered.

J.B. shrugged now that the sec leader was within earshot.

"Welcome," the short man said. "My name is Robards. I'm sec chief for Baron DeMann."

"Name's Ryan." He pointed his way around the group of friends. "This is Jak, J.B., Doc, Mildred and Krysty."

"Pleased to meet you all, and I know I speak for the baron when I say he will be delighted to meet you as well."

Eleander and Moira walked past Sec chief Robards, their heads down as if in shame. The other two sec men fell in line behind the two women, as though they were going to keep an eye on them all the way back to the ville.

"My dear Mr. Robards, as you might have noticed, I am getting on in years and I am not ashamed to say that I am not quite up to a long walk under this stifling sun." Doc wiped a bony hand across his forehead to emphasize the point. "And of course, young Jak's not doing so well, either. I am curious to know how far it is to this ville of yours because if it is any great distance, I would rather take a rest now and make the journey all in one go."

"Not to worry old-timer," Robards said with a smile. "You'll all be riding to the ville."

Robards led them through the trees, and as the forest first thinned and then came to an end, they came upon a large dirty yellow wag. There was no glass in any of the window frames and the sides had been reinforced with steel plate, but there were plenty of seats inside for all of them.

"It's an old school bus," Mildred said in disbelief.

"That looks as if it might do the job quite nicely," Doc said, nodding in appreciation.

"Wags, too," Ryan muttered when he was out of earshot of the sec chief.

"Whatever he's trading," J.B. commented, "he must trade a lot of it, or be a really good trader."

"Good, ruthless or dishonest," Ryan said.

# Chapter Three

The ride in the wag was bumpy, but the vehicle made good time on the washed-out dirt roads and open fields that led back to the ville.

Ryan had hoped to have the chance to talk with Moira or Eleander along the way, but the two women had been placed in the seats directly behind the driver and across the aisle from Sec chief Robards. No one was more disappointed with the seating arrangement than Doc, who had tried to take the seat next to Eleander, only to be politely told to move toward the back of the wag by one of the sec men.

"Don't tell me you've taken a shine to the woman," Mildred said, as Doc made his way back to where the friends were sitting.

For a moment Doc looked stuck for words. Finally, he said, "I find the lady attractive, yes. Any woman who ventured this far from her ville just to enjoy the pleasure of a naked swim in a cool river is...intriguing to say the least."

"Sure is curious," Mildred acknowledged. "Maybe even a bit strange."

"Lots strange about ville," Jak said through slightly clenched teeth.

J.B. was just about to comment when the wag crested a rise and the ville suddenly appeared before them.

It was a fair-sized ville in two distinct parts. On the edges were all manner of run-down and ramshackle dwellings, and several areas made up of tents. Ryan recognized a few of the structures as gaudy houses and canteens, and guessed that the rest were flophouses and shelters for the ville's bottom-feeders. Past the outlying ghetto was a section of the ville that was fenced in by a wall of burned-out wags, piles of broken cinder blocks and bricks, and rusty and twisted steel girders. If there had once been a city on this spot, its remains had been pushed, pulled and dragged into a mile-long circle of eight-foot-high rubble. The front gate of the ville was a ten- or twelve-foot gap in the wall, which was closed off by a pair of thick wooden doors that swung freely on two massive hinged wooden posts. Most likely they served as telephone poles in pre-Dark days.

A lookout in a crow's nest set atop the pole on the right acknowledged the driver of the wag as it approached, and the doors swung open slowly to let the vehicle inside the ville.

As the gap between the doors inched wider, Ryan studied the buildings inside the wall. Like the structures on the outside, most of the buildings inside looked slapped together, with a few looking as if they'd been made from the cargo containers. Windows had been cut into the sides of the big square boxes to make living quarters, while others had been fitted with pipes and exhausts that suggested to Ryan that the ville's baron was more of a manufacturer than a trader. In the distance, toward the back of the ville, Ryan could make out large glass houses similar to the kind once used on pre-Dark farms. So, in addition to making items for trade, the ville grew its own food. That would explain the well-maintained wag and a well-armed and organized sec force.

There were obviously things worth protecting inside the walls.

The wag pulled up in front of a stack of square steel boxes, each set on top of another like bricks. The door to the wag opened and one of the sec men got out, followed by Eleander and Moira. Doc and the others got up to exit the wag along with the women, but Robards put up a hand to stop them. "They get off here," he said. "You're going somewhere else."

The friends sat down.

Robards stepped off the wag and spoke with one of his sec men. When he was done, the sec man double-timed it down the road. Then the sec boss got back on the wag and it lurched forward as it slowly got back underway.

Jak let out a slight groan of pain as the wag was jostled by a bump in the road, then quickly said, "Not hurt."

"Yeah, I bet," Mildred responded.

The wag pulled up in front of another series of stacked steel boxes and Robards turned and pointed to Jak. "This is where he gets off. There are people inside who can help him. They know he's coming."

Jak got up from his seat.

Mildred stood up as well.

"Are you injured, too?" Robards asked Mildred.

"No, but I'm going with him," Mildred said.

Robards seemed to consider it a moment.

"She has some experience as a healer," Ryan said at last. "Especially with blaster wounds."

Robards nodded, a bit reluctantly, and stepped off the wag. He led Jak and Mildred inside one of the stacked steel boxes and the rest of the friends waited several minutes for him to return.

"Think Jak will be all right?" J.B. asked.

"Be back good as new with Mildred looking after him," Ryan answered.

"Knowing Master Lauren as I do, it wouldn't surprise me at all if he had several women fussing over him by nightfall, each one offering him their virtue more passionately than the one before."

Ryan smiled at that.

The door to the steel box opened and Robards returned to the wag. "He's in good hands now."

Again the wag lurched as it began to move.

On the left side of the roadway, Ryan noticed a strange sort of paddock area. It was basically an empty space with old oil cans, concrete barricades and several fences serving no apparent purpose scattered across the grounds. It looked like an obstacle course, and Ryan thought it might be used to train the baron's sec force.

On one side of the paddock was a high and wide concrete wall that had been pockmarked by blasterfire. Ryan had seen such walls before and knew that they were used mostly for executions. That would explain the darkest stains on the wall, but there were other stains—

bright yellows and oranges, and even a few of them green—on the wall and all over the enclosure that defied explanation.

"What do you make of that?" Ryan asked J.B.

"Firing squad?"

"Mebbe, but who bleeds green?"

The wag began to slow as it approached a brick-and-stucco building that towered three stories over the rest of the surrounding structures. There were plenty of blown-out windows, and large cracks in the walls that ran from the top all the way down to its foundation. The building had obviously survived the shock wave from a big blast miles away that had wiped out the rest of the ville. But while the building was still standing, it looked as if one more good bang would bring the whole thing crashing down. At least that's the way it looked from the outside. But despite the damage, the building was by far in the best condition of any inside the ville, and it was obviously the place where the baron lived. However, judging by the size of it, there had to be plenty of others who lived inside as well.

"Last stop," Robards announced.

"The baron lives here," Ryan said.

"Yes, and so will you for the next few days."

The muscles along Ryan's back tensed at the words. "You make it sound like we're prisoners."

"Not at all," Robards said. "That's merely the usual duration of the baron's hospitality. He grows tired of guests who don't capture his interest, but I have a feeling your group will be allowed to stay for as long as you like."

"When will we meet the baron?" Doc asked.

"He's tied up with a business matter at the moment, but he's assured me that he will be attending a small reception being held in your honor prior to this evening's dinner."

"A reception?" Doc quipped. "And I left my formal dinner jacket at home."

Krysty let out a slight laugh.

"Don't worry, Doc," J.B. said. "The food will taste the same."

"This way," Robards said, leading them into the building.

THE INTERIOR of the steel box was hot and smelled of rust and urine, feces and blood. The sunlight shining in through the open door forced the man chained to one of the walls to squint to protect his eyes.

Baron DeMann, dressed in an immaculately clean lab coat, entered the steel box and pinched the end of his nose to fight off the stench. "I thought you said this stinkhole was hosed down."

"Done last night," the sec man on the baron's left said.

"I want it clean just *before* I enter, understand?"

None of the sec men answered him.

Then one of the men said, "Mebbe he emptied his bowels this morning when we told him you'd be visiting."

The rest of the sec men laughed, but the baron wasn't impressed.

The laughter quickly died.

Baron DeMann stopped several feet from where the

prisoner was chained up by his arms. They'd hoisted him up onto the wall just high enough so that his feet were off the floor, and his arms had to carry all his body weight. After a few days in that position, his arms had stretched enough for him to get his toes onto the floor, relieving some of the load on his arms, but not the pain.

The baron looked at the man's feet touching the floor of the box. "Crank him up another six inches," he ordered.

Two sec men turned a winch handle that reeled in several links of chain, lifting the prisoner higher up on the wall.

The man screamed in pain, but even in the echo-filled steel box, the cry sounded weak and feeble.

Beaten.

"Now, you little rad-blasted bag of scum," the baron began, "have you had the chance to think about what you did?"

"Been thinking a lot..." the prisoner gasped.

"Yeah, about what?"

The prisoner's head shifted to the right, and he opened his eyes against the invading sunlight. His dry, cracked lips parted, and his tongue appeared over his bottom lip like that of a lizard. He tried to spit at the baron, but his mouth and throat were too dry to produce any moisture.

The baron just shook his head. "You've got a bad attitude, Des."

"Fuck you!"

The baron sighed. "And that disappoints me," he continued, as if the prisoner wasn't even there, "because I like you. Anyone who thinks they can get away with skimming jack off the top of my operation has either got the biggest pair of prunes in the entire ville, or he's the stupidest rad-blasted fuck alive."

The prisoner, Des, turned his head to the side, as if he'd heard the baron's spiel before.

"I know you're not stupid, because if you were, that would make me stupid for putting you into a position to rip me off. That means you've got to have Grade A plums in that scrotal sack of yours, and I like that."

Des said nothing.

"I like that, but it's not exactly a good thing for you to have. See, if by now you had told me you were sorry, I would have had to think about forgiving you. And if I'd forgiven you, then mebbe you'd already be dead, instead of hanging around inside this steel box waiting for me to let you die. But since you still haven't come around to being sorry for what you've done, I've gotta make an example of you so no other sec men get any bright ideas about trying to cut themselves a piece of my pie."

Des tried to spit again, but all that came out of his mouth was dry air that hissed as it passed through his lips.

"I guess that means you haven't changed your mind."

"Fuck you, you ass..." The man's words trailed off without being completed.

"You really want to live, huh? Hang in there as long as you can?" Baron DeMann laughed at that.

The sec men surrounding him laughed as well.

"Well, I'm gonna make sure you hang in a long, long

time, asswipe." He turned to the sec man on his right. "Bring it here."

The sec man moved forward, carrying a clear plastic bag filled with a clear liquid. There was a pale white rubber hose coming out of one end of the bag and a needle connected to the end of the hose. "This will keep you hydrated, Des. It'll be like you're drinking, but you'll never have the pleasure of feeling the water sliding down your throat."

The baron moved forward, climbed up onto a step provided for him by a sec man, then jabbed the needle into a vein in the prisoner's arm.

"No." The word escaped the man like a sigh. There was fear in his voice. Real terror.

"Oh, yeah. I'm going to keep you alive as long as I can, just to hear you scream." The baron moved in close to Des so there were just inches between their faces. "And when I get tired of that music, I'm going to add some junk to the bag, stuff I'm experimenting with that will eat away at your brain until there's nothing left but goo." He paused, savoring the moment. "Finally, when it's more work than it's worth to keep you around, I'm going to put a few crazed muties in this box with you and watch."

"No!" Des screamed loudly.

"Ah, that got your attention, eh?" the baron said, climbing off the step. "Good. Think about those muties crawling all over your body, looking for junk."

"No, no. I'm sorry...sorr-ee," Des screamed, his voice echoing eerily off the walls of the box.

But the baron wasn't listening anymore. He had turned his back on the prisoner and was on his way out of the box, followed by a half-dozen sec men.

When they were all outside, the sec men closed the steel doors in silence, all of them listening to the screams of a man who had just started down a very long and painful road toward his own death.

It gave them all something to think about, especially since Des used to be a sec man, just like them.

AT THE OTHER END of the ville, a door opened on a large steel box. From somewhere inside the box came a gnawing, high-pitched mechanical whine that rose in pitch, and then suddenly settled down into a staccato hum.

People outside the box turned to look in the direction of the sound.

And then all at once the sound lost its reverberation as a man atop a motorized, two-wheeled wag suddenly burst from the opening. The wag's engine whined as the vehicle sent a plume of dirt and dust into the air behind it.

The gate to the ville opened slowly, and for a moment it appeared as if the man on the wag would crash into it, but by the time he reached the gate there was just enough space for him to slip through the opening.

The wag's small engine rose in pitch again, screaming like an instrument of terror now as it raced toward the western horizon.

In seconds, the driver and wag were little more than a trail of dust in the distance.

The cry of the engine began to fade.

In minutes they were gone from view.

# Chapter Four

Jak and Mildred were led down a long dark corridor that smelled—if Mildred remembered correctly—of disinfectant. That, of course, was impossible, since the manufacture of such things as disinfectant and household cleaners died with the nukecaust.

Still, she sniffed at the air and caught the unmistakable scent of pine.

"Smell good," Jak said. "Clean."

"I guess we won't have to worry about conditions being sterile," Mildred commented.

When they reached the end of the corridor, the sec man guiding them opened a door that led into a white room that was well lit by windows and portals cut into one of the walls.

"A healer has been sent for," the sec man stated. "He should be here in a few ticks."

Mildred nodded her thanks. She helped Jak up onto a wooden bed covered with linen and, when he was comfortable, she took a look around.

The room was small, but at first glance it appeared to be well stocked. Mildred made a closer inspection of the room and saw a variety of bottles and vials that were labeled with names of medicines and drugs she hadn't seen, or even thought about in a long, long time.

There were bottles of cyanide, which she knew could be made from the seeds and pits of apricots, peaches, apples and wild cherries. Next to the cyanide were several vials of a whitish powder that Mildred guessed was arsenic trioxide. She turned one of the vials and read the label, proving herself right. Seeing the two poisons on the shelf gave Mildred a bad feeling, but further study revealed that this was a shelf storing nothing but poisons. There was another shelf in the room that appeared to be stocked with a variety of dried herbs that were often used for medicinal purposes.

She suddenly felt better about the setup.

The first one she picked up was dried echinacea, which was good taken internally against infections and externally for skin abrasions. Next to that were dried elder flowers, which were also good for skin ailments. Farther along were dried ginkgo leaves, good for a half dozen or so diseases, especially those to do with the mind. She continued down the shelf past Ginseng and Hops, Kava and Lemon Balm, St. John's Wort and Valerian. These were all wonderful herbs and useful for the treatment of mild ailments, but none of them were strong enough to fight off an infection from a bullet wound.

Mildred looked for something stronger, and found it locked inside a cabinet in one corner. The doors to the cabinet were wooden framed panels of chicken wire. Just behind the wire she saw jars of dried hemp leaves, more commonly known during pre-Dark times as marijuana or cannabis, which could be used as a sedative or a postoperative painkiller. Next to the hemp were containers full of poppy seeds, which were an essential ingredient in the production of opium, as well as painkillers such as morphine and codeine.

These were more of the types of medicine Jak would be needing.

Behind the poppy seeds, Mildred saw several bowls filled with large green and yellow fungi, some of them excreting a yellowish fluid from the ridges and folds of their surface. If Mildred remembered her botany and biology correctly, penicillin was basically an antibiotic compound taken from molds of the genus *Penicillium.* If she was right, and she was sure she was, then she was probably looking at the medicine's raw material.

"Seeds and leaves," Jak said, lying back on the bed, exhausted.

"They may just be seeds and leaves to you, Jak, but to someone who knows what they're doing, they can be made into powerful drugs."

"Jolt and dreem?"

Mildred shook her head. "There's no sign of that, but if the baron knows how to make good drugs like penicillin, then he can probably make the bad ones, too."

"Not want drugs," Jak said.

Mildred came over to his side and opened up the pressure bandage she'd put over his wound. "I think that's wise, Jak, but you might not have a choice in the matter."

"Make sure safe."

"Don't worry, my young friend," Mildred said, patting Jak on his good shoulder. "I'll look after you."

Just then, the door to the room opened and a tiny older man dressed in a clean lab coat came into the room, moving to Jak's side quickly. He had a thick mustache and thinning black hair combed over his hairless pate. "What's the problem?" he asked, almost sounding irritated.

"He has a flesh wound that needs some attention," Mildred answered for Jak.

"Playing with knives, eh?"

Jak looked at the man for a moment and wondered if he knew something about Jak's talent with throwing knives. "Mutie shot me," Jak said.

"Is that so?" The man unlocked the doors to the cabinet, then opened up the chicken-wire doors. After a moment's consideration, he took out several containers and began mixing items on a shiny steel square that sat on top of the counter. "Being stupe outside the wall, were you?"

Mildred noticed Jak reaching for one of his leaf-bladed throwing knives and put her hand out to stop the teen from doing anything foolish.

"Not that it's any of your business," she said, "but we're outlanders who came across a group of muties who were about to rape and chill two of this ville's women."

"Which women?"

"Eleander and Moira."

The man stopped mixing herbs and turned to face

Mildred. For a moment, he just looked at her and Jak in turn, then he said, "My name's Katz. I run the ville's pharmacy, so if there's anything you need, I'll see that you get it."

Mildred was startled by the sudden change in the man's attitude, but was glad he'd come around because now Jak would be less inclined to chill him where he stood.

"What are you preparing for him?" Mildred asked, doing her best to sound curious, but not reveal any of her medical knowledge.

"An antibiotic for the wound," Katz said, "and a painkiller to get him through the night."

Mildred was confused. "Aren't you going to fix the hole in his shoulder?"

"I'm what you'd call a chemist," Katz shrugged. "If he takes these medications long enough, he'll probably recover from his injury."

"No offense, Katz, but I'd like to be a little more sure than just *probably*. Do you mind if I work on him a bit first before you give him the drugs?"

"If you think you know what you're doing, then great. Easier for me."

"I'll need a few things."

"Like I said before, anything you need, I'll see that you get it…as long as we have it here in the ville, of course."

Mildred nodded. "I'll need a good strong needle."

"We've got plenty of those."

"Some thread or fine string, some boiled water and maybe a few sterile cloths."

Katz shook his head. "Not a problem."

"And then when I'm done, you can give him the antibiotics."

"What about a painkiller?" Katz asked.

Jak looked at Mildred.

Judging by the look in the teenager's eyes, he could use some.

"Maybe a small dose of morphine for now, just to see how he reacts to it."

Katz nodded. "Sure, whatever you say."

"WE HAVE FOUR ROOMS for guests," Robards said, opening the door to one of them. "I'm sorry we don't have more, or larger, or better rooms for you, but the baron isn't in the habit of hosting so many people at one time."

"This is fine," Ryan said, wondering what Robards was talking about. The rooms were better than anything they'd seen in months.

"First-class accommodations!" Doc exclaimed. "Five star!"

Robards smiled, and nodded. "Very well, then. The baron will be meeting with you in an hour. Spend the time as you wish."

The sec chief turned and walked back down the hallway in the direction they'd just come, leaving Ryan, Krysty, Doc and J.B. to examine their new surroundings.

The walls along the hallways outside their rooms also had stress fractures and cracks in them. It was possible that the only parts of the building that were cracked were the inside walls and outside bricks, and that the interior steel superstructure was undamaged, but that was unlikely. While the building would remain standing for as long as they'd be staying there, a single large blast in the right place and the whole thing might come down like a house of cards.

"Think it's safe?" Ryan asked J.B.

"Been standing for a hundred years, so it should be safe enough for the next few days." J.B. lifted the brim of his fedora and ran a hand over one of the cracks in the wall. "I wouldn't want to be a permanent resident, though."

Ryan nodded. "We'll leave as soon as we're resupplied." Then he continued inspecting their living quarters.

Their rooms were small and dark with sturdy wooden beds topped with mattresses made of dried corn husks and covered with old, but clean, blankets.

"Hey! There's a bed in here," Krysty said. "I don't know how long it's been since I've slept on a bed."

Meanwhile, Ryan and J.B. were busy examining the rooms for booby traps and locks. There was no evidence of either, which meant they couldn't lock their doors, but they wouldn't be locked into the rooms by their hosts, either.

"Impressions?" J.B. asked.

"Looks good so far," Ryan stated.

"Too good, you think?"

"It crossed my mind."

"Gentlemen, I, too, am astounded by our good fortune, but how many times have we rescued damsels in distress only to have that noble act of extrication be punished by imprisonment, threats of death and bodily harm or simple misfortune? Is it so inconceivable that for once in this forsaken hell of a land there might be someone who is actually grateful for our good deeds and wants to thank us with a reward that is actually in line with the magnitude of our deed."

J.B. looked strangely at Ryan.

Ryan glanced over at Doc and smiled. "I think he might have a point."

"Mebbe, but I'm still being cautious. In Doc's time there might have been people who were friendly like this, but I haven't seen many in the Deathlands. My guess is that the baron wants something from us, and it's not the pleasure of our company."

"So we'll be on alert and no one goes anywhere alone, or without a blaster."

J.B. nodded.

"Sage advice, my dear Ryan," Doc said. "In the meantime, I am going to take full advantage of the amenities. I want to be well rested for the reception."

"You expecting Eleander to be there, Doc?" Krysty asked.

"You read my mind, Krysty. What an absolutely charming gift you have."

Ryan stepped into the room he and Krysty would be sharing.

In the second room, Doc lay down on the large bed in the middle of the room, the only bed in the room.

J.B. cleared his throat.

"If there's something caught in your throat, John

Barrymore," Doc said, "I believe there is water in that jug on the table over there."

"Mildred will be back soon."

Doc looked at J.B. a moment, then glanced down at the bed he was lying on. "Oh, right," he said. "I shall take one of the other rooms."

J.B. nodded his thanks.

Doc stepped into the third room that had a single large bed—just a tad smaller than J.B. and Mildred's—and closed the door behind him. Then he lay down on the bed and fell asleep with thoughts of the lovely woman Eleander swirling through his head.

SEC CHIEF ROBARDS caught up with Baron DeMann when the baron returned from his visit with the prisoner.

"How is my old friend Desmond?" Robards asked.

"He's in terrible shape," the baron responded with a smile. "I think I'll let him live a little longer...till he begs me to let him die."

"It'll be a lesson for the rest of the men," the sec chief commented. Then added, after a pause, "We have visitors."

"Yes, I saw the wag come in. Who are they?"

"Outlanders. They happened upon Eleander and Moira down at the river."

"The river! What were they doing down there?"

Robards hesitated, knowing that telling the truth would likely warrant punishment from the baron, but also knowing that the truth couldn't be avoided. "Moira says she asked Eleander to take her swimming. They had planned to be back before anyone realized they were gone."

The baron abruptly stopped walking and turned to face the sec chief. "How did they get out?"

"I have men checking on that."

The baron nodded. "Were they really swimming?"

The sec chief nodded. "Moira said it was her idea."

"Do you believe her?"

The sec chief shrugged. "No, but they were naked, and in the water. They had no provisions with them other than two remade blasters."

"Perhaps they were using the outing as a test of the walls and of your sec force's brand of security."

Robards was silent, knowing there was nothing he could say in his own defense.

"Obviously you failed."

More silence.

"But even though they got outside the ville undetected, they can't leave. They *need* to be close to the ville for the rest of their lives."

Robards waited for the baron to punish him for being so careless with the ville's security.

"Eleander must be punished," he said at last.

"Thank you, Baron," the sec chief said, acknowledging the order. Then he said, "When the outlanders came upon them, the two women were about to be raped by a gang of muties."

"Muties? You're supposed to take care of them as well."

"We did our usual sweep, Baron. They must have found new places to hide, or these scum were new muties."

The baron sneered, obviously disappointed with his sec chief's performance. "So these outlanders saved them?"

"Chilled the muties like they were chilling flies."

"Then I suppose we owe them a debt of thanks."

"I've conveyed as much to them."

"Good, give them some jack and send them on their way."

Again the sec chief hesitated. It was the best he could do to let the baron know that he didn't exactly want to follow the order.

"What is it?"

"I've offered them a place to stay for a while. And you'll be meeting them in an hour at a reception."

The baron sighed. "I don't want to waste my time with outland garbage."

Robards lowered his head. "Your feelings on the subject are well known, Baron, but I would like to keep this group close by for the next few days."

"Why is that?"

"Well, for one, I'd like to test my men against them."

"Yes, I suppose that might be fun. I'll see if it can be arranged. What else?"

"The leader of the group is somehow familiar to me. I've sent a man to Indyville to check on something for me. He should return in a day or two."

The baron looked at his sec chief with an inquisitive eye. "All right, Robards. I trust your judgment enough to let you play this out. But, in the meantime, would you mind telling me what all this is about?"

"I'd rather not until I'm sure. Could be right, could be wrong."

"Will I like what you have to tell me if you're right?"

Robards shook his head. "I don't think so."

"Then don't tell me until I need to know."

# Chapter Five

Ryan lay back on the cot watching Krysty strip to the waist. There was dirt and grime on her skin, darker on her arms and shoulders, lighter but still present on her back, belly and breasts.

"No running water in here, lover," she said, running her hands gently over her body. "But they did leave us a few jugs of water, washcloths and a washbasin big enough to stand in."

"Very kind of them," Ryan said, admiring the firm shelf of Krysty's chest and the perky nipples placed high on each breast. The Deathlands had made her body hard, but it was hard and sculpted in all the right places.

"Would you like to wash my back?" she asked, slipping out of the rest of her coveralls, exposing her exquisitely shaped buttocks, and powerful thighs and calves.

Ryan knew that if Krysty felt comfortable enough here to wash up, then they were probably safe for the next little while. Ryan too felt safe for the moment, and he also knew that the feeling wouldn't last. It was best to take advantage of the moment and enjoy it while it lasted.

"How could I say no?"

He got up from the bed and approached Krysty from behind. She gathered her fiery red hair in her hands and pulled it forward around her neck and away from her shoulders to expose the base of her neck and top part of her back.

Ryan picked up a washcloth and dipped it into the lukewarm water. After squeezing out the excess water, he dragged the damp cloth across Krysty's shoulders and watched as the dirt and dust of the day flowed away, leaving her smooth, unblemished, and clean skin behind.

"Mmm." She sighed. "That feels good, lover."

Ryan said nothing in response. Instead, he rinsed the washcloth and continued bathing Krysty, moving down her back, over her buttocks and inside her thighs.

And then she turned so he could do the front.

Ryan started at her neck and shoulders again, moving slowly down her body, spending extra time on her breasts, enjoying the way her nipples responded to his touch, and that of the water. Next came the reddish thatch of hair between her legs, which she parted slightly to give him better access to her legs.

"You're right, lover," Ryan said. "This does feel good."

"Your turn now," she said, smiling.

Ryan stripped down, keeping the SIG-Sauer and Steyr within arm's reach. The water felt cool on his skin, and Krysty was careful to wipe gently over his scarred flesh to make it feel more like a lover's touch than a bath.

"Does that feel good?" she asked.

Ryan didn't answer at first.

Instead he turned around and let her see the aewas having on him.

"Oh, lover," she breathed.

Ryan took Krysty in his arms and carried her to the bed.

THERE WAS a knock at the laboratory door.

Eleander was hard at work in the lab, making insulin for an East Coast baron with diabetes.

"Just a minute," she said, trying to free her hands to open the door.

But before Eleander could answer it, the door burst open and Sec chief Robards was standing in the doorway. There was a look of evil on his face, as if he intended to hurt someone.

Someone like her.

"What is it?" Eleander cried, shrinking from the doorway. "What do you want?"

The sec chief took a few steps forward, pushing her backward and forcing her to crawl away from him, but running out of room in the tiny lab.

"You know why I'm here," he said.

"We were swimming, I swear."

"A good story for the outlander trash, but not good enough for me, or the baron. We know you were testing possible escape routes."

"No, that's not right," Eleander insisted. "Moira just

wanted to get away for a little while, just the two of us, alone. How could I refuse her?"

"You're supposed to have an escort anytime you leave the ville. You know that as well as anyone."

"And with the way your sec men look at us, who will protect us from them?"

The sec chief's hand came out of nowhere, hitting her hard on the cheek and knocking her off her bed. The flesh stung, but the sec chief was too good at administering beatings to ever let a mark show on her face.

"After so many years, I still can't believe you need to learn your place here," Sec chief Robards said.

"I'm a chemist, and Moira's mother—"

"All of which means nothing to me." Robards grabbed her arm.

"No, please don't..." And then she cried out, "I'm sorry," even though she hadn't done anything wrong.

The sec chief laughed. "Oh, *now* you're sorry. Your little adventure made a fool out of me in front of the baron."

"It was never meant to. I only wanted to spend some time with my daughter."

But the sec chief was no longer listening. He reached into a pocket on the thigh of his pants and took out a tiny syringe.

Eleander saw the needle and cried out, "No, please... I'll cooperate. Whatever you want."

But it was too late to change her mind.

The sec chief jabbed the needle into the base of her neck.

Almost instantaneously, Eleander's body went limp.

Robards tossed the needle aside and removed his belt.

"Teach you to fuck with me," he said, as he delivered the first blow.

MILDRED WYETH MADE one last check on Jak's wound. Although it wasn't much more than a flesh wound, there had been some tearing to the muscle tissue that had to be repaired before she could close up the hole in his shoulder.

Luckily, Katz had been able to provide her with a local anesthetic that deadened the area enough so that Jak wouldn't be in too much pain while she worked. He'd jerked his body a couple of times when she hit a nerve, but there were no major problems considering where they were and the conditions the surgery had been done under.

Jak wanted to sleep now, but Mildred wanted to join up with the others before letting him doze off. In a few hours his shoulder would feel as if it had been hit by a gren, and by then he'd be a lot harder to move.

Mildred turned to Katz. "I came here with Jak and four others. We're supposed to be guests of the baron—can you take us to where my other friends are staying?"

"I'd be happy to," Katz said. "Anything you need."

"Thanks."

"They're probably in the old sec men's quarters in the baron's mansion. I'm going there anyway."

Mildred helped Jak to his feet and together they exited the building and started walking down a dirt road that knifed its way between rows of small clapboard houses and large steel shacks.

"You do good work," Katz said as they walked.

"Thank you," Mildred answered.

"Mebbe you were a healer once?"

"I know some."

"Bet it comes in handy out there in the Deathlands."

"Couple of times."

"You know, if you're tired of being an outlander, and mebbe wanted to settle down somewhere, I know the baron would be thrilled to have someone like you around."

Jak, who had been struggling to keep pace, let out a slight laugh.

"You think?" Mildred said.

"Oh, I know it."

"Well, I've had similar offers before, and I've always turned them down. I'm not much of a healer really. More like a dabbler."

"A good one."

"I appreciate the offer, but I've been with my friends awhile now and we've become sort of a team. I'm not ready to break it up just yet."

"I understand," Katz said, nodding. "But if you ever change your mind, you'll be welcome back here."

"Thanks," Mildred said politely. "I'll keep it in mind."

"Here we are."

They came upon a pre-Dark-looking structure made of

bricks. Its three floors rose up from the ground, towering above everything else around it as if it were a fortress.

"Very nice," Mildred said.

"This is the baron's residence. The baron lives here, of course, but your friends are staying here, too."

"Very nice."

Katz caught the attention of a sec man outside the front door of the building. "They're guests of the baron as well. Take them to the others."

The sec men nodded. "This way."

Mildred said thanks and goodbye to Katz, then she and Jak followed the sec men inside, down several dark corridors until they came upon three rooms at one end of the building.

As they approached, the middle door opened slightly to reveal J.B. standing there with his Uzi in his right hand.

"Just us, John," Mildred said.

J.B. opened the door wide.

The sec men left Mildred and Jak in the hallway, then headed back to their post.

J.B. opened the door to the third room, where Doc was asleep on his bed. He helped Mildred take Jak to the bed on the far side of the room. The albino youth grimaced several times as he was eased onto the bed, but once he was stretched out, he closed his eyes and was asleep in seconds.

"How is he?" J.B. asked, as he and Mildred exited the room.

"Sleeping like a baby now."

"He'll be all right, then?"

Mildred nodded. "He'll have some pain in a few hours, and there's always a risk of infection, but he should be as good as new in a couple of days."

J.B. entered their room and put down his blaster.

"Were you expecting trouble?" Mildred asked.

"Not really. Just didn't want you to interrupt Ryan and Krysty while you were looking for a room for Jak."

"Uh-huh," Mildred said skeptically. She listened closely, and beneath the sound of Doc's snoring, she could hear the soft moans of pleasure coming from next door. "That sound been giving you any ideas?"

J.B. just smiled.

Mildred began to get undressed.

AFTER A SEARCH of the residence, Katz found Baron DeMann tending to some of his open-air plants behind the mansion. These were special projects that the baron was experimenting with. Most of them were new plants he'd grown from seeds traded for on their last trip to several eastern villes. Half the seeds had been planted in the glasshouses, while the other half had been planted outside in an attempt to see which conditions best suited which plants.

Based on the size of the outside plants, growing them inside the glasshouses seemed the only way they could be grown large enough to extract sufficient amounts of active ingredients.

Katz cleared his throat. "Excuse me, Baron."

Baron DeMann steadied himself on one knee and

looked up from the leaf he was examining. "What is it, Katz?"

"I've just come from the clinic."

"One of the guests was wounded, right?"

"Yes, Baron, a shoulder wound. He was tended to by another one of the outlanders."

"And he's doing fine now, I take it."

Katz nodded. "The dark woman who looked after him..."

"Yes?" The baron got up to his feet.

"I think we could use her talents."

"She wants to stay with us?"

"I made suggestions about it, but she politely resisted."

The baron considered this, then smiled. "Not to worry. They're not going anywhere for a while. I'm sure you'll have the chance to ask her again under more favorable conditions."

Katz smiled at that. "Thank you, Baron."

# Chapter Six

"Time to go," the voice said.

Ryan stepped up to the door and pulled it open enough to look out. A sec man was standing in the hallway, one Ryan hadn't seen before. "Time for the baron's reception."

The one-eyed man nodded and closed the door.

Krysty stretched lazily on her cot, getting the blood circulating again after a short but contented sleep. She turned to Ryan and said, "Can't we stay here a bit longer, lover?"

"Yeah, but I'm curious to meet this baron, and to find out how he keeps his ville running."

"I sure could do with something to eat," Krysty said. She rose up off the cot and ran her fingers through her long red hair as if they were combs.

Ryan moved out into the hall where J.B., Doc and Mildred were already waiting.

"What about Jak?" Ryan asked.

"Sleeping," Mildred said. "He'll be out for another couple of hours. I'll stay with him if you want."

Ryan considered it.

"We're just going down to the basement," the sec man

offered, overhearing their conversation. "You'll be free to come back and check on your friend anytime you want."

"I'll come down with you to meet the baron," Mildred said. "Then I'll come back and stay with him. Maybe bring him some food."

Ryan nodded, then noticed Doc shifting nervously from side to side behind J.B. He looked strange, different, as if he'd just passed a comb through his hair, then pasted it back with some sort of grease. His frock coat also looked cleaner, as if he'd hung it on a line and beat it with a stick to get all the dust out of its fibers.

Krysty was studying Doc as well. "Lookin' good, Doc," she said, joining the others in the hall.

"Thank you for noticing, my dear Krysty."

The sec man gestured to Ryan's SIG-Sauer and Krysty's Smith & Wesson and said, "You won't be needing your weapons."

J.B. shook his head as if to say he knew the story would be changing.

Ryan looked hard at the sec man. "We don't go anywhere without our blasters."

"All right by me." The sec man shrugged. "But the baron might have something to say about it."

Ryan said nothing. The baron could say all he wanted, but they wouldn't be giving up their blasters without a firefight.

The sec man led them down the hallway.

AS PROMISED, they were led into the basement of the mansion and into a large room that was set up as a dining hall. Paintings hung from the walls, and the floor was covered with a carpet around the edges and a hardwood floor in the center. There was a long, rectangular table on one side of the room with settings for twelve people.

On another table off to one side were pitchers full of fresh water and juices, and carafes of both red and white wine. There was also a series of small finger bowls, each one filled with different colored tablets. "Make yourself at home," the sec man said. "Thc baron and the others will be here shortly."

When the sec man was gone, the friends went to the table and sampled the water and wine. Both were clear. The water was tasteless, while the wine seemed a bit strong.

"What do you make of these?" Ryan asked Mildred, pointing to the bowls of multicolored pills.

Mildred shook her head. "I don't know. Don't recognize any of them."

"Considering that these items are offered in conjunction with some truly excellent wines, I can only assume that they must be stimulants of some sort," Doc said. "Perhaps even depressants."

"Rccrcational drugs," Mildred said. "In pre-Dark times, ecstasy was the drug of choice, especially among young people. Kids thought it was cool, but of course it was nothing but bad news."

"So the baron's a drug lord," Ryan said, holding one of the pills, a yellow one, between his fingers. "Fireblast!"

Krysty eyed a tablet that was almost as red as her hair. "That'd be my guess."

"Can't say it comes as all that much of a surprise," Mildred said. "He's produced a lot of healing drugs. If he can do that, no reason he can't make junk like jolt and dreem."

"By the Three Kennedys, that would explain what bang is…and smash!"

"And now we know why his sec men have such good blasters," J.B. offered.

"We're leaving," Ryan ordered. "Let's get Jak."

The friends turned to leave the dining room, but the doors at either end of the room opened up and sec men with blasters and scatterguns filed in.

"You can't leave yet," the baron said as he entered the room behind his sec force. He wore an immaculate lab coat and his clothes beneath it looked just as clean and fresh. "We haven't even met yet." There was a hint of disappointment in his voice, making it sound as if he were being sincere.

"We don't associate with drug lords," Ryan stated.

The baron put up his hands, almost in surrender. "It's true, I do deal in drugs, but I assure you, only healing ones."

Mildred gestured to the bowls of pills on the table. "Expecting some big headaches?"

"Ha, a sense of humor. I like that in my guests." The baron moved toward the table holding the pills. "I'm merely trying to be a good host. Since I didn't know what you liked, I simply offered you all that I have. I'm actually glad you don't want to sample any of the drugs, since I don't like them, either. Makes articulate speech rather difficult and compromises one's judgment, two things I can ill afford as baron." He waved his arms as if he were swatting unseen insects. "Take them away."

A sec man hurried over to the table, picked up the bowls and carted them away.

"Now, if you'll forgive my small mistake, let's all share a meal, shall we?"

Ryan wasn't in favor of joining the baron for dinner, but even if they wanted to blast their way out of the situation, they wouldn't get very far. The sec men surrounding them could throw up a wall of fire heavy enough to cut down a small forest. There would be a fight, Ryan knew, but this wasn't the time or place for it.

Reluctantly, he put away his blaster. The others followed his lead.

"Thank you," the baron said.

The sec men also lowered their weapons.

"I better check on Jak," Mildred said.

"Not to worry..." the baron's voice trailed off.

"Mildred," the doctor offered.

"Not to worry, Mildred. Your friend is fine, I assure you. Of course, you're free to return to him whenever you like, but I wouldn't be much of a host if I didn't encourage you to eat at least a little something first."

"I'll take it back to eat in the room."

"Fine, fine, now let's get started. I'm starved." The baron sat at the head of the table. Ryan and the friends took seats on either side of him.

At that moment, Moira entered the dining room, wearing a sundress and leather sandals.

"Ah, here she is now, the lovely Moira," the baron said, "who I believe you've already met, down by the river."

The friends watched the young woman enter the room.

J.B. leaned close to Ryan. "Sounds like they're more than friends."

"Mebbe she's a big jack gaudy slut," Ryan pondered.

"Isn't she a thing of beauty," the baron said, gesturing for Moira to take the seat next to him.

Moira appeared to hesitate, then reluctantly joined the baron at the table.

"She's charming," Doc offered.

Moira smiled in Doc's direction.

Ryan had to admit that she was a good-looking young woman, especially now that she'd had a chance to clean up and put on some clothes. And the fact that Moira was the baron's mistress explained why they had been treated so well since entering the ville. Any man would be grateful to the people who saved his lover from a gang rape. Still, if Moira was the baron's lover, then why had she been so afraid of Robards and the sec men at the river? Ryan had never met a baron's woman who didn't act as if she ran the baron's ville for him.

"Now that she's here, perhaps we can begin eating."

In minutes, a man and a woman were bringing in trays of food for them to sample. Most of it was grilled vegetables such as eggplant, zucchini and red and green peppers, but there was also some fresh corn bread, dried nuts and one small sausage each, the meat of which smelled like chicken but could have been anything from possum to snake.

Ryan was famished, and when the food began appearing on the table, he looked forward to eating his fill. However, something didn't seem right with the picture.

Doc pointed out the problem to all of them.

"Uh, excuse me Baron DeMann," Doc said, trying to be polite.

"Yes, sir," the baron answered.

"Oh, I appreciate the compliment, but I assure you I'm not a member of any House of Lords. My name is Theophilus Algernon Tanner."

"Theo..."

"Most people call me Doc."

"Doc? Are you a scientist?"

Ryan looked at Doc, curious to hear his answer.

"Not exactly," Doc said. "I have some knowledge of old sciences, and I dabble a bit in the new ones. I suspect I earned the nickname because I'm the only one in the group who can divide three-digit numbers without the use of a stick and patch of sand."

The baron laughed at that.

J.B. seemed to find it funny as well.

"All right...Doc. What is it?"

"Well, when my colleagues and I saved your lovely, uh, mistress from certain harm, she was with another, older woman..."

"Yes."

"Moira here referred to that woman as her mother…" Doc's voice trailed off, leaving the question unsaid.

The baron nodded.

"Well, if she is her mother, and we saved her from the muties as well this afternoon, I just thought that, well, it would be nice if she could join us, too."

The baron looked inquisitively at Robards.

"She's not feeling well," the sec chief said.

"But she was fine when she got off the wag this afternoon," Doc said.

"Yes, bring her here," the baron ordered. "I'm sure she'd enjoy the company."

The sec chief slowly got up from his seat. "I'll see if she's feeling any better."

"You do that," the baron said.

"Thank you." Doc nodded graciously.

"If you'll excuse me," Mildred said, piling some vegetables on a pair of metal plates, "I've got to check on Jak. If he's awake, I'm sure he'll be hungry, too."

"Give your friend Jak my regards," the baron said.

"I'll do that," Mildred responded, collecting a bit more food for herself and preparing a tray for Jak.

The baron turned his attention from Doc to Ryan. "Am I right to assume that you are the leader of this group?"

"Name's Ryan."

"Then you are the leader?"

"You can assume that if you like."

The baron said nothing for a moment. "As you've probably noticed, I've got a decent sec force here with plenty of well-trained men and some of the best blasters around."

"We noticed."

"Hard to come by," J.B. interjected. "Some of those blasters look right out of the box."

"Baron DeMann," Ryan said, "this is J.B. He's the weapons expert of our group."

"A man who appreciates fine craftsmanship and design, no doubt."

"Did you get your blasters new?" J.B. asked, avoiding any mention of the redoubt.

"I can't be sure," the baron replied. "I sell drugs. Good drugs that people need to survive. And when people are dying, they can get rather desperate. I can pretty well name my price for my drugs. I know that may sound hard, but I'm a trader and traders don't give their wares away when they can hang on to them and get top jack."

Ryan nodded. He'd seen top traders in action, and the baron's assessment was right on.

"So, if I'm in the market for anything, be it blasters or blankets, I make sure I get the very best available. The best blasters, the best blankets, the best food, wine..."

"Wags," J.B. said.

"Everything," the baron responded. "The best that jack can buy."

The baron paused and everyone took the opportunity to take a bite of food.

"I also like to think I have the best sec force of any ville in the area. They're the best equipped and well trained, but one can never be sure about such things."

"I've seen plenty sec men," Ryan said. "Yours look as disciplined as any."

"But are they the best?"

"Won't know that until they're tested in a firefight."

"Exactly," the baron said. Then he went silent, staring at Ryan a moment, as if expecting the man to comment.

"Not sure I follow you," Ryan said.

"I have a favor to ask of you and your friends."

Ryan shrugged. "No harm in asking."

"We have an obstacle course we use for training sec men. In addition to blaster practice, I also use it for pitting sec man against sec man in order to see where they should fall in terms of rank."

"Must make for a lot of dead sec men."

The baron laughed. "No, not at all. I have blasters that fire tiny balls filled with colored water. They're just like regular blasters, but can't chill people. A good tool for training, and for turning poor sec men into good ones."

"Point to all this?" J.B. asked.

"Well, my sec chief was wondering if you and your group might agree to test several of his best sec men in a contest."

Ryan shook his head. "No, thanks. We've had plenty of real firefights out in the Deathlands. We don't fight for sport."

"I can appreciate that, and I would have the same opinion if I were in your shoes."

"Then you know my answer."

The baron said nothing for a while, thinking through the problem. "Ah, you need a reason to fight."

"That's right, usually it's to keep from getting chilled."

"A wise position, but I'm not about to try and chill you just so you'll participate in my test. However, might I suggest that you agree to participate in exchange for the hospitality I've shown you and your friends."

Ryan gestured to the food on the table. "We didn't ask for any of this."

"Quite right." The baron nodded. "Then what if I said that if you bested my sec men, I'd be willing to provide you with as much ammo as you need when you leave my ville, as well as any medicines and supplies, uh, Mildred, might want to take with her. I'm sure those sorts of things are still useful to you in your travels."

Ryan looked to J.B. "Running low all around."

He turned to Krysty.

"Who knows?" she added. "Might be fun, firing a blaster and *not* chilling somebody for a change."

Ryan sighed. "All right, we'll play your game, but J.B. checks all the weapons before we begin, just to make sure we're all using the same ammo."

"Of course."

"When?"

"Is tomorrow afternoon too soon?"

ROBARDS WALKED slowly down the street to Eleander's residence. Thanks to one of the outlanders, he now had to bring the woman to the dining hall and have her eat and talk to the baron's guests.

Dammit!

This was an unfortunate turn of events, but not a problem.

There were ways…

The sec chief turned to the sec man following him. "Go find Katz. Tell him what the problem is and bring him to Eleander's home. And make it fast."

The sec man turned and ran, double time.

MILDRED TAPPED on Jak's door with the toe of her boot.

"Who there?" Jak asked. His words were followed by the sound of his .357 Magnum Colt Python being cocked.

"It's Mildred," she said. "Brought you some food."

There was a metallic click on the other side of the door and Mildred knew it was safe to enter.

"I figured you'd be hungry," she said, pushing open the door and entering the room.

"Guessed right," he answered. He was sitting up on his cot, one arm hanging limply from the shoulder, the other rubbing a hand in circular motions over his empty growling stomach.

She put the food on the rough wooden stand next to the bed, then sat on the empty bed next to him.

"How's your shoulder? Does it hurt?"

"No." Jak shook his head. "You fixed good."

Mildred lifted the dressing and saw that although there were still a few wet spots to the wound, it was generally healing nicely. She touched the bruised flesh with the point of her finger and Jak grimaced.

"You know, for someone who doesn't say many words, you're not a very good liar."

Jak smiled.

"I'll clean the dressing later. Right now you should eat. Build up your strength."

"Food good?"

"Oh, yeah." She placed a plate on his lap and gave him a fork. "Best we've had in months."

THE WAG HAD PERFORMED flawlessly, taking its rider across the rad-choked land between the two villes in less than six hours. He had stopped twice along the way, once to refill his tank with alcohol, the other to refill himself with food and water.

Now he was approaching Indyville, the engine still running smoothly as the dusty miles fell beneath his wheels.

The ville's lookouts would have spotted him by now, and the entire ville's sec force would be on alert. That was good, because by the time he arrived there, the baron would be aware of his approach and curious to know what he wanted.

Now, as he neared the ville's perimeter, the road got rougher. The surface of the road was spotted with holes and was covered with rocks and chunks of asphalt. He slowed the wag by half, the engine's song falling from a high whine to a throaty growl.

The gates to the ville grew larger in his sights. Sec men stood on either side of the rolling door made of rusty rebar and sheet metal. One of the sec men signaled to him to slow down by waving both his arms over his head.

He waved back with just his right hand.

The entrance to the ville was less than a quarter of a mile away, and he slowed the wag further. Closer in, there were dead things on the road—the carcasses and bones of long-dead animals, fallen trees, strategically positioned rocks and the odd corpse of a mutie who made the mistake of trying to get into the ville. It was a strange way to protect the outer edges of the ville, but it was doing a good job of it.

The driver was forced to slow to a crawl, just to find a way through the maze of death and ruin.

But at last he was at the gates of the ville. He brought the wag to a stop, but left the engine running just in case it might not start again.

"What do you want?" the sec man asked. He was armed with little more than a pointed stick, but in the towers on the other side of the gate were several batteries of large-caliber automatic blasters, some of which were aimed directly at his head.

"Greetings from Baron DeMann."

The sec man said nothing.

"I need to speak with Baron Schini."

"About what?"

"Sorry, but I must speak only with the baron."

"She's not seeing anyone tonight."

The driver nodded. He'd been told that he might be refused at the gate, and that's why he'd been given a gift to present to the baron.

"I've brought a quarter pound of bang to give to the baron." He took the small sack from his shoulder bag.

"I'll take it."

He quickly snatched it away before the sec man could grab it. "Sorry, it's for the baron only."

The sec man licked his lips, then sighed. He turned and raised his eyes to the top of the gate. "He's got bang for the baron—let him in."

After a few moments of silence, the large steel door started rolling to the left, giving him just enough room to enter the ville.

KATZ LOOKED at the body of Eleander lying on a cot in a corner of the lab. She seemed dead and lifeless, as if she wouldn't become conscious for another few hours yet.

Robards was rearranging her clothing, hiding the slight welts, in order to make her presentable enough to bring to the baron.

"I can wake her up, but there will be a dangerous mix in her system," Katz said. "If she takes anything else in the next twelve hours, it could chill her."

"I'll watch over her," Robards said, his voice emotionless.

"And of course, there will probably be some slurring of her words—that is, of course, if she can speak coherently at all."

"I'll tell them she's been drinking."

"That's probably best. She'll seem drunk, might even feel like it, too."

"Rad-blasted outland scum," Robards said. "One of them took a liking to this bitch. Asked the baron if she could join them."

"And the baron agreed?"

"The outlanders wanted to leave, and I instructed the baron to keep them here for a couple or few days, till my rider comes back from Indyville. And so when the old-timer asked to see her, the baron had no choice but to agree."

"You could always say she's turned in for the night."

Robards shook his head. "Tried something like that, but this outlander was persistent. Wouldn't take no for an answer. Probably come here to see her if she doesn't join them over there."

Katz produced a large plunge-type syringe from his bag. "This will bring her around," he said, then sighed. "But she's your problem after that."

Robards put a hand on his blaster and said, "Just do it!"

Katz gave Eleander the jab.

At first nothing happened, and then her eyelids fluttered open. "Where, what..." She put a hand on her forehead. "Headache."

"Thanks," Robards said.

"Don't thank me," Katz replied. "You're on your own. I want nothing to do with this."

Robards snickered. "You're already involved."

Katz shook his head. "You mention my name, and the baron will get the full story. About the others, too..." He closed his bag and left the room before Robards had a chance to respond.

At the sound of Katz's departure, Eleander's eyes opened wider. When she realized Robards was standing over her, she instinctively tried to move away from him, crawling backward like a spider.

"Relax," Robards said. "I'm not going to hurt you."

She looked skeptical.

"The baron wants to see you. Apparently, one of the bastard outlanders has taken a shine to you."

A sleepy smile broke over Eleander's face.

"Tidy up," Robards said, pulling back the blanket. "I don't want to keep the baron, or the outlanders, waiting."

# Chapter Seven

Baron Schini was a strong, powerful woman who had risen to power in Indyville by virtue of her cunning and keen sense of picking the right person for a job. Her sec force was strong and well trained, and led by a meticulous sec chief named Viviani who left nothing to chance and no detail overlooked.

But the baron was also a wealth of knowledge and information. Her memory was like a strongbox, and anything that she might have trouble remembering was filed in a collection of journal notes. The notes were part of a vast library housed in the center of the ville. Untouched by the nukeblast that devastated much of Indyville, the library had been the first thing the baron had sought control of when she was newly assigned to the previous baron's sec force. Schini found that by controlling knowledge she also had power, and by acquiring more knowledge, she would acquire even more power. And so the library grew and grew, adding valuable books on subjects as diverse as basket weaving and blaster design. There were books on how to have better sex, and how to fight without blasters, knives or swords—

even books on how to chill people with poisons...if you happened to have the right poisons.

The baron had a dozen librarians reading through the texts in the library, each one with a special area of expertise, such as geography, geology, chemistry, biology and history. Every so often, one of the librarians would be called upon to solve a problem pertaining to their area of expertise and, over the years, Indyville had become a very powerful barony, selling knowledge to those who needed it.

Like Sec chief Robards...

"So," Baron Schini said. "The sec man at the gate says you brought me a quarter pound of bang in exchange for some information."

"That's right, Baron."

"Well, what does Robards want to know?"

The sec man sent by Robards cleared his throat. "Baron DeMann is playing host to a group of outlanders—"

"I thought he hated the scum?"

"He does, but he's holding them for a reason."

Baron Schini nodded slowly.

"One of the outlanders, their leader in fact, goes by the name of Ryan. He's rather distinctive looking with a large scar on the right side of his face and a black patch covering his left eye."

"Plenty of outlanders have scars like that."

"Yes, but this one is unique. His band of six includes an albino teenager, an old man, a black woman, another woman, fair skinned with flaming red hair, and a thin man who wears wire-rimmed spectacles and a fedora."

"A motley crew to be sure, but why the fuck should I care?"

"Sec chief Robards thinks this Ryan may be the same outlander who chilled Baron DeMann's brother a few years ago in a gaudy house in Spearpoint."

Baron Schini suddenly appeared more interested in Baron DeMann's outlanders. If their leader was the one who chilled the baron's brother, then he's also the one who chilled her son in the very same gaudy house firefight. "What makes Robards suspect this outlander is the one?"

"Well, he remembered hearing something about a one-eyed outlander working for a man they called Trader, and he knew it was one of the Trader's men who chilled the baron's brother while the Trader was at Spearpoint working on a deal with Levi Shabazz."

"Why not just ask the outlander if he's the one? Or just chill them all and be done with it?"

"These outlanders are dangerous, and he didn't want to let them know he suspected who they were until he was sure they were the ones."

"And so he sent you here to me."

"Correct."

"And if this is the outlander who chilled the baron's brother, what does that candy-ass Robards plan to do about it?"

"Why, chill the scum and his friends on behalf of Baron DeMann, of course."

Schini shook her head.

"You disapprove?"

"Not at all," the baron said. "It's just that if this one-eyed outlander is the same one who chilled the baron's brother, then he's also the one who chilled my son, Luca. And if that's the case, I damn well want to be there to watch him die."

Robards had warned the sec man that this request was a possibility. "As you wish, Baron."

The baron smiled politely. "But first we need to know we have the right man, eh?" She turned to one of her sec men. "Take him to the archives and look up the journal entries on Luca's death. And keep me informed as to what you find."

The sec man nodded and led the messenger away.

THEY WERE ALMOST finished eating when Eleander entered the dining room.

"Ah, here she is," Baron DeMann said. "The mother of the beautiful Moira." It was obvious he had none of the same feelings for the older woman as he did the younger.

Eleander stepped slowly into the big room, as cautious as if she were walking over broken glass with naked feet.

"She was resting soundly," Robards offered in explanation. "I was sorry to wake her up, but when she knew she had been asked for, she insisted on joining you."

Doc smiled broadly, his eyes stuck on the older woman.

Ryan had never seen Doc so smitten by a woman before, though he had had a few liaisons. He had spoken countless times of the wife and children who had been left behind when Operation Chronos snatched him from his own era and brought him forward in time. But while he spoke of his dear wife Emily with fondness, romance, love and respect, he seemed to eye Eleander with a lust that was somewhat uncharacteristic of the man. But with his mind shaken so badly from the jumps in time, and emotional scarring, a person could never be sure of Doc's mental state. Ryan was glad that this time he appeared to be affected by lust, instead of the usual madness that bordered on lunacy.

"There's an empty seat here next to me if you like," Doc said, pulling back the chair and patting its seat as if that would make its hard wooden bottom more comfortable.

Eleander walked slowly toward Doc and took the chair with a slight nod. She smiled broadly at him.

"Right," the baron said, acting as if the woman wasn't even there. "I imagine you and your weapons man might want to look over the blasters you'll be using tomorrow."

Ryan nodded.

"I would like that very much," J.B. added.

"Let's go have a look, shall we?"

Ryan and J.B. got up to leave with the baron. Ryan looked to Krysty to ask if she were joining them.

"I think I'll stay behind with Doc."

Ryan glanced at the old-timer, who was already making conversation with Eleander. "I don't think he needs a chaperone."

"No, but it wouldn't hurt to keep an eye on him."

Ryan couldn't argue with that logic.

"Later, then," he said.

Krysty smiled coyly. "I'm looking forward to it, lover."

THE LIBRARIAN was an old, old man, hunched over a gnarled wooden walking stick and moving about with a considerable limp. His right leg was twisted strangely to the left, and it looked to be a few inches shorter than his other one.

"You say you want the volume documenting the death of the baron's son at Spearpoint?"

"That's right."

"Any particular reason?"

"I want to see the description of the scum who chilled him."

"Might not be one there, you know."

"But the journals must have recorded the eyewitness accounts of that time."

"Sure, sure…but there might not be the exact description you're looking for. For all I know it might just say the baron's son was killed by some outlander. Nothing more."

"Even if the outlander has several distinguishing features?"

"Well, if he had just one arm, it might be written in the journals. I'm just saying we may not find what you're looking for. You might be disappointed."

"I'll take my chances. Besides, your baron's got an interest in this, too."

The librarian perked up at the mention of his baron

as he no doubt realized that if his journals were short of the information she wanted, he might be held accountable for it.

"Here it is. Journal 52."

The librarian turned the pages of a ragged oversized book that was two feet long and a foot and a half wide. The pages were stark white and covered with tiny handwritten scrawls, each letter no bigger than a drop of water. "We bleach the pages of the books whose information isn't valid anymore. Then one of our scribblers who can write in very small letters records new information on the pages." He was looking over the book's type with a magnifying lens that was the size of a bottle bottom.

"Spearpoint, you say, eh?"

"Yeah, where Baron DeMann's brother, Joshua, and Baron Schini's son Luca, were both chilled by an outlander in a firefight."

The librarian continued to pour over the handwritten text in silence, now deeply engrossed in his task.

Every once in a while he blurted out a few words as he read.

"...confrontation with Vernel, crew leader for Levi Shabazz, in gaudy house over fat dancer named Big Dumpling. No, that's not it."

He continued reading, mumbling a few words every so often as he went.

Then, after a few minutes...

"Mebbe this is it." The librarian adjusted the lens and reset it over the page.

"Members of Trader's crew stole several wags. Made a run for it after rescuing several captured members of their group. Firefight with members of Baron Zeal's sec force."

"Joshua and Luca were both members of Zeal's sec force."

"What's the brother and son of barons doing as members of someone like Zeal's sec force?"

"They were young, free-spirited," the messenger said with a shrug. "Way I was told, they were out looking for adventure, excitement."

"Humpf," the old man laughed. "Seems they got more than they could handle."

"Is it there?"

"There's something here…just a minute." The librarian adjusted the lens again and began to read.

"Joshua DeMann and Luca Schini both chilled by outlanders in an attempt to rescue members of their crew."

"Is that all?"

"Patience!"

The messenger made himself comfortable and waited to hear from the librarian.

"Escape attempt led by three members of Trader's crew. The men—First man, tall, muscular, black curly hair, blue right eye. Carries Ruger Blackhawk blaster. Second man, short, stocky, thick mustache, long hair usually tied in knot. Third man, older, muscular, called Poet."

The librarian turned to the messenger. "Is that any help?"

"Yes and no. The first description sounds like the outlanders' leader, but he carries a SIG-Sauer, not a Ruger, and his right eye is blue, but is there no other mention about his eyes? Two of them?"

"I read everything that's here."

"And the descriptions of the other two don't fit his companions. There is an older man, but he's called Doc, not Poct."

"Mebbe he got some new friends."

"Yeah, mebbe. Is there any mention of other outlanders? Any women?"

"Yes, in the entry about the gaudy house. Now where is it? Ah. Woman, green hair, carries double-barreled shotgun. Man, tall, skinny, wears hat and spectacles, carries Browning Hi-Power Mark 2. Another man, named Sam, carries 9 mm H&K P-7."

The messenger shook his head in frustration.

"Something wrong?"

"There's two women with this outlander now, and one of them has red hair—very beautiful red hair—not green. One of the men in the group is a match, the one with the hat and glasses, but there's no mention of the black woman or the albino."

"Albino?"

"Yeah, a teenager, white hair, red eyes. Albino."

"Would've mentioned something like that in the journal if he'd been there."

"That's what I figured."

"But this is from a few years back. If he's a teenager now, then he would've been a little kid."

The messenger considered the information he'd been given. He was almost sure that the outlanders' leader was the same man who was mentioned in the journal. Sec chief Robards recalled just such a man, and there were too many similarities to dismiss it as coincidence. But he needed to be sure. If they decided to chill the outlanders, there was a good chance many of their own would likely be chilled in the process.

"Is there anything else? Anything?"

"Hmm, let me see… Ah!"

"What is it?"

"The Trader's crew blew up Baron Zeal's refinery with copious amounts of C-4. The one-eyed man—" he paused, knowing this was a definite clue for the messenger "—orchestrated the escape of Trader's party and the theft of most of Zeal's wags." A pause. "Sez here the name of the one-eyed man is…"

The librarian's voice trailed off and the messenger became anxious. It was almost as if he were teasing the messenger.

"Tell me, you old fucker, or I swear I'll chill you where you stand."

The librarian ignored the threat. He had what the man wanted, and he wasn't going to chill him before he delivered the goods.

"The man's name is Ryan Cawdor."

"Ryan."

"That's right."

"Then it's him! He's the one."

The librarian took a sheet of bleached paper from a stack at the corner of the table. "I'll copy the information for you to take back to Baron DeMann."

"Yes, thank you."

There was a smile on the old man's face as if his entire existence had just been validated.

"I'VE NEVER SEEN anything like it," J.B. said, turning the blaster over in his hand.

"It fires balls filled with colored water," the baron said, handing a second identical blaster to Ryan. "The balls come in two pieces and break open on impact, leaving a colored stain on the target."

"Heavy," Ryan said, lifting the blaster in his hand like a deadweight.

"That's the ammo. Since it's mostly water, a loaded blaster can get a bit heavy."

"An overweight blaster that doesn't chill?" J.B. said in disbelief. "What good is that?"

"We've found it very useful. As you can imagine, it can be expensive and dangerous to train sec men with real ammo, but these rounds can be reused. We just clean them up, fill them up and press them together again."

Ryan pointed the blaster at a mark on the wall of the small room next to the arena. There were all sorts of colored marks on the walls where others had tested their blasters. Ryan squeezed the trigger of the blaster and it *pocked* in his hand. A glistening splash of blue was now on the wall in line with the blaster's muzzle.

"It's powered by compressed air. Originally they had to be loaded with carbon dioxide cartridges, but we figured out a way to rig them to work with simple compressed air." The baron was obviously proud of the technical prowess he'd shown in keeping the blasters operational.

Ryan could only think he had to be very well armed and secure in his position to devote such time and energy to worthless nonlethal blasters.

J.B. held up his blaster, squeezed off several rounds, and the wall came alive with bursts of red, green and yellow.

"Excellent," the baron said. "Obviously you know how to handle blasters of different types. I'm sure you'll give my sec men a good test."

J.B. put down the nonlethal blaster. "You said we'd be getting ammo."

The baron smiled. "I can see why you're the weapons expert. Blasters and ammo must always be on your mind." He led them into another room, which was stocked floor-to-ceiling with ammunition and a few lesser-quality remade blasters that had at one time been Colts and Smith & Wessons.

"Impressive," Ryan said. If the baron's sec force lacked any fighting skills, they'd be able to more than make up for it in firepower.

There were an assortment of ammo boxes like the ones they'd seen dozens of times in the redoubts, only these were devoid of the plastic wrap and wax that usually preserved the contents against the elements. They also looked scuffed up, as if they'd been emptied and refilled several times over the years. The boxes were labeled with crude but clearly legible black letters denoting boxes of .357-, .44- and .38-caliber rounds. There were also boxes of 9 mm rounds, both regular and Parabellum. There were even a few ammo belts for .50-caliber machine blasters. Although Ryan hadn't seen such a big blaster in the ville yet, he had no trouble believing the baron had one stored somewhere safe.

"We found an old military installation not far from here," the baron said.

Ryan and J.B. looked at each other, but said nothing.

"It was stocked with many useful items," the baron continued. "Burners and hoses, beakers and large glass bottles. I took everything that wasn't nailed down, and a lot of it turned out to be useful in the creation of my medicines and drugs."

"Did you find all of these weapons there, too?" J.B. asked, examining a very well-crafted remade blaster.

"No, there were a few broken blasters, some ammo that we couldn't use, and a bunch of other supplies, but it looked to us as if someone else had already been through the place, taking the most useful and valuable blasters and leaving behind whatever they didn't need, or couldn't use. I suspect they had to leave in a hurry, judging by the condition of the inside of the place. Several firefights damaged a lot of items I probably could have made use of."

Ryan wondered if the Trader had been through the redoubt before he and J.B. had joined up with him. And if not the Trader, then someone else. That would explain the condition of the redoubt, and why the mat-trans chamber was damaged on the outside, but not the inside.

Lucky for them it was in good enough condition for one last jump.

"So—" the baron clapped his hands together "—what will you need?"

J.B. recited a list of ammo used by each member of the group. When he came to Doc's LeMat, he faltered. "And Doc will need, well..."

"Yes?"

"His blaster is old—ancient really. He'll need a supply of bulk gunpowder, cotton wadding and lead."

The baron simply nodded.

"Copper primer nipples would be helpful, too."

The baron smiled. "My chemists can take care of that, and I have people who can manufacture just about anything given the proper specs. We have a supply of pre-Dark pennies, which I imagine could be remade into excellent primer nipples. If your man, Doc, is it, provides the proper instructions, then we can make them for him."

J.B. just shook his head.

"Is something wrong?"

"I keep thinking the old man is a crazy fool for hanging on to that museum piece, but as odd a blaster as it is, he's never been short of ammo for it."

"It has character," the baron said. "Like the man."

Ryan smiled. "He's a character all right."

"When will we get the ammo we need?" J.B. asked.

"Arms are always on your mind, aren't they?"

"When?" J.B. prodded.

"You'd make a good sec man, you know that."

It was obvious the baron was ignoring J.B.'s question.

"We'd like to have it ready, and where we can see it, *before* we play your little game."

The baron smiled, but it was an empty smile holding no promise.

"I'll see what I can do."

J.B. didn't press the point, since it was obvious there was no point in doing so.

"Shall we rejoin the others?"

The baron led them out of the armory.

BARON SCHINI was sitting at her dinner table, the remains of her meal in front of her. Several shiny white bones were scattered about the plate, stripped clean of every last scrap of meat. The messenger had seen plenty of animal bones before, but he didn't recognize any of them. They looked…almost human, and reminded him of the condition they often found the muties to be in, living on the outskirts of the ville. The only difference was, the muties had some skin to go along with their bones.

"Well," the baron said commandingly, "did you find what you were looking for in the library?"

"I did, Baron."

"And?"

"It is him."

The baron's mouth dropped open.

"Most of his crew are different now, and he wasn't the leader of the group back at Spearpoint, but the journal talks of a one-eyed man named Ryan, and that's the outland scum's name."

"And *he* killed my boy?"

"Yes, Baron. The journal is very specific on that point."

Baron Schini let out a long sigh. For a moment it looked as if she might shed a tear, but none came. "Thank you for letting me know you've found the outland bastard."

"If you'll excuse me, Baron, I must be getting back. Sec chief Robards wanted me to return as soon as I could. If I leave now, I could be back before morning."

The baron looked sternly at the messenger. "Do I look like a fool to you?"

The messenger was unsure of what had just happened. He decided he needed to answer the question with a lie since the baron looked to be somewhat unstable at the moment. "No, Baron, not at all."

"Do you think I became baron of Indyville by letting things slide, by shrugging things off, by turning the other rad-blasted cheek?"

Baron Schini was one of the most ruthless barons for hundreds of miles in every direction. She'd been known to cut her enemies to pieces, instructing her librarians to remove pieces of their bodies just to see how much pain and mutilation they could endure before they expired. One man, caught holding back some of the baron's jack, had lived for a week until he'd managed to snatch a blaster from a sec man and shoot himself in the head to end his misery.

"No, Baron. I don't think that at all."

"So if you have the man who killed my boy, don't you think I'd want to be there to see him die?"

"Of course, Baron." The messenger was doing his best to be humble, knowing it would probably save his life. "I'm sorry, I wasn't thinking."

The baron got up from the table, walked over to the messenger and moved slowly around him, sizing him up. When she stopped, she was standing directly in front of him, a hand on her holstered blaster.

The messenger trembled slightly.

"You didn't think," she said.

And then her right hand came up and struck the messenger in the face. Two of his teeth were knocked loose, and his lip cracked open. The split in his mouth glistened scarlet.

"That's all right," she said, smiling now, as if feeling better. "I like sec men who don't think." She turned to one of her own security men. "Give him a room, something to eat, and a man or a woman for the night, whichever he wants."

"But Baron DeMann—"

"Fuck Baron DeMann. You're in my Indyville right now."

The messenger lowered his head. "Yes, Baron."

"We'll all leave in the morning," she announced. "You, me and my sec force. I'm sure Baron DeMann and Sec chief Robards are quite capable of chilling the outlander, but I want to be there when it happens. I want to feel the scum squirm under my fingers as I strangle the life out of him. I want him to tell me he's sorry. I want him to beg me for his life, and then I want to chill him as painfully as possible."

"I'm sure Baron DeMann will be happy to have your

assistance," the messenger said, doing his best to sound sincere.

Again, she slapped him hard, only this time on the other cheek, puffing up his face equally on both sides.

"Bullshit! DeMann is going to be pissed off when he hears I'm in his ville, but he'll have to let me in. I have a family death to avenge, just as he does."

The messenger was speechless, not daring to say another word.

Baron Schini smirked. "Take him away, and give him whatever he wants. I like him. He's a good boy."

The baron's sec men led the man away.

The messenger seemed relieved to be out of the baron's presence. He was already asking if there were different women for him to choose from.

When he was gone and out of earshot, Baron Schini called over her sec chief, Viviani.

"Yes, Baron."

"Gather twelve sec men for the morning. They'll ride with me. The rest of your force with leave a half hour later."

"The purpose, Baron?"

"I've been wanting to take out DeMann for years. This thing with the outlander is just the excuse I need to get inside the ville, and once I'm in, I'll open it up for your force so we can take him from inside."

The sec chief smiled. "Very good, Baron."

Baron Schini let out a long, hard laugh. "It's better than good. The grieving mother seeking justice." She laughed again. "It's perfect."

# Chapter Eight

"I am sorry I roused you out of bed," Doc said, sitting across the table from Eleander.

"That's all right," she answered with a pained smile. "I turned in too early anyway. If I'd slept any longer, I would have spent the middle of the night pacing the floor."

"Well, then, I am glad you decided to grace us with your company."

"Us?" She looked around the dining hall. "I haven't said two words to anyone but you since I got here."

"I have to admit I have been monopolizing your time, Eleander, but understand that in travels with my companions it is not often that I come across a woman with as much grace, charm, good looks and...well, class, as you possess."

"You're too kind," Eleander said.

"No, I am not being kind at all. I believe you to be truly wonderful, and I have but only begun to scratch the surface in regards to your charms."

Eleander just smiled. She seemed tired and rundown, but Doc was unable to see it.

"Tell me...what do you do here?"

"I'm a scientist," she said.

"By the Three Kennedys. Of course you are."

"I don't understand."

"Not only are you beautiful, graceful and charming, but you are also a whitecoat. A woman of science who has tasted fruit from the tree of knowledge. Where did you study?"

Eleander looked at Doc strangely. "Why, here, of course."

"There is a university, a school, in this ville?"

"No, the baron taught me how to make the drugs himself. His father taught him, and his grandfather taught his fathcr, all the way up the line. The knowledge of drug making is like a family secret in the DeMann family. The baron has taught people here to make insulin and penicillin. I can make those, and other kinds of drugs."

"To help other people." Doc's eyes were wide with enchantment.

Eleander looked away. "Yes, although I don't always think of it in those terms."

"Toll mo, do you like to read?"

"When I can."

"The classics?"

"I've read some Shcrlock Holmes, some Wells and Verne."

"Have you read *The Time Machine?*"

"There's a copy here in the baron's library, but I haven't read it yet."

"Oh, you must read it," Doc insisted. "It will tell you a little bit more about who I am, and where I came from."

"Then I will read it first chance I get."

Doc put his hand on top of hers and held it for a long, long time.

A while later, Ryan and J.B. returned from the armory. "You must be tired after your adventurous day," the baron said. "Which is just another way of me saying, it's time that you return to your rooms for the night. I want all of you well rested for the challenge tomorrow."

"I guess this is goodbye," Doc said, rising from his chair. There was disappointment in his voice.

"Perhaps," Eleander said, getting to her feet and staggering slightly when she was upright.

"Are you all right?"

"Just tired." She steadied herself by grabbing Doc's shoulder. "Go now, and tomorrow I'll cheer you on. My knight in shining armor."

Doc smiled at that. "I assure you, I am no knight."

"But you are, truly. Or was it someone else who came to the aid of a young damsel and her matron in distress?"

"Two damsels, my dear lady," Doc said, bowing slightly and kissing the top of her hand. "Two finc damsels."

"Are you coming, Doc?" Krysty asked.

Doc hesitated.

"I'll see you tomorrow."

"Every minute will seem an hour."

She kissed him on his cheek, then turned away.

Doc, a smile painted on his face, joined the friends and headed back to his rooms.

WHEN THE OUTLANDERS were gone, Eleander stumbled toward a chair and fell down into it.

She was tired, weak and unsure of where she was.

"You did well," a voice said.

It was Sec chief Robards. She could recognize that vile, detestable voice anywhere.

"I think that old outlander has got eyes for you."

She didn't want to answer, but couldn't stop herself from saying a few words in Doc's defense. "He's kind and polite is all. You could learn a lot from a man like that."

The sec chief's hand rose above his shoulders as if he were going to strike Eleander, but Eleander didn't flinch.

"Go ahead," she said, "beat me here and now, in front of the baron. And see what he thinks."

Robards's hand returned to the table.

"I know you've got plans to overthrow the baron," she said. "I can see it in your eyes, the way you watch him, envy him, want all that he has. I also know that you're skimming jack from the operation." That was a guess, but not an outlandish one, since sec chiefs in De-Mannville were notorious for pocketing a little extra jack whenever they had the chance. It was one of the reasons why they never remained sec chiefs for long. The accusation seemed to be bang on as the confident sneer on the sec chief's face suddenly fell away.

"But let me tell you, Sec *man* Robards, it takes more than an iron-hard fist to be a baron. You might take over from him someday, but you won't last long."

Robards just looked at her, wondering how she'd been able to have such insight. Perhaps the combination of drugs, one down, one up, had unlocked a part of her mind, brought thoughts and ideas from deep inside the brain to the forefront. Whatever the reason, it had him worried.

He wasn't ready to overthrow Baron DeMann just yet, but he couldn't afford to let Eleander talk. It would have been better to let her escape with Moira, because now she'd have to be chilled before she had a chance to make trouble for him with the baron.

"Can I walk you to your room?"

Robards looked behind him and saw it was Moira, the baron's mistress.

"One of my sec men will take her," he said.

"You're welcome to send one along if you like, but I want to talk with my mother about the handsome stranger."

"Of course." The sec chief smiled awkwardly, knowing that crossing the baron's mistress was a sure way to cause trouble with the baron.

Mother and daughter left the dining room, arm in arm.

Robards signaled to one of his sec men. "Follow them. And let me know when Eleander's alone."

The sec man nodded, and hurried to catch up to the two women.

MILDRED SAT by Jak's side, watching the albino teenager struggle to get some rest despite the searing pain in his shoulder. He was also a bit feverish, and there was a good chance that the wound had become infected. She didn't want to give him too much medication, since she couldn't be sure of its quality, but it was obvious that she had to do *something* to help Jak.

She lifted a huge stainless-steel syringe—something that looked as if it had come from Doc's time—off the tray by Jak's bed and began filling it with morphine. He could probably use more than the small amount she'd be giving him, but she didn't want him to become addicted to the drug. She gave him a little more than half of what he could handle.

She cleaned a spot on his arm, jabbed the needle into his flesh, then slowly depressed the plunger.

"Will help?" Jak asked through tightly clenched teeth.

"I'm just giving you something for the pain," she said. "It might help with your fever, too."

Jak nodded.

In minutes, it was obvious that the medicine was working. Jak lay still, no longer jerking back and forth in fits of pain. His breathing had evened out, too, and it looked as if he were going to fall asleep.

Mildred remained by his side.

"Go," Jak said.

"What?"

"Go to J.B."

Mildred smiled, caught a little off guard by Jak's intuition. "I said I would look after you—"

"No need watch sleep."

Mildred considered it. Jak really didn't need anyone to watch over him. He'd be fine sleeping alone for the next few hours, and the friends were safe as guests in the baron's home. Besides that, Doc would be joining him in the room soon, so Jak wouldn't have to be alone. "Well, I could come back and check on you in a few hours, or Doc could watch over you for a while."

"Either way," Jak said. "Not matter. You go. Hello to J.B. for me."

"I'll do that, Jak."

"DID YOU HAVE TO invite that bitch to the table?" the woman said as she unbuttoned her serving smock. She had served the party food during the reception, and now she was serving Sec chief Robards as his own personal gaudy slut.

"One of the outlanders asked for her to join us," the sec chief replied. "The baron couldn't refuse the man. He saved the baron's mistress, after all."

"Saved her," the woman sputtered. "What was she doing outside the ville?"

"I don't know," Robards said, rankled by the question. "Perhaps I should ask a few of my sec men how it was possible that two women were able to get outside the wall unnoticed."

The woman was naked now, smiling coyly. "It's not the fault of any sec men. They're men after all. If those two slipped out of the ville it's because that hag fucked a sec man to open the gate."

"It's an interesting theory," Robards said, rising up from a chair and moving to the woman's side.

While she was in the middle of stroking the brush

through her hair, the baron grabbed a handful of hair and twisted it around his fingers.

"Ow, hey!" she screamed.

"A very interesting theory," the baron repeated. "How often have you done that yourself?"

"What? I don't understand."

"How many times have you fucked a sec man to get what you wanted?"

"Never," she said. "I'm yours."

"My what?"

"Your own personal slut."

"Then how do you know this about Eleander?"

She didn't, but she couldn't back down now. "I've heard the rumors, that's all."

He pulled harder on her hair, almost lifting her off the chair. "And if they turn out to be anything more than rumors, and I find out you're lying to me, I'll string you up and give you a continuous supply of bang so you'll be good for nothing except begging in the street. And the baron's got no use for beggars."

Clumps of hair were beginning to come loose in his hands.

And she was crying now from the pain, tears leaking out from the corners of her eyes.

Still, she dared not argue with him.

He lowered her back onto her chair and popped two tiny yellow pills into her mouth.

She struggled at first, but he forced her to swallow them. In minutes she was looking at him with a pair of glassy eyes.

"I'm sorry, baby," she said, her voice soft and sultry. "I just don't like it when other bitches are around. Can I help it if I want you all to myself?"

"Say what you want about her, but from what Baron DeMann tells me, Moira services him like a champion gaudy slut, which is more than I can say about you."

"Oh, but I want to, Sec chief," she cooed. "You want to try now? C'mon babe, make it with me." She began crawling across the floor toward him. "Give me all you've got."

The sec chief smiled.

"That's more like it," he said under his breath. "All you needed was a slight attitude adjustment."

MOIRA ACCOMPANIED her mother all the way to her mother's quarters. As a whitecoat, and mother to one of the baron's three mistresses, Eleander was given living space that was generous, but kept far away from the baron's residence.

"I think I might have said a little too much to Sec chief Robards tonight," Eleander said, as the fog she'd been under as a result of the drug began to wear off. She was weary, but still able to recollect all that had transpired tonight.

"Too much, how?" her daughter asked.

Eleander checked to see that the sec man following them was well behind. "I told him I suspect him of wanting to overthrow the baron."

Moira smiled. "What sec chief doesn't?"

"I know, but his response was troubling. I think he really *is* planning something."

Moira brought her mother in close. "Mebbe you shouldn't stay in your own quarters tonight."

Eleander glanced back at the sec man. "I think you might be right."

RYAN HELD Krysty tightly in his arms. It had been a while since he'd been able to take his time loving her, and after the frenzied passion of their first session following dinner, Ryan now wanted to rediscover his lover's body slowly.

His hands roamed leisurely over the sculpted muscles of her shoulders and arms, down the small of her back and over the well-formed mounds of her buttocks. Meanwhile, Krysty was making explorations of her own, caressing Ryan's thighs, running her fingers through the tightly curled hair on his chest and eventually finding the thick shaft that jutted from the junction of his legs.

"Oh, lover." She sighed, contented.

Ryan took firm hold of Krysty's hips and brought her closer to him. He wanted to love her slowly, sensually, but his instincts were betraying him. Ryan had learned during his years in the Deathlands to make the most of the moment, because he could never be sure what the future might hold for him. As a result, their lovemaking had always been intense and passionate.

Then, suddenly, blasterfire erupted somewhere outside.

Somewhere close.

In moments, Ryan was on his feet and dressed, the

SIG-Sauer in his hand. Krysty followed him outside into the hall where they were met by J.B. and Mildred.

Shouts and orders were being barked throughout the building.

"J.B., Mildred," Ryan said. "Check on Doc and Jak, then meet us outside." He ran to the end of the hallway where there was a window overlooking the street in front of the building.

"Escape attempt?" J.B. asked, already on the move.

Ryan looked out the window and down the street. "Nope. Looks more like a mutie invasion."

# Chapter Nine

The invasion turned out to be more like a slaughter.

And it was over in minutes.

At the south end of the wall, about a block from the baron's residence, a group of about two dozen muties were scaling the wall, climbing over the rusting hulks of wags in a suicidal attempt to get inside.

By the time Ryan and Krysty had reached the wall, several sec men had taken up positions behind buildings and old oil cans scattered in the street, and were busy trying to pick off the invaders as they crawled down the jagged slope of the walls.

Although a few of the sec men were decent shots, the majority of their blasterfire was missing the mark by a wide margin.

Ryan and Krysty took cover inside a doorway about twenty yards from the wall and began to fire single shots at the muties that had made the most progress climbing over the wall.

Ryan chilled the first one, an old man dressed in ragged clothes that hung off his skin and bones like something that was dead. As the old man cried out for "Bang!", Ryan put a round into his open mouth, sending a chunk of brain matter flying out the back of his head that knocked down the mutie standing behind him.

Krysty waited for that mutie to get to her feet before putting a round from her Smith & Wesson into the woman's chest.

More flowed over the wall.

The longer the firefight went on, the more erratic the sec men's shots became until it was taking them four and five rounds to take down a single mutie.

"Waste of ammo," J.B. said, as he and Mildred joined Ryan and Krysty on the firing line.

"Or else it's bad ammo," Ryan suggested.

Mildred began to fire at the oncoming muties and took one mutie out for every round fired.

"Where's the sec chief?" Ryan asked.

"Haven't seen him," J.B. answered. "Mebbe this is a regular thing, and he doesn't need to show up?"

"It doesn't make any sense!" Mildred exclaimed, still firing at the muties. "They're like lemmings."

"What?"

"Lemmings," she repeated. "Rodents that used to be found in countries like Sweden and Norway. They breed until they run out of food, then they move across country, tearing up everything along the way. When they reach the sea, they just keep on going until they become exhausted from swimming in the water and die...all together."

"That sounds crazy," Krysty said.

"What else would you call muties who scale a wall only to meet a certain death?" Mildred raised her Czech-built target pistol and took aim at a mutie who had made too much progress while she'd been talking. She squeezed the trigger and hit the mutie in the forehead, snapping its neck and sending the body reeling backward.

"It's crazy all right," Ryan said with a nod. "But nothing in this ville makes much sense."

Just then a wag pulled up with Sec chief Robards riding in the back behind the driver. He stood and leveled what looked to be an MP-40 on the gang of muties. It was a remade SMG fashioned out of a combination of solid forgings and stamped steel pieces welded into position.

Robards began firing, sending 9 mm rounds into the muties at a rate of 500 rpm.

"Like killing flies with hammers," Krysty said, between bursts from Robards's gun.

"Or he has more ammo than he knows what to do with," Ryan said.

"Ammo or brains," J.B. quipped.

And then the blasterfire ended.

The muties were strewed across the ground, or hung up on the wall like dead bodies in a war zone.

"Secure the outside perimeter of the wall," Robards shouted. "Check for any stragglers."

The sec men fanned out, looking for any muties who'd made it into the ville and gone into hiding.

Minutes later, the baron arrived on the scene on foot to inspect the carnage. "Well done," he said.

"Thank you, sir," Robards said.

"No, I'm talking about our guests here," the baron stated. "I was watching from my balcony and saw how they were chilling these damn muties. One round, one mutie. It's a lesson I wish a few of your sec men learned before they bankrupt me and this ville."

"Yes, sir." Robards nearly spit the words out of his mouth.

The baron turned toward Ryan. "You wouldn't be looking for a job as a sec chief, would you?"

"Never," Ryan answered.

"Somehow I knew you'd say that." The baron turned and began casually walking back to his residence.

When the baron was out of earshot, Robards had his driver ease the wag over to where Ryan stood so he could have a word with him. "Enjoy it while it lasts, outlander."

Ryan wanted to ask the sec chief what he'd meant, but the man was gone before he had a chance, his wag sending up a huge plume of dirt as it pulled away.

The flying dust forced Ryan to close and cover his eye. When he opened it the sec chief was gone.

WHEN THE MUTIES had begun their invasion and the blasterfire had erupted, Robards had held one of his sec men back from the action.

"The muties," Upward had said, "they're breaching the wall!"

But rather than scramble to seal the breach, the sec chief had grabbed his arm and held it tight. "Relax," he instructed. "There are more than enough sec men on watch to handle the muties. I've got a special job I want you to do for me."

And now, with the sound of blasterfire little more than an echo in the distance, Upward was moving slowly down a hallway, careful not to make a sound, or otherwise betray his presence.

Robards had given Upward a length of steel angle iron, a favorite mutie weapon, and had told him to use it on the troublesome whitecoat named Eleander. He'd told him that the baron had grown tired of her, and today's suspected escape attempt had been the last straw. The baron wanted her gone.

When Upward had questioned the sec chief about it and asked why the baron wasn't giving him the order himself, Robards seemed to grow angry. "The baron doesn't want to alarm his mistress, Eleander's daughter. If she knows that he's capable of having her chilled, it would put a strain on their relationship. He wants it to look like an accident. This attempted invasion by the muties is the perfect cover."

Upward nodded at that and headed off with the weapon in his hand.

The story was going to be that one of the muties had escaped the barrage of blasterfire and gotten into the ville. While looking for bang, the mutie came upon Eleander's room where he chilled her and took her valuables, escaping over another part of the wall. The sec chief even said that he'd be putting torn bits of clothing, and one of Eleander's valuables, somewhere on the wall to provide further evidence of the story's truthfulness.

Upward didn't understand why the mother of the baron's mistress had to be chilled, but there were a lot of things he didn't understand about the baron, the sec chief and the way the ville was run. It seemed like continuous chaos to him, with very little order and routine.

And now he was going to be adding the death of a whitecoat to the mix. If all went according to plan and people believed the sec chief's account of what happened, mebbe there'd be some order in the ville for a while.

Or, mebbe all hell would break loose.

He came upon Eleander's door and stood there in the hall for half a minute while he caught his breath. It was one thing to chill a mutie in defense of the ville, or a whitecoat trying to escape the wall, but this was something different. This was premeditated, cold-blooded chilling. Upward knew that if he did this job he would be a favored sec man in the sec chief's eyes and be promoted quickly through the ranks.

But could he do it?

Yes, he could.

He was a sec man, and he'd been given an order by his chief. It was a no-brainer. If he was guilty of anything it was of thinking about it too much.

He tried the door.

It was unlocked.

He pushed it open. Luckily, the door swung silently on its hinges.

There was a form lying on the cot, fully covered by sheets and a blanket.

Her head was near the pillow.

He would strike there first, silencing her with the opening blow and making the rest of his task that much easier.

Upward held the angle iron in both hands and slowly raised it above his head.

The heavy piece of steel wavered there, as if he were considering not going through with the chilling one last time...his last chance to change his mind.

But then he shook his head slightly and brought the steel down onto Eleander's head. There was a loud *crack!* of bone and a simultaneous *thump!* of flesh as the angle iron connected with the bony plates of her skull.

And then, silence, except for Upward's ragged breathing as he stood over the body waiting for it to move, to twitch, to cry out in pain.

But there was nothing.

No sound.

He kept looking at the bed for a splatter of blood, the stench of fresh gore.

But there was none.

He brought the steel down on the body again. There was another loud *thump,* a tiny *crack,* but nothing more.

No blood.

He pulled the sheet back and saw that the figure he'd thought was Eleander had been nothing more than a down pillow, some extra clothing and a few sticks of kindling wood.

Eleander wasn't there.

At first, Upward felt relief, knowing that he hadn't chilled the woman and wouldn't have to do the deed tonight. But then other thoughts occurred to him, troubling thoughts.

First of all, if Eleander had gone to such lengths to make it appear she was in her room, she probably knew that someone was out to chill her. And second, and perhaps worst of all, Upward was now faced with the task of telling Sec chief Robards that Eleander wasn't in her room.

That she hadn't been chilled.

The sec chief wouldn't be pleased, to say the least.

THE FRIENDS returned to their rooms, more than ready for a good night's sleep. The incident with the invading muties hadn't been much of a fight, but it had come at the end of a long day.

Mildred went into the fourth room to check on Jak and relieve Doc. She could sleep well enough in the room with Jak, and Doc would appreciate spending the rest of the night in his own room.

"How has he been?" Mildred asked.

"Sleeping soundly," Doc answered.

She stood over Jak, felt his forehead to check for fever, and listened to his breathing. His fever had gone down, and his breath was regular. He was sleeping fine.

"What was all the fuss about outside?" Doc asked.

"Bunch of muties tried to breach the wall."

Doc looked confused. "I am not much of a military strategist, certainly not anywhere in the same league as Ryan or J.B., but it strikes me that such an invasion would be doomed to fail. Perhaps even termed suicidal."

"It was," Mildred said. "It was like a shooting gallery out there."

"What would make mutants want to commit such an act?"

Mildred sighed. "There are drugs inside these walls. And whether it's in pre-Dark times or after the blast, drugs have been known to make people do some pretty strange and desperate things."

"Well, I bow to your knowledge of such things, my dear Mildred. While my own knowledge is limited on the subject, I do recall the character of Alice in Lewis Carroll's books having quite the adventure thanks to pills and pipe-smoking caterpillars."

Mildred just shook her head.

"What is it?"

"Funny you should mention that book," Mildred said. "This ville is like an *Alice in Wonderland* situation. A lot of things we've seen are absurd and defy logic, yet somehow the whole thing seems to work."

"Not to worry. We shall be on our way soon enough."

"Right now wouldn't be soon enough, if you ask me."

BY THE TIME Doc made it back to his room, he was looking forward to a good night's rest.

In the morning he'd be meeting Eleander again, and hopefully they would be able to spend some time together.

The thought of the woman brought a smile to Doc's face. He hadn't felt this way in, well, a very long time. It was as if he were a teenager again, filled with excitement and lust over a woman he couldn't wait to get his hands on.

How things had turned. Usually it was Jak who managed to capture the interest of the ladies on their various journeys, but here he was, Theophilus Algernon Tanner, feeling like a schoolboy again, and loving every minute of it.

He opened the door to his room, and immediately felt there was someone inside it, waiting for him. Without a moment's hesitation he unsheathed his swordstick and took up a fighting stance in the doorway.

"I know you're in here," he said, holding the swordstick in front of him. "I suggest you come forward and reveal yourself, or my blade will be the one to discover your whereabouts."

"Doc? Is that you?"

It was a female's voice.

"Eleander?"

"Yes."

"What are you doing here?"

She stepped out of the shadows, and was absolutely radiant in a long-sleeved white nightgown that hugged her body closely, yet was thin enough to be see-through. "I...I didn't want to spend my night alone."

"Well, I, uh, well, in addition to being speechless, I am flattered. Oh, more than that, I am thrilled."

"I hoped you would be."

"How could I not be, in the company of such a lovely, lovely lady?"

"You're too kind," she said, undoing the string that kept the front of the nightgown together.

Doc watched her pull aside the halves of the gown, exposing fully rounded breasts that were capped by a pair of pert nipples.

"In addition to being kind, I can be naughty, too," Doc said.

"Of that, I have no doubt."

Doc closed the door behind him.

It didn't open again until morning.

# Chapter Ten

Baron Schini was up before the dawn.

She had three sec men riding with her in her wag. The wag was shiny, big and black, and although it was missing two of its four doors, it was still an impressive vehicle.

The messenger's two-wheeled wag had been serviced by the baron's mechanics and had been topped up with alcohol.

"Ready to go?" the messenger asked.

The baron leaned up against her wag and moved her head in the direction of one of her sec men.

"His name is Slade," she said. "I wanted you to meet him before we headed out."

Slade was a big and dirty man with long scraggly hair, and several missing teeth.

The baron nodded in the man's direction. "He's carrying a Gewehr 43. Ever heard of that make of blaster?"

The messenger shook his head.

"'Course you haven't. With that sight on top it's an excellent sniper's weapon. So if you think we'll just rumble out into the Deathlands and you'll take off on that little machine of yours, just remember that Slade here is good with the blaster and will blow a hole through your head before you're able to put twenty yards between you and my wag."

The messenger swallowed, and licked his lips.

The baron smiled sardonically. "Do you understand?"

"Yes, Baron, I understand."

"I thought you might." A pause, then, "All right, then let's move out."

TWENTY MINUTES after the baron and the messenger had left Indyville, Sec chief Viviani gathered together a group of six wags and led them out of the ville. Five of the wags carried sec men while the sixth vehicle was a war wag with a .303-caliber machine blaster on a swivel mount.

The plan was simple.

Baron Schini would get inside DeMann's complex. When the baron was told that his guest was the same outlander who murdered his brother, he'd become incensed. Then, while Baron DeMann was busy getting rid of the outlanders, Sec chief Viviani would enter the ville and take it over from the inside.

There was going to be a bloody firefight, but Baron Schini had had her eye on DeMann's operation for years, and this seemed like the best time to make her move.

She had the blasters.

She had the element of surprise.

And there would be six outlanders who would be keeping DeMann's sec men busy while Baron Schini took control of the ville.

Sec chief Viviani smiled at the thought of his baron's plan. With the baron taking over from DeMann, it would leave him as the second in command who controlled Indyville for Baron Schini.

How long would it take, he wondered, to take full control of the ville and have Baron Schini chilled?

It was an interesting thought, one that kept the sec chief's mind occupied for almost the entire journey.

MILDRED CHECKED on Jak in the morning and found he was doing better. He was a still a little hot, but the wound looked to be healing nicely.

"Hungry?" Mildred asked him, stretching out the stiffness that the night on the cot had given her.

"Could eat horse."

Mildred smiled. "The baron here has got plenty of things, but I haven't seen one of those yet. You might have to settle for stale bread and an apple."

Jak licked his lips. "Be good, too."

"I'll see what I can find."

ELEANDER LED the friends to the kitchen where several people were already busy serving breakfast to the baron's sec force. They were each given a bowl of what looked like cornmeal, a slice of bread and cup of water flavored—or perhaps just colored—with fruit juice.

"Not great," J.B. said, cleaning the bottom of his bowl with his slice of bread. "But not bad."

"Had worse," Ryan said. "A lot worse."

"I don't think this is what Jak had in mind when I mentioned breakfast, but I don't think he'll complain."

As the friends made small talk, several of the sec men

seemed to grow interested in their conversation. The previous night's episode at the wall hadn't made Ryan and the others any friends among the ville's sec force, and it seemed the sec men were looking for a reason to start a fight.

"Something wrong with your food?" one of the sec men, a dirty black-haired man with a thick beard and big nose, said. What few teeth remained in his mouth were yellow and rotting.

"On the contrary, my hirsute friend," Doc said. "We have not had gruel this good in months. I'm tempted to ask for seconds."

The sec man was moving closer to the group of friends. "You got a smart mouth, old man."

Doc nodded graciously. "I shall take that as a compliment, but while I appreciate being called 'smart,' my mouth merely says what my brain tells it. So in fact, what you are saying is that my brain is smart, and I have known that for years...thank you."

The sec man continued to approach Doc, his hand on the butt of his blaster.

Ryan watched the sec man closely, taking out his SIG-Sauer and keeping it concealed under the table in case he needed to use it in a hurry. Around the table, he knew that the rest of the friends were doing the exact same thing.

"You've got a big mouth, too, I see."

Doc shrugged. "No larger than most. Over the years I have found it to be large enough to allow sufficient quantities of food in, and a sufficient number of words out. Some might say more than a sufficient number of words, but I have never had any trouble making myself understood."

Everyone in the room seemed to be on triple alert, and the situation was seconds away from erupting into a firefight.

"You think you're all better than us?" the sec man said. "You think you're something special, don'tya?"

Eleander moved to get up from the table, but Doc put his hand on her shoulder to keep her seated at his side.

"Better? Not at all." Doc shook his head. "But, my good sec man, I do happen to be a very *special* human being, several hundred years old, as a matter of fact."

The sec man stared at Doc with a confused look on his face, as if he wasn't sure if he should laugh or be insulted.

"I was alive when your great-great-great-grandfather was still in diapers and the world was a much kinder and gentler place."

A couple of sec men at the tables laughed, but it turned out that the sec man confronting Doc had no sense of humor. "I've had about as much bullshit from you as I can stand, old man," he said, racing forward with a clenched fist.

Ryan and the rest of the friends raised their weapons and aimed them at the charging sec man.

The other sec men also had their weapons out, each one leveled at Doc's head.

But rather than pulling out his LeMat, Doc unsheathed his swordstick and held the blade horizontally before him in the path of the charging sec man.

The sec man stopped in his tracks, as if the blade was a line in the sand that would bring dire consequences if crossed.

For a moment the room was deathly silent, neither side wanting to make the next move, a move which would undoubtedly end up with people getting chilled on both sides.

"Put the blasters away," a voice said with a mixture of tiredness and irritation.

Ryan turned to see the baron standing in the doorway.

"I'm happy to see tensions running high," he said. "A genuine dislike of the opposition will make for a great game this afternoon."

Blasters were lowered, then replaced in their holsters.

"Linsley," the baron said, "save it for later."

The sec man took several steps backward, but never took his eyes off Doc. "Yes, Baron."

Doc nodded to the man, then put away his blade. "I look forward to testing our skills in good-natured sporting competition."

Sec man Linsley turned and joined the other sec men at the table without another word.

"Did you really mean what you said?" Eleander asked, when everyone returned to their meals.

"About what, my dear?"

"About being hundreds of years old."

"How old do you think I am?"

She looked at him a long time. "Not a day over fifty-nine."

"You're very kind," Doc replied. "But I have always

believed that you are as young as you feel, and while my actual age can at times be the subject of great debate, you have made me feel positively young again."

Eleander laughed like a young girl. "Would you like to go for a walk, or a tour of the production facilities?"

"Yes, I would like that," Doc replied. "I would like that very much."

MILDRED RETURNED to Jak in the friends' quarters, bringing the injured albino teen his breakfast.

"What this?"

"It's cornmeal, sort of. It'll make you stronger."

Jak took a spoon of the gruel and sampled it. Then he shook his head, making sure not to move his shoulder too much.

"What's wrong?"

"Not taste like chicken."

Mildred just looked at him.

And then Jak smiled, and continued to eat.

RYAN, J.B. AND KRYSTY went to the game arena after breakfast to check the setup and develop a battle plan for beating the baron's sec men.

J.B. paced out the arena and learned it was roughly thirty yards wide and seventy yards long. The wall around it was chest high and was curved evenly in each of the corners. The dirt floor surface of the arena was dissected by several lines crossing the width of it in the middle and almost at the midway point between the middle and each end. Apparently, the center of the arena was a neutral zone, while each end was either a defending zone, or an attacking zone, depending on which team you were on. There were also several obstacles strewed about the arena floor, such as concrete walls, burned-out wags, and trapdoors set into the floor, some which led under the arena and connected with other trapdoors, and some which led a few feet and then stopped abruptly at a dead end, making the trapdoors aptly named. Exits were situated at each of the four corners and led out into the ville. Finally, on the south side of the area was a line of targets, the splatters of which they'd seen from the wag when they'd entered the ville. On the other side of the arena was a line of stalls where the sec men stood while shooting at the targets.

"It's like the ruins of a rad-blasted ville," Krysty said, giving a black hulk of a wag a push with her boot, only to discover that the thing still rolled on its wheels.

"Been in places like this plenty times before," J.B. remarked. "Only it was no game."

"Let's check all of the trapdoors," Ryan commanded. "I want to know where all of them lead. And I want to know where these exits go, too, just in case we have to use one to get away."

"Expecting trouble, lover?"

Ryan shook his head. "Are you?"

Krysty was silent, searching her feelings for any hint that they were in danger. "Nothing."

"Then I'm just being cautious. If we're going to play this game, then we might as well play to win and take as much ammo with us when we leave as we can."

"Go hard, or go home," J.B. barked.

"You think we might lose?" There was surprise in Krysty's voice.

Ryan shook his head. "Not a chance."

ELEANDER SLIPPED a coat over Doc's shoulders and smoothed out the creases in the fabric.

Doc took a moment to feel the crispness of the garment and run his fingers up and down the sleeve. "It is so clean."

"Has to be," Eleander said. "The baron's operation wouldn't work if things got dirty. He's developed chemicals and cleaners that make things white. I hope it's all right."

"It is fine."

She led him inside a large white room that was filled with all sorts of beakers, burners and vats. Two other people were in the room dressed in lab coats, busily moving trays from one part of the room to another.

"This is where we make insulin for a person with diabetes," Eleander explained. "We used to make it from the pancreases of dogs, but that was very expensive and we went through a lot of dogs just to make a little bit of it. Then he realized that with so many muties dying in and around the ville, why not make it from human pancreases. It makes for a better insulin and we make more of it, and more cheaply."

"That's..." Doc searched for the word. He wanted to say disgusting, but that was just an initial knee-jerk type of reaction. The baron was actually showing himself to be quite resourceful. Perhaps even a genius. "That's amazing," he said at last.

Eleander shrugged. "The baron's ancestors were all great whitecoats. And he has access to some pretty big pre-Dark books. He says that if he has the raw material, he can make any medicine that the pre-Dark whitecoats could. That's why he spends so much time in his garden growing different things."

"But how many diabetics are there to trade with?" From what Doc knew about the disease it was unlikely that anyone born with a severe case of it in the Deathlands would survive very long, just as it had been with diabetes during his time. That would leave type-two diabetics who contracted the disease later in life. If they survived, and had the jack to pay for the insulin, it was possible they'd be able to survive, lucky to be alive.

"Just one. There is a baron in an East Coast ville that has the disease. All of this production is for him. We make shipments each couple of months."

"And he pays?"

Eleander let out a little laugh. "Of course he pays. If he doesn't have it, he'll die."

Drugs, Doc thought. There was always someone desperate enough to pay the price, no matter what the cost.

She showed Doc around the room, explaining how the insulin was made and stored. She also let him feel and touch the equipment as much as he wanted.

Doc pointed his swordstick at a door at one end of the room. "Is there another laboratory in there?"

"You can't go in there!" Eleander exclaimed.

Doc was speechless. Such outbursts were uncharacteristic of the woman.

"Is it secret?"

"Yes. As a matter of fact, it is."

"Say no more," Doc said, raising his hand. "I have been around my share of secret laboratories to know that if you don't want me to know what's in there, then I probably don't want to know, either."

Eleander seemed relieved.

"Just tell me one thing. Is it possible that the thing on the other side of that door could harm people, people such as my friends and I?"

"No, what's in there doesn't hurt. It only makes a person feel good."

BY MIDDAY the group traveling with the messenger were nearing DeMannville. The trip had taken twice as long as it should have, slowed by Baron Schini's insistence on making the trip a leisurely drive between villes.

A couple of times the messenger had thought about revving the engine of his wag and shooting off across country and leaving the baron in a pile of dust, but every time he turned, Sec man Slade had the Gewehr 43 pointed at his back. The damn blaster never wavered. If he did try to run, he'd be lucky to make it ten or twenty yards before his back would be torn to shreds.

A quarter mile outside the ville, the messenger stopped and let Baron Schini's wag catch up.

"I'll go on ahead," the messenger said, "and inform

the baron of your arrival so he can properly greet you when you enter the ville."

Baron Schini smiled and slowly shook her head. "That was a good try, but I think we'll all enter the ville together. DeMann doesn't have exclusive rights to the grief this man Ryan has caused our families, and I've got just as big an interest in his execution as anyone."

The messenger nodded, started up his wag and led the baron the rest of the way to the ville.

At the gate, the messenger was stopped by the two sec men on duty.

"What's that bitch doing here?" the smaller one said, spitting into the dirt to show his contempt.

"She wants to see the baron."

"Well, the baron don't want to see her," the second sec man said. He held his longblaster in one hand, the butt of it resting against his right hip.

The messenger sighed and nodded in agreement. "The baron won't, but Sec chief Robards will."

The two sec men at the gate suddenly became more interested in the visiting baron.

"Get the chief," the second sec man said.

The smaller one turned to enter through the small door to the left of the gate, but was stopped by Robards, who was standing in the doorway and had been listening to the exchange on the other side of the gate.

The chief was uninterested in the presence of Baron Schini, and wanted only to talk to his messenger. "Well," he grunted. "Is he the one?"

"Yes, Chief. He did the baron's son, too."

Robards smiled demonically. "Let her in, then," he said.

The two sec men looked at each other in confusion—it was no secret that Robards hated Baron Schini—but they opened the gate as they were told.

Moments later, Baron Schini entered the ville, the procession of wags looking very much like a triumphant motorcade entering a newly conquered ville.

# Chapter Eleven

"So, you're sure it's him?" Robards asked.

The messenger nodded. "The journal was pretty clear on the matter. The outlander that killed the baron's brother was named Ryan Cawdor."

"Anything about his eye?"

"Only that his right eye is blue."

"That's good enough for me," the sec chief said. "And I think it will be good enough for the baron, too. Good job."

"What about Baron Schini?"

"Right. I suppose she wants to be the one to chill the outlander."

"She might, but so far she's said she only wants to be there to see him suffer."

The sec chief was silent for several moments, as if thinking. "Sure, we can do that for her."

"Got a plan, Chief?"

"The outlanders will be competing against some of our men in the arena this afternoon. Make sure Baron Schini has a place of honor for the contest next to our own baron. She might prove to be a useful scapegoat if something bad should happen to the baron."

The messenger laughed.

"Now, let's not keep the visiting baron waiting."

They left the sec chief's office and went outside, where they met with Baron Schini and her two sec men.

"Baron," Robards greeted her with a gracious nod. He offered his hand to shake, but she ignored the gesture.

"I was expecting Baron DeMann, but it's about time *somebody* came to greet me."

Robards smiled. "We're busy getting ready for a contest in the arena this afternoon."

"A contest? Who's challenging?"

"My best men, and the outlanders."

Schini's eyebrows arched in surprise. "Including the bastard who chilled my son?"

"The very one."

"Mmmm, I'll enjoy watching him die."

"Perhaps, but these outlanders happen to be very good at staying alive and chilling their enemies."

The baron grew angry. "You don't have to tell *me* that. They wouldn't have been able to chill my dear sweet Luca if they weren't."

Robards paused. Luca Schini had been little more than sewer scum, which is why he'd been a sec man for someone like Baron Zeal and not his own mother. Still, the baron's anger was an asset. He'd be able to use it against the one-eyed outlander as well as Baron DeMann.

"Luca was an excellent sec man," Robards lauded. "I would have been proud to have him in my service."

"Cut the crap, Robards, and take me to see Baron DeMann. I'm sure we'll have plenty to talk about."

"Of course." Robards smiled. "This way."

LESS THAN TWO MILES from DeMannville, Sec chief Viviani turned the wag train off the main, weed-choked road and led them into the woods far enough so that the brush and trees would keep them all hidden from view.

When all the wags had stopped and the air was filled with the ticking sound of cooling engines, he called out the names of his two best sec men. "Sherman and Roy!"

Two young men appeared at his side.

"I want you to head the rest of the way to DeMannville on foot."

The two sec men nodded. "Yes, Chief."

"If anything happens in the ville I should know about, one of you delivers the message back to me while the other remains back watching the ville. If Baron Schini gives the signal, then you both return and join us for the invasion."

The sec men remained still and silent, waiting to be dismissed.

"Depending on how fast you can travel on foot, we should be slipping in through the gate and into the ville no more than twelve minutes after the baron's signal."

"How about ten minutes?" Sherman said.

Viviani nodded. "All right, ten."

Sherman and Roy headed off through the trees in the direction of DeMannville. Their footsteps could be heard for a minute before they faded into silence.

"What about the rest of us, Chief?" someone asked.

The sec chief pulled a partially smoked cheroot from a pocket on his sleeve and lit it with a butane lighter.

"We wait," he said, puffing on the cheroot.

ROBARDS CALLED Katz into his office.

Katz seemed frightened when he entered. Being called in to the sec chief's office was never a good thing. "You wanted to see me, Chief?"

"Ah, there you are."

"I do something wrong?"

"No, not at all."

Katz let out a sigh.

"I wanted to see you because I've got a little job I want you to do for me."

BARON DEMANN WAS busy working in his garden.

In the past six months he had been trying to grow a hardier variety of poppy, or *papaver somniferum* as it was called in one of his books. While he'd had little trouble making opium from the plants, the unripened seeds contained several alkaloids including morphine, a very powerful painkiller, and codeine, a milder painkiller, but still very effective. The poppies he'd been growing up until now had produced few seeds, or else dried up before coming to term, and as a result he could only make opium and a small amount of morphine from the crop. However, each of the last few generations of poppy plants had done better than the one before, and it looked as if the current set of plants were close to being right for the production of morphine and codeine on a large scale. If he was able to produce more of those drugs as well as the ones he'd been making for years, he might be able to sell in villes farther down the East Coast. There were a few in Virginia that were wide open and ready for his wares.

"Excuse me, Baron DeMann."

It was the voice of his sec chief.

The baron, on his hands and knees between the rows of plants, looked up. "I'm busy, what is it?"

"Baron Schini is here to see you."

"What the fuck does that bitch want?"

Robards inhaled a deep breath. "Do you remember when the outlanders arrived, I told you there was something about them I needed to check out?"

"Sure."

"Well, I sent a rider to Indyville to look through the journals Baron Schini has in her library there."

The baron rose off his knees and was now standing between the plants and wiping the dirt from his hands. "And?"

"I sent him there to check on the death of your brother—"

"He died at Spearpoint, a stupid sec man with more balls than brains."

"I know that, Baron. What I was checking on was the identity of the man who chilled him."

"It was an outlander working for the Trader who fought back when that asshole Zeal tried to rip him off."

"That's the general story, yes, but I wanted to check

to see if there were anything in the journals about the deaths of your brother and Baron Schini's son."

The baron looked at his sec chief with an intense gaze. "And now she's here. What did you find out?"

"Well, I'd remembered hearing people talk about Spearpoint being leveled by Trader and his men. The Trader had plenty of men working for him, but one of them had just a single eye."

"One eye?"

Robards nodded.

"And you think our guest, Ryan, is the same man?"

"The one that chilled your brother, and the baron's son."

DeMann said nothing for the longest time. "So this one-eyed bastard has been staying in my ville, enjoying my hospitality, eating my food, fucking in the bed I provided for him, and all the time he's the one who chilled my brother."

The sec chief nodded.

"That takes some balls."

"The biggest."

"And that's good work." The baron slapped his sec chief on the back. "How did you remember?"

Robards shrugged. "I just recalled hearing stories about a one-eyed man. When he showed up outside our ville, I figured it was worth checking out."

In truth, Robards had once been Sec man Robards on Baron Zeal's sec force at Spearpoint. He'd remembered seeing a one-eyed man in the Trader's party and knew he was responsible for the deaths of a lot of Zeal's men.

It had been a long shot that Baron Schini's journals made mention of Spearpoint, but Robards had decided long before he'd sent a messenger that he would tell his baron that the outlander named Ryan had chilled the baron's brother. It was just the sort of diversion the sec chief needed to chill the baron and start devoting all of the ville's resources to making a lot more of the jack-making drugs like jolt, dreem and bang.

DeMann clenched his fists, turning the knuckles white and stretching the skin taut over his fingers. "None of those outlanders leave here alive."

"Of course not, Baron."

"I want them all chained up in the hot box where I can watch them die slowly, and in great pain."

"I remind you that Baron Schini is here to watch the outlander die. If you chill him slowly, it means she may remain here for a week or more."

"Right." The baron nodded. "Then a .38 round through the forehead for the one-eyed bastard, or maybe one through his good eye so he can see it coming. But that's only after I put one in his foot, in his kneecap, both hands and shoulders… The rest of them get one behind the ear."

"That's good, but…"

"But what?"

"I've got another idea. Perhaps it's even a better one."

"What is it?"

Robards told him.

It brought a smile to the baron's face.

JAK WAS ALONE in his room.

At his insistence, Mildred had gone to meet with

Ryan and the others to talk about the challenge they'd have in the arena in the afternoon. She said she'd be back in a few minutes, but she'd already been gone for quite a while now.

It somehow sounded wrong to Jak—blasters that didn't chill. The only reason anyone used a blaster was to chill and to be able to point a blaster at someone, squeeze the trigger and know that person wouldn't die, wouldn't even be hurt, wasn't right. If you used a blaster that didn't chill, then you could get careless with it, using it when you didn't have to, or hesitating when your life was in danger.

Every time Jak held a blaster to someone's head, the only reason he did it was to blow the person's head apart. Not to scare them, not to hurt them, but to chill them. If he just wanted to hurt someone, he could always use his knives. With his assortment of leaf-bladed throwing knives, Jak could cut someone, chill someone, even poison the blades so they died days later. Knives could do all those things, but blasters…blasters were meant for chilling.

But, as crazy as he thought this contest was, at least after they'd won it, they'd be on their way with all the ammo they could carry. Jak was down to less than a dozen rounds for his .357 Colt Python, and in a firefight twelve rounds wouldn't last more than a few minutes. It would be good to feel the heavy tug of ammo pulling on his pockets and belt, but it would be even better to be gone from this place. Even though they'd been well treated and well fed here—and Mildred had been able to fix him up with the help of some of their medicines—Jak didn't like the place. There seemed to be little order in this ville—so many people doing whatever they pleased and chaos seemed to erupt too often without warning. It was like paradise one moment, a hellhole the next, and you could never be sure which one it was going to be or for how long.

As far as Jak was concerned, it would be good to be out in the Deathlands again.

The sooner the better.

Just then the door to his room opened and the whitecoat named Katz entered. He had a small metal box with him, the outside of it a shiny chromed steel that reminded Jak of the chromed guns he'd seen people carry in some of the eastern villes. Flashy, clean, but nothing anybody who knew anything about blasters would use.

"How are you feeling?" Katz asked, flipping open the lid of the box.

"Good. Where Mildred?"

"Oh, uh, she's with your other friends, getting ready for this afternoon's challenge. She said she'd be busy for the next little while so she asked me to come by and give you your medicine."

Jak didn't believe that. Mildred would never send a stranger to do her work. None of the friends ever passed off responsibilities to anyone other than the people in their group.

Nobody else could be trusted.

Jak slipped his left arm inside his jacket and pulled out one of the leaf-bladed throwing knives hidden there.

At that moment two sec men entered the room.

Katz took the shiny steel syringe from the box, lifted the pointed end toward the ceiling and depressed the plunger until a thin stream of reddish liquid spurted out the tip of the needle.

He moved toward Jak.

"What that?"

"It will help with your pain, and your fever." A smile appeared at the corner of Katz's mouth. "It will make you feel real good."

Jak shook his head.

The sec men grabbed him, one on each shoulder.

A searing pain burned in his wounded shoulder as the sec men pushed him back onto the bed.

Katz neared.

Jak kicked him with his right leg, the toe of his boot connecting with one of his kidneys.

The whitecoat's smile was gone. His teeth were bared now and he looked evil, and a little bit mad.

One of the sec men punched Jak in the side of the head with a beefy fist. The blow stunned the youth, but he remained conscious.

"Hold him still."

"Fucker's stronger than he looks," the sec man on the left yelled.

The sec man on the right punched him again, only this time he hit Jak's shoulder, causing the albino teen to see sparks of pain behind his eyes.

The whitecoat was over him. The red liquid from the syringe was leaking onto the sheets, leaving tiny brown stains...like blood.

Jak's left hand appeared from beneath his jacket.

He flicked his wrist and caught the whitecoat in the throat.

The man screamed and grabbed at his neck, rich red blood leaking through his fingers.

But while Jak had injured the man, most likely fatally, the whitecoat was still able to stab the needle into his thigh and depress the plunger.

Jak felt a coolness enter his leg. The thigh muscle tingled, and that tingly feeling quickly began to spread. His right leg went limp, feeling as if it were—he searched his mind for the word—enchanted. Yes, that was it, his leg felt enchanted, as if it had been touched by magic.

The rest of his body began to feel the same thing. Down to his feet, and over his penis and testicles, his stomach, arms, wrists, hands, fingers...all enchanted. And then his face tingled and his head...his head felt as if it had detached from the rest of his body.

He saw stars and butterflies.

He saw women, all that he wanted. There was food—beef and corn and fruit.

He saw Christina and Jenny. He spent time with them on the shores of a lake loving each other...like a family.

"Enjoy it while it lasts, freak," the whitecoat said, the blood still pouring from his neck.

Jak was enjoying it.

He lay back on the cot, relaxed.

And wishing that this feeling would never end.

"THERE WILL BE four on our team," Ryan said. He jabbed his chest with his thumb, then pointed to the others. "Me, Krysty, J.B. and Mildred."

Doc coughed an "ahem." "I have no question about your leadership of this group, my dear Ryan, but I would not be much of a member of it if I didn't complain about not being invited to the party." Doc stood with his swordstick in front of him and both hands on top of its silver lion's-head handle.

"You'll be watching us, Doc, with Jak and Eleander."

Doc nodded, suddenly pleased with the assignment. "Oh, I see... Well, excuse my little outburst. As usual, you have made an excellent leadership decision, and I ask that you excuse my ignorance for not seeing the logic of it immediately."

"No problem, Doc."

"I will make our little trio the best cheering section ever," Doc said. "Why, I remember cheering the Oxford eights in a victory of Cambridge. I was so hoarse afterward that I could barely speak a word for a week."

"Something to look forward to, then," J.B. quipped.

"Let's get our gear together and have it all ready to go after the challenge. I want to load up on ammo and leave as soon as we're done, so make sure nothing gets left behind."

"I'm not sure Jak will be ready to travel," Mildred said.

"He'll have to be," Ryan countered. "The longer we stay here the less I like it."

"I'm with you, lover."

"All right, then. Let's get packed."

ROBARDS LED Baron Schini on a circuitous route through the baron's residence, making sure to take her up and down as many flights of stairs as possible.

"Where the fuck are you taking me?" she demanded after they'd gone up two flights of stairs and gone down one.

"The building is being refitted. There are rooms that are best avoided until they're done."

"Bullshit! You're just having your fun with me, and I don't like it. If I don't see the baron soon, one of my sec men will open a window and start taking out citizens of this festering little ville of yours with his blaster."

Robards ignored the threat. "Ah, here we are." He opened the door to Baron DeMann's office, then walked right through to the door that led to the back room.

The large back room was outfitted like a pre-Dark pharmacy, only not as clean. The shelves on all four walls were lined with dozens of plastic jars and bottles of different shapes and sizes. Some were filled with capsules, some with roughly made tablets, and still others with powders of varying color and texture. At one end of the room there was a noisy pre-Dark refrigerator that looked as if it had been remade several times, the last time fitted with a compressor taken from a cooling unit that had to have been four times bigger than the refrigerator. Cables snaked out the window to a noisy electrical generator outside. In the center of the room was a long freestanding island, holding beakers, burners and trays filled with medicinal cultures and viruses. It was marked with a faded and worn, black-and-yellow card that read "Biohazard."

Baron DeMann stood at one corner of the island, wearing a pair of crudely made black rubber gloves. He held a glass beaker in his hands. Inside the beaker was a cloudy liquid that looked a lot like milky water.

"Still looking for the fountain of youth, DeMann?"

The baron didn't look up from his work. His eyes fixed on the beaker as if it would do strange things if he took his eyes off it for even a second. "Baron Schini," he greeted. "Pleasure to see you, as always."

"I'd have less trouble believing you if you actually looked at me when you said that."

Baron DeMann's gaze remained on the beaker. "If you'll excuse my rudeness, I happen to be working with a significant amount of hydrochloric acid, which among other things is highly corrosive."

"Did you say acid?"

"Yes, a highly corrosive aqueous solution of hydrogen chloride. In pre-Dark times it was used industrially to remove zinc from galvanized scrap iron and in the production of chlorides and chlorine."

Baron Schini laughed nervously. Like many barons, she never quite understood what DeMann was up to with his chemicals and concoctions until it was too late.

One story she'd heard about Baron DeMann had him solving a dispute over jack owed to DeMann by a baron in Florida by tainting the water supply of the baron's ville with a type of bacteria. Forty-two people died and more than two hundred and fifty got deathly ill. The dispute was resolved less than a week later.

"Usually the acid is diluted in water and might burn through clothing or cause minor skin irritation. This is pure, or as pure as I can make it, and it could eat through your flesh, muscle and bone like a mutie rat, only faster and more painfully."

Baron Schini swallowed, but showed no other outward sign of her discomfort, knowing DeMann would be all over any perceived weakness. "What are you going to do with it?"

Baron DeMann poured some of the acid into a half sphere of plastic and then pressed a second half sphere over the first, creating a perfectly round ball filled with hydrochloric acid. "Let's just say it's a surprise for the one-eyed asshole who murdered my brother."

Baron Schini was silent. She had wanted to chill the outlander who had killed her son herself, but a round from a blaster didn't seem to be as fitting as what DeMann had in mind.

"You wanted to talk to me about something?" Baron DeMann said, filling a row of balls with acid.

She shook her head. "Not as much talk to you, as tell you that I appreciate you allowing me to watch the outlander suffer."

The baron finished filling the balls and had a few

drops of acid left in the bottom of the beaker. He poured them out onto the wooden top of the table, and the wood bubbled and smoked as an inch-deep line was burned into the surface. "Oh, he'll be suffering all right, because his death is going to come oh, so slowly."

WHEN MILDRED RETURNED to check on Jak, the albino teenager was sleeping soundly and sporting a slight smile on his face. She put a hand over his forehead to gauge his temperature.

He felt normal.

"You're doing better," she said.

At first Jak didn't stir, but when she repeated her words, his eyes fluttered opened. They were a bit red, and shinier than usual, but she attributed that to everything he'd been through these past couple of days.

"How do you feel?"

"Good."

"We'll be heading out later today," she said. "After the challenge. Think you're up to it?"

"No problem."

She flicked her head toward the door. "We're all going to the arena now. You'll be watching with Doc and Eleander."

"No problem."

That seemed like an strange response from Jak. Even though he was still recovering from his injury, Mildred would have expected Jak to want to be in on the challenge. Instead, he was content just to sit on the sidelines and watch. That wasn't like him, but then again, maybe he was growing up and maturing, knowing his limitations.

"C'mon," she said. "I'll help you down off the bed."

Without a word, Jak rolled over and got onto his feet. He struggled to stay upright, and had to put a hand onto the bedpost to steady himself, but after a few moments he was standing on his own.

"You're doing better than I thought."

Jak just smiled.

Mildred found the smile curious. It wasn't the smile of someone who was pleased with his progress. It was the smile of someone who was somewhere else....

In another world.

"Let's go," she said uncertainly. "Doc will take you to the arena."

ELEANDER MET UP with Doc and accompanied him on his way back to their room to collect Jak and bring him to the arena. Doc greeted the woman with a hug and a kiss and took the time to smell her hair, which seemed as if it were scented with ambrosia.

"The baron makes his own soaps," she said. "Flowers for the women and musk for the men."

"Scented soap," Doc boomed. "Amazing. In all my time in the Deathlands, I have never come across anyone who was so enterprising in his reclamation of some of the more subtler aspects of civilization."

"The baron is a bit of a mad genius."

"He would have to be to put so much effort into making things smell good." Doc took a step back so he could look Eleander in the eye. "But I am grateful to the man, or should I say 'DeMann,' ha!...for making such a beautiful flower smell as good as she looks."

Eleander's face turned a pale shade of red.

As they turned to start toward Doc's quarters, Eleander grabbed Doc's arm. "You know, it's not all flowers and sunshine here."

"Of course not. Nowhere is, but from what I have seen it is a better life than most can ever hope for in the Deathlands."

"From what you've seen..." she reminded him.

"That's right."

Eleander looked up at Doc. "But there is a lot you haven't seen. A lot you don't know about."

"What are you saying?"

"Do you recall yesterday when you asked what was behind the door in the laboratory?"

"Yes, of course. You didn't want me going in there and I understood that completely. I know that some things are meant to be kept secret. If the baron is doing research into new chemicals, he would not want people poking around in his work without his knowledge. It is simply a matter of respect, and I am perfectly content to give the man his due." Doc let out a sigh. "Believe me, I would have appreciated it immensely if people had not tampered or experimented with my own research."

Eleander was silent for a long time.

"What is it?" Doc asked. "Have I offended you in some way?"

"No, not at all. On the contrary, you've actually shamed me."

"Shamed you? Oh, please accept my humblest apologies."

"No need to apologize. Indeed, I'm the one who should apologize to you."

Doc shook his head. "I am afraid I do not understand."

They sat down on the concrete wall of an ancient flower bed long overgrown by weeds.

"I haven't been telling you the whole truth about this ville, and I feel badly for it."

"Whatever you've kept to yourself, I am sure you've had your reasons."

"The baron doesn't only produce medicines here. He also grows and refines a lot of drugs, bad ones like wolfweed, jolt and dreem. And there's others who have tampered with what he's accomplished to produce even more potent drugs."

Doc nodded knowingly. He paused a moment, then continued. "I appreciate your candor, my dear sweet Eleander, but I suspect Ryan and the others have already arrived at that conclusion and therefore that is why we shall be leaving this ville immediately after we're done with this silly little game the baron has arranged for us."

"The baron deals in jolt and dreem, and even though he's addicted to both, he doesn't allow it to be traded freely inside the ville."

"A foolish and wise man all at the same time. But if there are drugs produced here, there's no way he could prevent them being bought and sold on the black market."

"But the baron isn't the dangerous one in the ville. The one you have to be careful of is Sec chief Robards."

"Oh."

"He doesn't know anything about making drugs, but he's persuaded a bunch of whitecoats to create new drugs for him, new and deadly drugs, including a powerful hallucinogen called bang."

"Bang? That's what the mutie wanted from us."

"The sec chief has been experimenting with the drug on people on the fringes of the ville. He gives the drug away and, it's highly addictive…

"And it acts on their central nervous systems," Doc chimed in. "Producing changes in moods and hallucinations."

"Yes," Eleander said.

"And it produces suicidal feelings, too, does it not, which would explain why those so-called muties climbed the wall last night when they knew they'd be slaughtered."

"Yes, and lately it's even been causing mutations in long-term users."

"And you think this monster of a sec chief is out to hurt us? Surely he could have chilled us all a dozen times over if he wanted."

"I can't be sure what he has in mind, but I do know that he's plotting to get rid of the baron. I think he's going to try to use your friends as a scapegoat."

"But how? The baron won't be in the arena, and the blasters used in the challenge are little more than toys."

"I said I don't know exactly how, but I have a feeling the challenge is a small part of a larger plan to overthrow the baron. You see, the baron has never been very fond of outlanders, since it was a group of outlanders like yours that chilled his brother at Spearpoint. Things like your staying overnight and the challenge in the arena are, well, unusual for this ville."

"Spearpoint?" Doc whispered. "I've been to Spearpoint, or rather, I was there to see it blown to kingdom come."

Eleander put a hand on Doc's shoulder. "Promise me you'll be careful today."

"I assure you my lady," Doc said, rising to his feet. "If I am anything, I am always careful."

"I'm glad."

"Come now!" He extended his right arm so that Eleander could hold it as they walked. "We must warn the others."

BARON SCHINI made herself comfortable on one of the bleacher-style seats that had been brought to the edge of the arena on the back of a wag. Baron DeMann, the baron's mistress Moira, Robards and a few other specially invited VIPs would be using the seats. And, she'd been told, so would two of the outlanders and one of the ville's whitecoats that one of the outlanders had taken a shine to.

"When do you want to signal the others?" one of her sec men asked.

Baron Schini lit a cheroot she'd carried with her for several weeks waiting for a special occasion. The painful death of her son's killer was just the sort of event she'd been waiting for. "Not yet," she said into the sec man's ear. "Things are too quiet right now. Let's wait to see how this challenge goes. I have a feeling things are going to be all fucked up in this ville by the time it's over and done with."

The baron took a few puffs on the cigar and made a sour face. The tobacco had turned bad. She tossed it aside and it bounced off the bleacher, then tumbled onto the ground where it burned slowly, sending two thin tendrils into the air.

The two sec men accompanying her jumped from their seats and raced each other for the burning butt. The smaller of the two reached it first, picked it up and clenched it between his teeth.

Then he returned to his seat, puffing proudly.

THE FRIENDS had gathered outside the arena.

"O captain, my captain," Doc said, capturing Ryan's attention, but speaking to the entire group. "The fair lady Eleander has brought something to my attention that I feel should be shared with the rest of you immediately."

"You're in love, Doc," J.B. suggested.

"That is besides the point, John Barrymore. What she has brought to my attention is that in addition to all the beneficial drugs and medicines made by Baron DeMann, there are also operations within these walls which produce the more sinister variety of stimulants and narcotics such as wolfweed, dreem and jolt."

"I knew it," Mildred said, slapping her thigh. "There's

no way someone operating out here alone could be so altruistic."

"Did a good job hiding it," Ryan said.

Eleander stepped forward. "He uses the medicines as a cover for his drug operations. With every shipment of insulin or penicillin that goes out, a package of jolt or dreem goes along with it."

"So anybody wanting medicine for their ville has to take the bad drugs along with the good."

"That's sort of how it works."

"We all suspected it," Ryan stated. "And it's why I want to leave as soon as we can, but why are you telling us this now?"

"Robards produces a drug called bang that I think the baron is still unaware of. I know Robards has plans to overthrow the baron and take control of the ville, and your arena challenge might be a part of his plans."

"That seals it, then," J.B. barked. "Forgot this stupe challenge. We leave now—fuck the ammo!"

Ryan nodded his agreement. The one-eyed man had seen plenty of internal power struggles turn ugly, and he didn't want to get caught up in one here. "We go!"

"Hold on there, Ryan." It was the voice of Baron DeMann. "We had an agreement."

"Changed our minds."

The baron sighed. "And here I thought you were an honorable man of your word."

"Talk's cheap, Baron. Your sec chief told us we could leave anytime we wanted."

"Hmm... I'll have to have a word with him, lying like

that. Next he'll be stealing and cheating me out of my jack."

"Mebbe he already is," J.B. said.

"Mebbe," the baron said, deflecting the comment. "But this isn't about my sec chief, it's about you. If you leave now, I guarantee you won't be getting very far, especially without ammo."

"Take our chances."

"But *I* want you to stay."

"Sorry, we're leaving."

DeMann shook his head, and as he did, sec men appeared behind him. A moment later, sec men appeared on the wall surrounding the arena. Finally, a pair of sec men showed themselves on the tops of nearby buildings, each sporting a longblaster with a scope pointing down at the group of friends.

"Perhaps you didn't hear me." The baron bared his teeth in a smile. "I said, I want you to stay, and it is my ville after all."

The door leading into the arena opened up on the friends' right.

"All right, Baron," Ryan said. "We'll do your challenge, but not with those toys you showed us last night, but with real blasters."

None of the friends blinked.

However, a few of the assembled sec men gasped and muttered in protest. Ryan had not only anted up, but he'd raised the stakes to a level that most of Baron DeMann's sec men weren't exactly comfortable with.

"Bravo, but that won't be necessary. I want to test

your group's skill against that of my sec men. I'm not interested in losing sec men for the purposes of entertainment. I think we'll stick with the paintballs this time."

Ryan didn't want to step inside the arena, but they were surrounded by the baron's sec men and there wasn't anywhere they could move to without getting torn apart by a hailstorm of hot lead. Their best chance was to partake in the challenge and hope an opportunity for escape presented itself while they played. "All right, we'll play your game, but after we win, we walk out the front gate of this ville with your blessing. Agreed?"

"Oh, absolutely, agreed."

The friends headed for the open door that led into the arena. "Uh, one last thing," the baron said. "I'm afraid you'll have to give me your weapons. We can't have you tempted to use them during the challenge."

"Fuck you," J.B. said. "Blasters stay with us."

"Oh, I like your spirit, J.B., but you haven't changed my mind. Air-powered guns only inside the arena."

"What about your sec men?"

"The rules apply to them as well, of course. And you'll be free to check them and their weapons before we begin."

"Doc and Jak hold our blasters, then," Ryan stated.

"Of course, whatever you wish. I assure you I already have more than enough blasters for all my men."

Of that Ryan had no doubt.

"All right, people," he said. "Give your blasters to Doc." He looked at Doc, but said nothing while he and the friends put their blasters in the care of the time traveler.

"I assure you, my captain, I will guard these blasters with my very life."

"I'd prefer you guard them with your LeMat," Ryan said.

"As you wish, Ryan."

Doc, Jak and Eleander collected the friends' blasters, then headed for the seats where they would watch the contest.

The rest of the friends reluctantly entered the arena.

# Chapter Twelve

The arena had been modified slightly by the baron's sec men and now featured several wooden buildings and ramps that would be useless at providing cover against blasters in the Deathlands, but gave solid protection against the paintballs used inside the arena.

"It's a little like a maze," Mildred commented, walking through the recently erected structures.

"Plenty of places for sec men to hide," J.B. added.

They walked into the center of the arena where there was a large open space and the dirt on the ground was level. The walls surrounding the arena were now topped with spectators. Most of them were people from the ville, workers in Baron DeMann's laboratory, but there were still sec men scattered throughout the crowd. The few permanent seats set up around the arena were taken up by whitecoats, who obviously enjoyed special status in the ville. Ryan noted that there were no addict muties in the crowd, and wondered what it would take to get them streaming over the wall into the ville.

Robards followed the group into the arena and joined the friends in the center. A sec man assisting Robards came up behind the sec chief pushing a wheelbarrow containing a steel strongbox. Robards opened the box and handed a blaster to each of the friends.

"Light," Krysty said, hefting a blaster in her hand.

"It's not loaded," J.B. told her, as he accepted his blaster from Robards. "When the balls go in the hopper, it gets pretty heavy. Best to keep between one and two dozen balls in the blaster. More than that and you won't be able to move the blaster fast enough."

Robards handed blasters to Ryan and Mildred. Then the sec chief went back to the wheelbarrow and picked up several sets of plastic goggles.

"What are those?" Ryan asked.

"Protection for your eyes," Robards said. "The balls won't hurt you, but if you get one hitting you just right you could lose an eye. Want them?"

Ryan just stared at him.

They had been in firefights in which hot lead had zinged past their eyes, in front of their eyes, and just over their heads. Now that they were playing a game, protection against water-filled balls seemed ridiculous. "No, thanks."

Robards tossed a pair of goggles to each of the sec men, then handed them each a blaster.

Ryan noticed that the blasters the sec men were getting looked new, or at least better maintained, while the friends' blasters were scratched, pitted and stained. It was only the outward appearance of the weapons, but if they hadn't been maintained on the outside, then they probably hadn't been looked after properly on the inside.

"Mind if my man inspects those blasters?" Ryan said.

"Not at all," Robards answered.

Ryan looked at J.B. and flicked his head in the direction of the sec men.

J.B. walked over to one of the sec men carrying the dirty, well-worn blaster he'd be using in the game. He tested out the older-looking model, making sure the action on it worked properly and the pressure charge on it was full and didn't bleed off extra pressure with each shot. The blaster responded well with a smooth and even *pock, pock, pock* sound with each squeeze of the trigger.

Then he tried the sec man's weapon and although looking cleaner and newer, it worked in precisely the same way.

"No difference in these two," J.B. reported. "I'd like to check them all, though."

"Be my guest," Robards said.

The sec men gave up their weapons and J.B. looked all of them over and compared them with the blasters to be used by the friends. In the end, J.B. decided to keep his blaster and the one to be used by Krysty, but exchanged Ryan's and Mildred's for the two best blasters belonging to the sec men.

"Satisfied now?" Robards asked.

J.B. nodded.

"All right, then, here's your ammo." A second sec man entered the arena pushing a green wheelbarrow filled with two mesh sacs, one red and one blue. He lifted the red sac first and brought it over to where the friends were standing, then carried the blue sac over to the sec men.

Robards beamed. "I assume that's more than enough ammo."

Ryan nodded. "It'll do."

J.B. stepped forward. "Mind if I check the ammo, too?"

"Why would I mind?"

J.B. dug a handful of blue balls from the sec men's sac and dropped them into his blaster. Then he raised the weapon and fired a line of balls against the wall, putting four blue splotches on the wall with a foot between each one. He walked over and looked closely at the stains, making sure they were just colored water.

"Looks all right," he reported when he returned.

"I'm almost offended that you didn't trust me."

"Just being careful," Ryan said.

"Of course you are. It's exactly why your little group is able to survive out in the Deathlands, and why the baron wants you to test your skills against our sec force."

"You sure those are the only reasons?" Ryan asked.

Robards ignored the question. "Since you are our guests here, I will leave it to you what type of challenge you'd like to partake in."

"You mean we've got a choice?"

"Well, yes and no. Between sec men we often engage in Last Man Standing, but since that could end up pitting my sec men against each other, instead of against you, your only real choices are Capture the Flag or Covert Ops, where you either attack or defend a specific target."

"How about we just chill your four sec men," Ryan said. "And then you can stick your flag up your ass!"

"Very well, then," Robards said. "You've made your decision."

"Let's just get on with it."

"All right, but before we begin, there's one last thing."

"What?"

"Since the blasters aren't fatal, a referee is required to resolve matters of near misses and grazings—"

"Give you three guesses who the referee is going to be," J.B. muttered, "and the first two guesses don't count."

"—and *I* will be that referee."

Ryan just shook his head. He knew that the challenge would somehow be skewed in the sec men's favor, but he'd thought it would have at least been unseen. This had become a farce, but at least the sec chief would be in the arena where Ryan could get at him if he had to.

"Let's get on with it."

Robards grinned. "All right, load up and take your positions. The challenge will begin in five minutes."

SHERMAN AND ROY took up a position just under a mile from the front gate. They had wanted to venture in farther, but they hadn't anticipated the outer edges of the ville being inhabited by so many addicts and muties. There was no way they'd be able to fit in and mingle among the population. They'd either be swarmed by a gang of muties and torn apart by addicts, or someone would spot them and call in DeMann's sec men.

So they hung back and watched.

But even from this distance it was obvious that something different was going on inside the walls. There was none of the usual activity going on in the ville, like people moving about, or wags making deliveries. It seemed as if everything had come to a stop.

"Sure would like to know what's going on in there," Sherman said, watching the ville through a cheap plastic telescope he'd found in the ruins of an elementary school in what was left of the pre-Dark ville called Muncie.

"Why don't you go down there and take a look around?"

"With those muties all over the place?"

Roy smirked. "They don't look too dangerous."

"No, not much. Just the kind that would slice open my belly to eat my breakfast."

"So what do you suppose we should do?" Roy asked.

"Sec chief told us to wait for Baron Schini's signal and that's exactly what I intend to do."

"What's the signal?"

"Don't know right now, but I figure I'll know it when I see it."

BARON DEMANN JOINED Robards on the arena floor. The baron wanted to speak to each of his men personally before the challenge, and the sec men seemed pleased that the baron had taken such a personal interest in what was for them just another challenge.

"This is something more than what you're used to," he began. "This is a test of two vastly different ways of life. Ours and theirs… Villelife versus the Deathlands… Sec men versus outland scum… Order and chaos…"

As he talked, DeMann walked back and forth in front of the four-man team, looking each man in the eyes, checking to see if the man was focused on the task ahead of him, and to see if anyone was about to do the challenge all doped up on jolt or dreem. Because the challenge blasters were nonlethal, several sec men over the years had participated in challenges high on drugs. The result was a reckless attack that put the sec man and his whole team at risk. But ever since the penalty for such drug abuse had become a slow tortuous death by, first, overdose of bang, and then a protracted deprivation, which brought on madness and eventually, some would say mercifully, death, drug use by sec men had gone way down.

DeMann was glad to see that the eyes of all the men were sharp and clear.

"I know you'll do this ville proud," the baron continued, "because you've had the best training of any sec force for hundreds of miles in any direction. You are the best, and your victory will be a message to the surrounding villes and outland scum that might wander past—don't mess with DeMann."

A slight cheer arose from the four-man team.

DeMann continued to walk in front of the sec men, but now he stopped before each one to shake hands. "Best of luck, Rodriguez," he said, extending his hand.

There were six balls in his hand, their shade of blue slightly lighter than those he'd given the men earlier.

"I want the one-eyed outlander dead," he whispered.

Rodriguez nodded, knowing exactly what the off-color balls were for. He slipped them into the plastic-lined pocket on the outside right thigh of his fatigues.

The baron moved onto the next sec man and whispered his instructions.

The sec man nodded silently, knowing what to do.

They all did.

"ALL RIGHT, EVERYONE," Ryan said, standing in a circle with the other friends at the far end of the arena. He began pouring out balls into the pockets and waist belts of each of the friends. "Keep your ammo in the blaster down below two-dozen balls." He paused a moment to feel the wind on his face. "And with the way the wind's blowing, these blasters won't be accurate past fifty yards, so bring them in close before firing."

"You think Robards will call his men out when they're hit?" Mildred asked, raising and lowering her blaster in her extended hand to check its weight and balance.

Ryan just looked at her. "What do you think?"

Mildred shook her head. "Can't trust a sec chief to go against his own men."

"That's right," Ryan continued, "so we're going to have to make our rounds count. Shots to the head and trunk only. Anything else and the sec men will probably argue it."

"What about leaving?" J.B. asked. "Case something goes wrong."

"I intend to play this game out and walk out of the arena a winner. But since we're dealing with sec men, I want everyone to make a note of where Doc is sitting as soon as we get out there so you can find him if and when you need your blaster. There are four exits from the arena, and a few of them are partially obscured by wooden structures, so if we have to get out in a hurry, those would be our best choices."

"What about on the outside of the arena? The streets of this ville are like a maze," Krysty stated.

"One thing at a time, but we'll probably have to blast our way out…if it comes to that."

J.B. shook his head. "I don't like this."

"None of us do," Ryan answered.

"We've been in worse spots," Mildred suggested.

"At least then we had real blasters, not this shit." J.B. held up his weapon as if it were a play thing.

"Any idea about how we're going to capture their flag?" Krysty said, reminding everybody that they had a mission to plan.

"Mildred will stay back and defend our flag while the rest of us will fan out and go on the offensive."

"We gonna try for the flag."

Ryan shook his head. "Best way I know to get the flag is chilling their whole team first."

J.B. nodded approval.

"So we're going to take them all out, then pick up their flag."

"Want to set a trap for them?" Krysty suggested.

Ryan leaned in. "What have you got in mind?"

"YOU SIT HERE!" a sec man told Doc, Jak and Eleander.

"A nice enough view, but I would prefer something a little closer to the arena floor."

"You'll sit *here,*" the sec man repeated, "until the baron or the sec chief say otherwise."

"If that is the way you feel about it, then very well."

The sec man turned and took a few steps back.

Eleander smiled at Doc. "We should be able to see everything from here."

"That is not what I am worried about, dear lady. If my friends get into trouble, I would prefer to be close enough to hand them their blasters."

"I see. Well, perhaps I can get us moved down closer to the wall."

"Much appreciated."

Eleander got up and went to talk to the sec man in charge.

"Isn't she something?" Doc said to Jak.

Jak had a strange smile on his face. It had been the same expression for the past half hour, and it was starting to nag at Doc. Jak was a young firebrand who would have wanted to be in the thick of the fight no matter what his physical condition. But here he was on the outside of the arena, content to sit in silence and stare blankly out onto the arena floor.

Sick or not, something was wrong. Doc decided he'd inform Mildred of the problem as soon as he had the chance.

"Are you all right, my friend?" Doc said, shaking Jak by his good shoulder then waiting for a response.

There was no answer from Jak. Just that same, unsettling grin on his face.

"It is unfortunate that we were not challenged to a knife-throwing contest. You would be the champion, eh?"

"Knives for survival," Jak muttered. "Not for games."

"Ah, so there is some life behind those two glassy ruby eyes of yours."

"Too bad not talking contest. You win easy."

"Ha!" Doc exclaimed. "Touché, my white-haired friend." Doc breathed a sigh of relief, happy to know that whatever unusual behavior Jak was exhibiting was a result of his wounds, and nothing more. He would be back to being his own irascible self in no time.

A few minutes later Eleander returned.

"We're moving," she said.

"But how?"

"Let's just say that you don't live in a ville for years without learning a few interesting bits of information about the sec men around you."

"Blackmail," Doc said, slightly astonished. "My dear woman, I had thought that a lady such as yourself would be above such messy endeavors—"

"We can stay here if you prefer."

"—but I wholeheartedly approve of your ability to determine when such underhanded methods need to be employed, and I appreciate your tact in administering them so judiciously."

"Does that mean you want to move?"

"Of course."

"This way, then."

"On your feet Jak, we will be taking up a position closer to the action."

"Knife range?"

Doc hesitated a moment, then nodded. "I do believe we will be close enough for that. Yes."

The trio moved closer to the arena wall.

MONTE SHARK WAS doing good business taking bets on the challenge. As early as last night, heavy jack had been flowing on the ville's sec men. After all, who knew the challenge better than the men who practiced on it daily.

But with the morning, a few brave souls had put money on the outlanders, liking the odds just a little bit too much. Monte had revised the numbers before noon, but that had done little to change the flow the bets were moving in.

Mebbe it was something about the look of the outlanders' leader. Monte sure found the man attractive. He was tall and rangy, powerfully muscular with black curly hair and a deeply set and intensely brilliant blue eye. And then there were the facial scars and the eye patch, giving him so much mystery and intrigue. The man was obviously tough, and probably an excellent fighter. But most of all, just looking at him told you he was a survivor. That was probably a characteristic that was missing from most of the ville's sec men. They joined the sec force so they could carry a blaster, have free access to jolt and dreem and to women who wanted to fuck a sec man for the security it provided them.

Thinking it through, Monte didn't blame people for putting money on the outlanders. All things being equal, they would probably kick Robards's ass.

But that was the thing, wasn't it?

All things being equal.

Monte had been around long enough to know when there was a fix on, and this little challenge stank of a fix like bear shit in a black plastic bag.

The baron and sec chief were planning something big, but he didn't know what. Others felt it, too, but even so, decent money was still coming in on the outlanders.

Pretty soon the odds would be one to one.

"Hey, Monte," a customer called. "What's the action like on the outlanders."

"Even jack."

"If I place a bet and the baron pulls a fast one on them, do I get my jack back?"

Monte had never been in the business of returning people's jack. "Fuck no!" he said.

The customer considered it, then began shaking his head. "Okay, but I'm still gonna go with the outlanders. You see their leader? Bet he's chilled his share of sec men over the years."

Monte took the woman's money. "Yeah, he does at that." And, he thought, maybe he'll be chilling some more, real soon.

THE BARON ROSE to his feet.

And everyone around the arena fell silent.

"Welcome and good day," he said, his voice cutting through the silence like the dull blade of a knife.

"The following challenge will be between a group of outlanders and four of our best sec men. There will be three ten-minute periods of play with a five-minute break between periods. The team that successfully captures the other team's flag will be deemed the winner. If neither team captures their opponent's flag, then the team with the larger number of active players at the end of time will be named the winner. If the teams are of equal numbers at the end of time, then a public vote will determine which team is the victor."

The baron paused. The wind swept over the arena, whistling like death itself.

"Any questions?" he said.

Ryan put a hand to his mouth. "Can we get on with this?"

A slight chuckle washed through the crowd.

"Very well, then. Contestants take your positions."

In moments the four members of each team vanished from view, like spiders running for the shadows the moment a light has been turned on.

The baron said nothing for several moments, making sure everyone had enough time to take up their positions.

"Let the challenge begin."

# Chapter Thirteen

Ryan slipped behind a piece of sheet metal that had been cut to resemble some sort of bush. It was one of the few obstacles that was strong enough to stop a round from a real blaster, and he made note of its location on the arena floor.

Although he couldn't see all of them, Ryan knew that the other friends were spread out on either side of him with ten to fifteen paces between them. On his left, Ryan could just make out Krysty's left leg as she stood behind a ramshackle wooden shed. On his right, J.B. and Mildred were hidden from view, trying to get a bead on one of their opponents.

Their strategy was simple. They would advance in pairs, one trying to draw out a sec man, and the other taking the sec man down. They wouldn't be making an attempt at capturing the flag until they'd knocked at least two sec men out of the game.

The arena was quiet.

The wind swept through the arena, churning up tiny clouds of sand and dust. Ryan felt the wind in his face and realized he was downwind of the sec men and would probably be able to smell them when they neared.

He sniffed at the air now and detected nothing. They were hanging back, waiting for one of the friends to make a move.

Ryan decided he had to do something to draw the sec men's fire.

He tossed a pebble in Krysty's direction so that it *ticked* off the side of the shed she was positioned behind. In an automatic response to the sound, Krysty swung around and had her blaster pointed at Ryan's head.

Ryan signaled her to watch for sec men. When she acknowledged him, Ryan took off his coat and hung it over the barrel of his blaster. Then, after bumping up against the sheet metal bush to make his presence known, Ryan held out his blaster so that his coat was visible to the sec men.

Three shots rang out in quick succession.

The first glanced off the barrel of Ryan's blaster and slammed against the arena wall behind him. The other two hit the sheet metal with a wet *pang*.

Then, in the time it took the rest of the sec men to find their target and aim and fire, multiple shots were fired. Judging by the sounds, several shots hit wooden obstacles, but at least one had a much softer landing, followed by a yelp of pain from one of the sec men.

"Scratch one sec man," Ryan whispered under his breath.

"It was not a mortal wound," Robards decreed. "Sec man Kuharski remains in the challenge."

"Fireblast!" Ryan exclaimed.

"Mebbe we have to brain them with the butt of our blasters to knock them out of the arena," Krysty said.

Ryan nodded in agreement. He would prefer a fight in close quarters over this. At least if he cut a man with his panga he could watch him bleed and know exactly where he stood.

This was arbitrary, a game...even worse, it was a game of chance. Well, if the shots needed to be fatal to knock a competitor out of the arena, then it would free him up to take a few more chances. If Mildred, J.B. and Krysty hadn't been able to make a head shot at this distance, Ryan doubted that any of the sec men could do better.

He got to his feet and put his coat back on. Then, once he had Krysty's attention and she was aware of what he was about to do, Ryan took one look over the metal bush and ran across the arena floor.

The arena echoed with the sound of the sec men's blasters.

*Pock, pock, pock.*

Spouts of dirt erupted in front and behind him, but not one of the sec men's rounds had hit him.

Ryan kept running, and moments before he reached the line of stalls at one side of the arena, he dived to the ground and somersaulted once into the safe zone behind one of the stalls.

The crowd cheered the bold move, knowing that the stalemate had been broken and things would be happening more quickly now.

Ryan checked his body to make sure he hadn't been hit. His body was clear, but it looked as if the outside heel of his right boot had been clipped. The leather heel had turned a little blue, but Ryan was unconcerned about that, since the hit probably wasn't even caught by Robards. No, the thing that bothered Ryan was that the leather heel was bubbling, as if it were being eaten away by the liquid that had been inside the ball.

It was strange, but he couldn't dwell on it. The last thing he needed was to lose this challenge and end up a prisoner in this rad-blasted ville.

He rubbed the heel of his boot into the dirt of the arena floor. The bubbling stopped, and the blue tinge was gone.

Ryan was ready to shoot some sec men.

"RYAN'S DRAWING OUT the sec men," J.B. said. "If I can get to that trash can over there, I'll be able to pick them off when they come for him."

Mildred took a moment to judge the distance. "Won't be easy getting there. Sec men will be ready for you now."

"You cover me?"

She held up her blaster. "Best I can with this piece of crap."

"On three, then. One…two…"

On the third count, Mildred was standing and firing her blaster in the direction of the sec men's last appearance. She was trying to catch the edge of the wooden wall the sec men were hiding behind so that the paintballs would break on contact with the walls and send a spray of water in behind. While it wasn't enough to put any of them out of the game, it would keep them behind cover until J.B. was in position.

While she fired, Mildred was careful to keep an eye on the rest of the arena to make sure a sec man didn't pop up somewhere unexpected.

None did.

J.B. slid the last few yards to the trash can and hunched behind it while he twisted his body so that he was facing the sec men and ready for an attack.

Ryan saw J.B. prepare himself and nodded approvingly.

Mildred and Krysty were now the two who were hanging back protecting the flag, while Ryan and J.B. would be moving forward.

Ryan waited several minutes for evidence of movement among the sec men, but there was none. They seemed content to wait for the friends to come to them. Well, if that was the way they wanted it, then Ryan and the rest would gladly take the fight to them.

Ryan signaled J.B. and told him what he was planning with a makeshift sort of sign language they had developed over the years.

Ryan would make his way up to the shack where the sec men were waiting. He would move around the left side of the building, his blaster leading the way. That would force the sec men to come out the other side, where they would be caught in fire from J.B. and Krysty. With any luck they would be able to pick off one or two of the sec men with solid shots to the head and body.

When J.B. nodded in understanding, Ryan made his move.

With speed uncommon in such a big man, Ryan

crossed the open ground between the stall and the shack in just a few seconds. As he ran, he could make out the face of a sec man looking out from behind the shack, but Ryan was too quick for the man to get the outlander in his sights.

He paused a moment to catch his breath and to give J.B. a chance to move into a better position.

When all was set, Ryan moved around the left of the shack, the blaster always in front of him and ready to fire.

As he neared the last corner, he could hear the sec men talking.

"Robards won't be calling you out unless you get nailed right between the eyes—" one of the sec men said.

"Bastard," Ryan muttered silently.

"—and just one of these rounds will knock the outlanders out of the arena, maybe even on the last train west."

Ryan didn't understand what he was hearing—all of the paintballs were supposed to be identical. Mebbe it was just the sec men being a little overconfident. Whatever it was, the friends had to play out this challenge and get out of this ville as soon as possible.

Without further hesitation, Ryan switched the blaster to his left hand and moved around the last corner of the shack.

Two sec men were crouched there, both of them looking rather surprised to see him.

Ryan squeezed off two rounds, the first hitting the sec man in front of him in the forehead, the second hitting him in the left cheek. In the Deathlands, the man's head would have been gone in a spray of gore and gray matter, but here, in this game, he merely had a pair of red welts and a face and head stained red.

Before the first sec man could be called out of the arena, the sec man standing behind the first raised his blaster and pointed it directly at Ryan.

Ryan leaped back around the corner as two blue balls zipped past his head.

But instead of striking the wall, the two balls hit a third sec man who had positioned himself behind Ryan in one of the stalls against the wall on the left.

The two rounds hit the sec man in the neck and chest, but instead of staining the man blue, his skin began to sizzle and smoke, just like Ryan's boot had done moments before.

The man began to scream, slapping at his neck and chest as if they were on fire.

A low rumble of voices swept through the crowd, as if they were unsure what they were seeing, as if the rules had been changed.

"SOMETHING'S WRONG," Eleander said.

"I would say so." Doc nodded. "That sec man's skin is disintegrating, as if he has been doused with some sort of acid. Sulphuric or hydrochloric acid."

"We have both in the ville," Eleander acknowledged.

"And all Ryan and the others have to fight back with is colored water?"

"It looks like it."

"Well, that does not seem sporting at all," Doc declared.

"It's obvious that we shall have to even the score somewhat."

"What can we do?"

Doc took a quick look around. Everyone seemed to be caught up with what was happening down on the arena floor. If there was ever a time to move, it was now.

"Can you get us to that end of the arena?"

"There are several ways of getting there."

"Under the circumstances, I shall forego the scenic route and opt for the shortest possible passage between the two points."

"Follow me," Eleander instructed.

"Jak," Doc said, "We are moving."

Jak smiled. "No, wait me."

And they were off.

All eyes around them were still on the screaming sec man.

RYAN LEFT the sec man's zone and retreated back to the safety of the other end of the arena. "What kind of bastard sec-man trick are you pulling on us, Robards?" he shouted.

"Sec-men's paintballs must be filled with some kind of acid," J.B. stated. "Burns your skin."

"Not a sec man trick," a voice said.

Mildred gestured toward the stage overlooking the arena. "Sounds like the baron."

"What is it then?"

"Payback time, Ryan!"

"Payback? For what?" Ryan couldn't imagine what

the problem was. They'd saved one of the ville's citizens from a mutie attack, and had helped fend off a group of muties who'd tried to scale the wall. What reason did they have to receive retribution?

"You remember Spearpoint?" the baron asked.

The screaming sec man was dead.

The crowd had grown silent, listening to the baron closely.

"That was years ago."

"Mebbe, but you murdered people there, people who were close to me."

"And me," a second, female voice said.

"We've never murdered anyone," Ryan said. "Only people we chill are the ones who want us dead. Chill or be chilled."

"No, you one-eyed prick," the baron shouted. "At Spearpoint, you *murdered* my brother."

"And my son."

"Allow me to introduce Baron Schini," DeMann said. "As you've already heard, you also murdered her son."

Ryan shook his head in disbelief. During all his years with the Trader and on his own with the friends, he had probably chilled dozens, or scores, maybe even hundreds of norms and muties, but he'd never murdered any of them. Murder was something you thought about, planned and committed in cold blood. He'd chilled, but always to save his own life, or the lives of others.

Ryan wasn't about to apologize for his past, or any of his actions. If he had chilled DeMann's brother, and the other baron's son, it was only because if he didn't they would have chilled him without a second thought.

"Don't remember chilling your brother…or your son," Ryan told them, "but if I did, then they were probably low-life scum that deserved to die."

"Glad you feel that way," the baron said. "It'll be so much easier to watch you suffer."

The baron raised his hand and the arena erupted in blasterfire.

People in the crowd started screaming.

Some ran for cover.

Others tried to get away as quickly as they could.

The entire ville was blanketed in chaos.

A SEC MAN STOOD in the aisle, blocking Doc's passage. "Where do you think you're going?" he asked.

"My hope would be forward," Doc mused.

The sec man shook his head.

Behind Doc, both Eleander and Jak remained silent, allowing Doc to do all the talking since, after all, it was what he did best. "That is truly unfortunate, my good man, because I fully intend to go forward. Now, whether it is around you, through you, or over your dead body, that is entirely up to you."

"You're not going anywhere, asshole outlander."

Shots continued to be fired into the arena. The friends could see that Ryan and the others were scattered around the arena floor. The number of blasters drawn against them seemed to be on the rise.

Doc, however, was unflappable. He slowly raised his LeMat and pointed it at the sec man.

The sec man started to laugh. "You can actually fire that relic?"

"I assure you it is in perfect working order."

As the sec man considered Doc's words, the smile vanished from his face. "Then put it down and get back to your seat."

"I am afraid I cannot do that. You see, my friends are currently caught in a firefight in which they are armed with toy blasters and their opponents are armed with the real thing. I beseech you, is that fair?"

"I said put the blaster down."

Doc was defiant. "No."

The sec man cocked his blaster, a remade Colt with a gray and pitted barrel.

"Last chance."

Doc said nothing.

A moment later the sec man was clutching at a leaf-bladed throwing knife that had suddenly lodged in his neck. A giant rent opened up in the flesh, and blood was gushing out in a torrent.

"Thank you Master Lauren," Doc said, picking up the sec man's blaster and tucking it inside his waistband.

"Waiting for you shoot him."

"I told him my blaster was in perfect working order.... Unfortunately, I happen to be out of ammunition for it at the moment."

They hurried on.

Blasterfire continued to rain down into the arena.

INSTINCTIVELY the friends dived for cover, safe for now, but vulnerable to blasterfire the minute the sec men had a chance to changc thcir positions.

"Let's get out of here," Ryan said.

"No argument here," J.B. agreed.

Ryan looked for Doc, Jak and Eleander but couldn't see them. "There's a door in the corner of the arena. We'll try for that and hopefully we'll meet up with Doc and get our blasters."

Without another word, the friends made a run for the arena door.

# Chapter Fourteen

"Don't let them get away!" Robards shouted.

The outlanders had made their way to the north end of the arena and seemed to have vanished from sight. They were good at surviving and would probably make it out of the arena, maybe even out of the ville. Robards was counting on them getting away, since that would bring the firefight out into the ville where it would be possible for the baron to catch a round from one of their weapons, or if not one of their blasters, perhaps from Robards's own. After all, once the baron was gone, who would challenge his authority over the ville? If he declared the baron dead by one of the outlanders' blasters, that would be the end of the matter.

"Patskou!" Robards called out.

Almost at once, a sec man and three juniors came running up to the elevated platform.

"Yes, Chief!"

"Circle around the south end of the arena, and take as many men with you as you can find. I don't want them doubling back on us and slipping out the back door."

Sec man Patskou nodded and left at double-time, his

three men trailing behind, and more joining the train as he circled the outside of the arena.

Robards watched approvingly.

Thc outlanders probably didn't need his help getting away, but there was no harm in helping to making sure everything went according to his plan.

BARON SCHINI watched as chaos reigned around her.

The episode in the arena had been awkward and careless. If DeMann and Robards had wanted the outlanders dead, why didn't they just tie them up and take their heads off with a volley of blasterfire?

She looked at Sec chief Robards and listened closely as he sent his men to the opposite end of the arena from where the outlanders had last been seen.

It all seemed so wrong.

Unless…

Unless Robards was working on something, and was using the outlanders' escape as a diversion.

"Perhaps I should retire to my residence. It will be safer there," Baron DeMann said.

"No, Baron, that might be seen as a sign of weakness by citizens of the ville," Robards countered. "Besides, the outlanders know where your quarters are, and they might seek you out in revenge for the double cross in the arena. Better to stay here with me so my men can protect you."

The baron eyed his sec chief suspiciously. "All right, but I'm warning you, if you let the one-eyed outlander escape, you won't live to see the morning. Is that understood?"

"Yes, Baron," DeMann said.

Baron Schini looked at Baron DeMann for a long time knowing that whether by her hand, or that of Sec chief Robards, he would probably be the one who wouldn't live out the night.

ELEANDER LED Doc and Jak to the north end of the arena. Ryan, Krysty, J.B. and Mildred were waiting for them there, eager to get their blasters back and a chance to shoot their way out of the ville.

Ryan checked his SIG-Sauer and the small cache of 9 mm rounds he had for it. There were barely a dozen rounds in his lone spare clip. He also had barely a half-dozen rounds for his Steyr.

He looked around at the others in the group. "How we doing for ammo?" he asked.

"Eight rounds," Krysty said, snapping the wheel of her Smith & Wesson in place.

"I'm out," Doc reported.

"I've got fourteen rounds," Mildred said.

J.B. shook his head. "Clip and a half for the Uzi, mebbe ten rounds for the scattergun."

Eleander watched and listened in fascination, marveling at the military efficiency the group utilized when they prepared for battle.

"What about you, Jak?" Ryan asked.

"Dozen rounds," he said. "Plenty knives."

Ryan noticed something strange about the albino teen. He seemed listless and slow. "You all right?"

"Shoulder bastard sore."

Ryan nodded. That would explain it, although he'd seen the young man wounded worse than he was now and still able to jump, run and shoot faster than most men.

Eleander stared at Jak for a long time and a look of fear and sadness crossed her face, but she said nothing.

"Eleander," Ryan said, grabbing her attention, "we need ammo to blast our way out of here. Either that or a wag."

"The armory is too far from here, but the wag pool is just around that building. There are a few machines kept ready throughout the day. If you get to one of those, there should be some ammo on board."

"Wheels *and* ammo," J.B. said with delight.

"Then we'll head for the wags," Ryan commanded. He looked at Eleander. "Take us there!"

BARON SCHINI had her weapon drawn, a snub-nosed Browning .38, but kept the blaster close to her side. Things seemed to be happening fast, and she wasn't about to tip her hand until she knew exactly what was going on.

She called one of her sec men.

"Yes, Baron," the man said.

"Do you have the flare?"

The man nodded.

"Make your way to the wall and get ready to light it. I have a feeling a hole is going to open up in the wall around this ville very soon."

The sec man ran off, slipping unnoticed into the crowd.

THE FRIENDS RAN single file through the narrow streets of the ville, Eleander leading the way, Ryan and J.B. covering their rear.

"Mildred," Eleander called without stopping.

"Right here," the physician responded.

"I'm worried about Jak."

"He'll be fine."

Eleander shook her head. "His wound is almost healed, yes, but I'm afraid he's been given something. Something bad."

"Like what?"

"Can't be sure, but just from looking at him, I think he might have been given some bang."

"Why would they do that to him?"

"Revenge would be my guess. If Ryan killed the baron's brother, then he probably had Jak injected with bang to get back at him, slow down the group."

Mildred turned to look at Jak. The albino teen was keeping pace with the rest of them, but the usual spark was gone from his eyes. It was as if he were going through the motions, nothing more. "What will happen to him?"

Eleander held back her answer as the group turned a corner.

At the end of the line, Ryan sent a few rounds from his SIG-Sauer down the alleyway, catching a trailing sec man in the chest. The man clutched at his chest and as he died, he momentarily blocked the alleyway. Other sec men appeared behind the man and used his bleeding body as a shield. J.B. fired a few more rounds, pushing the sec men back and chilling the lead man, sending him reeling backward onto the alley floor.

"When the drug is first administered," Eleander continued, "the feeling is euphoric. The world is a beautiful place and a person can stay motionless in one position for hours at a time."

Mildred recalled Jak had been strangely quiet that morning. At the time she had thought he'd just been getting some much-needed rest.

"When he's finished with that stage, he'll act pretty much normal for a few hours. That's what he's going through now. He'll be able to function, but his eyes will get increasingly glassy..." Her voice trailed off.

"And then?" Mildred prodded.

"And then when he comes completely down from the high, he'll want more of it. He'll scratch your eyes out for it, even kill for it, and won't stop until he gets it."

"Damn!" Mildred said. "We've met up with a few muties like that."

"They weren't muties, they were bang addicts, but they might as well have been muties. Sec chief Robards is still working on the drug. He wanted it to be addictive, but not this powerful. It's already wiped out a quarter of the ville's residents so far, and more are dying every day."

Eleander began to slow.

"How can I get him off it?"

"If he can get through the first few hours of need, he'll have a bastard headache and will never want to touch the drug again."

"Doesn't sound too bad."

Eleander shook her head. "When he asks for bang, tie him down. Make sure he can't move, and can't get at anyone. He'll kill them looking for the drug."

"Anything else?"

"Yes, let him scream all he wants. The madness is only temporary."

"Oh, great."

They continued on in silence, J.B. and Ryan keeping their rear clear of sec men.

"That's it over there," Eleander said, stopping in front of a gate that was locked with a small lock and thin gauge steel chain.

Krysty pulled on the padlock. "Looks like it's locked."

"Not for long," J.B. said as he approached from the rear. He leveled the Smith & Wesson M-4000 at the padlock and waited a moment so everyone could take cover, then he squeezed the trigger.

The padlock and much of the chain vanished in an instant under a cloud of smoke and dust, and the steel of the gate behind it was bent and broken by the blast.

The gate slowly swung open.

"Key to the ville," J.B. said, slapping the barrel of the scattergun.

The friends headed toward the wag pool.

# Chapter Fifteen

The wag pool was a large barn standing a block and a half northeast of the baron's residence. It was made of wood that had been worn and weathered by the elements, but the outside walls had been strengthened by sheet metal and aluminum signs collected from the surrounding countryside. Over the entrance was a rusted sign for something called Coke, and between the large overhead door and a small window was a blue road sign that read "St. Louis 150."

Positioned out in front of the barn were two sec stations built up with bags of dirt and loose earth. The sec men in each bunker were armed with large-caliber blasters and a healthy supply of ammo.

"Are there sec men around the back?" Ryan asked Eleander.

"There's one, but only because there are no doors on that side of the building."

"Can always make an entrance if we need to," J.B. said, slapping the butt of his scattergun.

"If we get rid of the sec man, can we get in from behind?"

Eleander shook her head. "The back wall is even more reinforced with metal plate."

Ryan nodded. He needed to come up with a plan in a hurry, since every available sec man in the ville was looking for them and it was only a matter of time before they figured out the friends would be looking for a wag to escape with.

"Ryan?" Krysty asked after several moments.

"Okay, here's the plan," he said. "Jak will take out the sec man behind the barn, real quiet. Then when he's got the man's blaster, he'll make as much noise as he can. When the two sec men out front come around the building to see what's going on, J.B. and I will take them out."

Jak nodded, as did J.B.

"Then Doc and Mildred will take up the positions at the front two posts, doing their best to look like the two dead sec men. That should give J.B. time to select a wag from inside and get it running."

Ryan looked around to see if anyone had anything to add.

No one said a word.

"All right, let's move!"

"WHERE ARE THEY now?" Baron DeMann shouted. "I want a report!"

"They are somewhere in the ville," Robards assured him. "Probably laying low, waiting for dark for a chance to scale the walls. When that happens, we'll shoot them like ducks in a gaudy-house arcade."

"Your men couldn't hit a duck if it was quacking at

the end of their blaster," the baron said, obviously disappointed in the performance of his sec squad of late.

"Not to worry, we'll have them," the sec chief promised.

Without warning, the baron reached over and pulled the blaster from Robards's hands. The move caught the sec chief by surprise, and he looked at the baron with an open mouth, unable to speak.

"I doubt that," DeMann said, turning the blaster around until it was comfortable in his left hand. "First, two residents escape the ville under the noses of your sec men because they wanted to go for a swim. Then you bring these outlanders into the ville and convince me to allow them to stay for a few days. But it was a good thing I did, because they helped stop an invasion of muties that your men seemed unable to control. You had your chance to chill them in the arena, but even that was too much of a task for your so-called highly trained men. And now you've lost them inside the ville, outlanders who've never walked its streets before." The baron shook his head in disgust. "Face it, Robards, you did all right when all you had to deal with were muties and a few drunken villagers, but you've gone soft on me." He shook his head in disgust. "You and your force are no match for hardened outlanders like these."

Robards said nothing.

"Are you?"

"I've kept the peace and been loyal to you for the past four years, Baron." The sec chief spoke slowly andcalmly.

"Loyal," the baron said. "That's an interesting word."

"What do you mean?"

"Well, a loyal sec man wouldn't do secret work on a new drug without informing me about it, would he?"

"I don't know what you're talking about, Baron."

"Oh, I think you do."

Robards pressed his lips together in a thin white line and his breathing became heavy.

"And before you go thinking about who it was that turned you in, I'll just tell you that I heard the news from four different sources."

Robards's face turned white.

Baron Schini's hand moved over the butt of her blaster…just in case.

"I assure you, Baron, I was going to turn the new drug over to you once it was perfected."

"Ah, a gift for me?"

Robards nodded. "Yes, precisely."

The baron's left hand shot forward and the barrel of the Heckler & Koch caught Robards on the chin. The sec chief was thrown backward, stumbling a few times before landing on his rear.

"I know you've already been selling it, turning the usually manageable junkies surrounding the ville into bang-starved killers. It's too addictive, too powerful, but of course you don't have the brainpower to figure that out. You'd keep going until all of your customers were gone. Then who the fuck would I sell the regular junk to?"

Robards opened his mouth to speak, but Baron De-

Mann kicked him in the chest before he could get a word out.

"This episode with the outlanders was your last chance to redeem yourself. If you hadn't screwed up with them, I might have let you live, or mebbe thrown you over the wall into one of the mutant hordes you've created, but no...you screwed this one up, too, didn't you?"

And then a look of realization and horror broke across the baron's face. He reached over and pulled his brightly finished Colt Mark IV from his shoulder holster. The barrel gleamed in his hand as he brought it to bear on Robards's head.

"Or mebbe you were planning on using this whole thing to get rid of me...like a diversion. Yeah, I bet that was it. The outlanders get their blasters and one of them is lucky enough to take out the baron, leaving you in charge of the ville."

The baron's eyes narrowed as the sec chief's plan became clearer in his mind.

"I bet you've even been giving extra jolt and dreem to your men, too, so they'd be loyal to you and wouldn't think too hard about how I was chilled under your watch."

The baron moved his blaster closer to the sec chief's head.

Just then a sec man came running up to the podium.

"Sec chief," the man cried, "we think they've gone inside the baron's residence..." His voice trailed off.

"The sec chief's busy at the moment," Baron DeMann said, pointing the Heckler & Koch in the sec man's direction while keeping the Colt Mark IV on Robards's head.

The sec man's mouth moved, but no words escaped his lips. He was obviously too shocked at the sight of the baron holding a blaster to the sec chief to do anything but gape.

"Continue your search," the baron said, not moving his blaster from Robards's head. "I'll be along to supervise in a few minutes."

The sec man didn't move.

"That will be all."

The sec man nodded, then turned and left the scene running. In no time, news of what was going on would run through the sec force faster than a bad batch of dreem.

The baron had to end this confrontation now so he could concentrate his efforts on finding the outlanders and maintaining control of his ville.

"What was it?" Baron DeMann asked. "You had free access to all the best gaudy houses. More jack than you knew what to do with. Your choice of blasters. A handpicked sec force. What more could you have wanted?"

Robards swallowed once, then said, "To be baron."

"Then you should have left and started your own ville somewhere else."

Baron DeMann positioned his Colt Mark IV directly over the crown of Robards's head and pressed the barrel against his skull.

And then a blaster boomed.

# Chapter Sixteen

Jak Lauren felt strange.

His arm and shoulder were still sore, but that wasn't the problem. He'd had worse injuries in the past, but he'd never felt his body hum and spasm like this. It was as if his whole body was hungry for something. But what? He could manage at the moment, but he had a strong feeling that it would be getting worse, and soon.

Shaking away the thoughts of his own condition, the albino teen moved quickly around the right side of the barn that housed the wag pool.

He peered around the corner and just as the woman had said, there was a sec man in a bunker in the middle of the back wall. Taking him out would be difficult, since the man seemed to be on triple alert with all the noise coming from the rest of the ville. He wouldn't know what was going on, but he'd know enough to think that *something* was up and that would make it double hard to get in close.

Double hard, but not impossible.

Around the other corner of the barn, Ryan was pitching pebbles against the wooden siding, making just enough noise to attract the sec man's curiosity, but not enough to make him leave his post to investigate.

While the sec man was looking in Ryan's direction for the source of the sound, Jak moved silently through the grass and weeds behind the barn.

The sec man was well trained. Despite his attention being focused on Ryan, he still took the time to look behind him at regular intervals. Jak began counting and realized he would look back every five to ten seconds.

Jak moved forward three seconds at a time before vanishing into the grass. He wanted to get closer, but the grass had been worn down around the bunker for twenty yards in every direction.

The albino teen pulled a leaf-bladed throwing knife from one of the hidden pockets inside his jacket and focused on his target. Twenty yards was a tricky throw at the best of times, and with the way Jak was feeling, it would be that much more difficult.

He waited for the man to look back, then when he turned to stare in Ryan's direction, Jak threw the knife.

It was low and off target, sticking into a sandbag.

The sec man spun and called out, "Who's there?" He raised his longblaster and opened his mouth to utter a challenge, but before he could get another word out, a second knife had pierced his throat.

At first he just stood there with a shocked expression on his face as blood poured out of his neck like water from a faucet. Then he grabbed at his throat and the blood streamed between his fingers in tiny rivulets. Finally his eyelids fluttered, his head wavered and he fell backward, dead.

Jak hurried into the bunker, picked up the sec man's

longblaster—a remade with a decent firing mechanism but a rough hand-carved stock and makeshift sight.

Jak raised the weapon and began firing it into the air three times while he shouted a few choice sec-man phrases.

"Hey you!"

"Stop!

"Come back!"

And then he crouched low in the bunker and waited.

ROBARDS WAS covered in blood.

Baron Schini's snub-nosed Browning .38 was smoking.

And half of Baron DeMann's head was missing from the corpse that was laid out in front of them.

Baron Schini moved her blaster onto Robards.

The sec chief was breathing in ragged gulps as he wiped DeMann's blood and brains from his face and shoulders. "What do you want from me?" he asked.

Baron Schini considered pulling the trigger and taking off Robards's head like she'd done with DeMann, but if she chilled both of them, Robards's sec force wouldn't let her get twenty paces before putting a dozen rounds into her back. The ville was hers for the taking, but she needed to play it smart.

"An alliance," she said. "A partnership."

Even though Robards was still on his knees, he was smart enough to know he was dealing from a position of strength. "I've got a drug operation. What have you got that I want?"

"Strength and stability. Baron DeMann is dead, but that doesn't automatically make you baron. I'm sure there are plenty of people in this ville that've got an eye on the position, some of them probably more worthy of the job than you."

Robards said nothing.

"You cut me in for say…a third of your operation, and I won't try and take this ville over while you're trying to solidify your hold on it."

"What will you do for your third?"

"Transport and delivery. I've got three or four wags that could make the run to the eastern villes, and I've got horses that could expand your markets over the badlands to the west. That would leave you free to concentrate on making the stuff…and beating back the muties and addicts."

"And if I say no?"

"Mebbe I'll shoot you right now and take my chances with your dreem-soaked sec force, or mebbe I'll call in my own sec force and take over the ville without your help."

Robards hesitated. He had provided so much junk to his men that they might not be able to withstand an attack from Schini's forces, especially not while their attention was already focused on a band of hardened outlanders.

"All right, you can have a quarter of the operation, and the right to expand the market westward as far as you like. I'll give you the junk at cost plus fifteen percent, and leave it up to you what you want to sell it for. Deal?"

A sly smile appeared in the corner of Baron Schini's

mouth. Even though it was just a first step toward controlling the ville outright, she'd never dreamed it would be so easy. "Deal," she said.

They each grabbed the other's right arm at the wrist. Baron Schini pulled Robards to his feet.

And then they shook on it.

RYAN CROUCHED in the grass and weeds on the right side of the wag-pool barn. Jak had gotten rid of the sec man stationed behind the building and was now firing off the man's weapon to attract the attention of the sec men around front.

Ryan waited.

The shooting and shouting had stopped behind the barn and all had turned quiet.

But the sec men weren't going around to investigate. Ryan figured they were either scared, or they'd been told never to leave their posts. Having seen the sec force in action, Ryan couldn't imagine they were that good at following orders.

"Ahhh, help, help me!"

Jak let out a scream of agony. If this didn't summon the others, then they were poor excuses for sec men.

Just then, one of the men turned the corner of the barn, moving cautiously toward the rear of the building along one of the side walls.

"Jerry," the man called out.

Jak responded with a scream.

The sec man started to run and just as he was about to pass Ryan's position, the one-eyed man sprang from the grass and caught him in the neck with his panga. The long knife sliced into the fleshy part of the man's neck, cutting the spinal cord and leaving the head to loll to the right as blood flowed freely from the wound in his throat.

Without wasting any motion, Ryan wiped the blood off the panga and sheathed it. Then he dragged the body into the grass and kicked dirt and dust over the pool of blood the dead man had made. Under the cover of the grass and weeds, Ryan took the man's ammunition, as well as his ball cap, green vest and longblaster. After he'd hid the body as best he could with whatever was at hand, he ran around to the front of the barn and passed off the sec man's belongings to Doc, who was already positioned in the dead man's post, with Eleander providing a second set of eyes.

"I would have preferred a pith helmet," Doc said, examining the faded blue baseball cap that had the faded words Ole Opry stenciled into the front of it. "But as a disguise I think this will do nicely. Who else would wear such a repulsive bit of clothing than a sec man?"

Ryan said nothing to the old man, letting him ramble on, not caring what he said as long as he made a convincing sec man.

When Doc was set, Ryan wondered if J.B. was having trouble chilling his sec man, but as he started toward that end of the barn, J.B.'s wiry figure came around the corner carrying a jacket, western-style hat and a double-barreled scattergun.

"Come with me," Ryan told Eleander.

The woman hurried out of the sec man's station and followed Ryan as he ran to meet J.B. at the second station, currently manned by Mildred and Krysty.

"Put up a good fight," J.B. said, "but not a very long one."

The Armorer handed the clothing and blaster to Mildred, who along with Krysty was already inside the sec man's position, keeping watch.

"Was the sec man white or black?" she asked.

"White."

Without a word, Mildred handed the clothing to Krysty, who bundled up her fiery red hair and tucked it up inside the western hat before slipping into the jacket.

Ryan nodded his approval, satisfied that the outside of the wag pool would be secure for a short time while they worked inside.

"Stay with Krysty, Mildred," he said. Then he turned to Eleander. "Take us inside."

She nodded, then led J.B. and Ryan into the wag pool.

# Chapter Seventeen

At the sound of gunfire, several sec men had rushed the podium where Baron Schini and Sec chief Robards had been arguing with Baron DeMann.

"One of the outlanders," Robards shouted. "The shot came from the upper floors of the baron's residence. Send a squad inside and flush them onto the roof."

Three of the sec men came to a halt and looked strangely at Baron DeMann's body. A large part of the baron's head was missing, and a lot of the flesh looked to be charred. The wound had all the markings of a round shot at close range, not from the rooftop of a building across the street.

"What are you looking at?" Robards asked, scowling.

"The baron's dead," one of the sec men said.

"That's right, and one of them outland scum did it, and I want him dead or alive."

"How'd they get so close to shoot him in the head like that?" another sec man questioned.

"I told you," Robards asserted. "The shot came from an outlander positioned over there." He pointed to the baron's residence.

The sec men looked at the dead baron, then at the building several hundred yards away.

It was obvious what the sec men were thinking. The outlanders were all excellent shots, but this was an impossible shot, especially for just a single round. Perhaps if it had been automatic fire…

"It's true," Baron Schini said. "The bullet zipped past my ear just as the baron was expressing confidence to Sec chief Robards about how his sec force wouldn't allow the outlanders to escape the ville."

Robards nodded and gave a humble smile. Baron Schini had said just the right thing at the right time to instill pride in the sec force and diminish their curiosity over the story about the baron's death.

"He said that?" one of the sec men asked.

"Yes, he did. So what are you waiting for!" shouted the sec chief. "Remember the baron and let's get those bastards."

The sec men ran toward the baron's residence yelling war cries and screaming about avenging the baron's bloody murder.

"I owe you one already," the sec chief said.

"Two actually," Baron Schini said. "One for getting rid of the bastard, and another for saving your ass just now."

"Two then."

"Not to worry," she said. "I keep a very precise ledger…Baron Robards."

Robards smiled. "Yes, Baron Robards."

"Sounds good, doesn't it?"

"Right, now let's get rid of these stupe outlanders. They've served their purpose, now it's time they were eliminated."

THE INSIDE of the barn was empty.

Too empty.

"Any mechanics working in here?" Ryan asked.

Eleander took a look around. "There are usually three or four men working on the wags, but they must have taken the afternoon off to watch the challenge in the arena."

Ryan nodded. The challenge had been a major distraction for the ville and the daily routine had been thrown out of order. "Well, J.B.?"

The Armorer stood by Ryan's side with a familiar expression on his face. It usually appeared inside a redoubt when they came upon a weapons store that had been untouched over the years, and they would be spending the day digging through oily blasters and shrink-wrapped boxes of ammo and supplies. But there were no weapons here, only wags.

A half-dozen wags of all makes, models and purposes.

There were large cubed wags that the baron used for delivering his goods, and a couple of general-purpose vehicles with gun mounts to escort the larger wags.

The bus was there, too, up on blocks and in pieces, as if it might be due for some routine maintenance.

But there were also some dedicated wags that had probably proved to be quite handy in the construction and maintenance of the ville and its wall of crushed vehicles. There was a backhoe that would be useful in digging trenches, moving earth and, with the hook bolted onto the end of its shovel, moving metal hulks into position on the wall. It was a nice heavy piece of equipment, but it would never carry all of them comfortably, or provide them any protection once they got out into the streets of the ville.

But J.B. hadn't even considered the backhoe, or any of the other vehicles for that matter. As soon as he'd seen the collection of wags, his gaze locked on one in particular. It was a construction vehicle.

"The dump truck," J.B. said, pointing to the large wag with ten wheels and a huge steel box on the back of it.

"Is that what you call it?" Ryan asked.

"We call it the up-down," Eleander offered.

J.B. smiled. "The box on the back lifts up and down to dump whatever material it might be carrying, like dirt."

"It brought a lot of wags to the wall from the outlying flatlands."

"And it's going to get us out of this ville."

"Be vulnerable from above," Ryan said. "One gren in that box will chill us all."

"Better to be vulnerable to one gren than a hundred blasters."

Ryan nodded and approached the vehicle. "Check the fuel tanks!"

J.B. unscrewed the cap of the large steel tank on the right side of the wag and grimaced at the smell of the fuel inside it. "Not diesel. Some kind of alcohol, grease-oil mix."

"Will it run?"

J.B. shrugged.

"It burns black and stinks, but it runs," Eleander offered.

"Can you get it started?"

J.B. climbed up into the cab and looked at the dashboard as if he were lost. There were wires hanging loosely from the panel, instruments smashed and several pieces just plain missing. There were also a few modifications, the most perplexing one being a light switch of the type you might find in a pre-Dark home.

J.B. turned to Ryan and shook his head. "Too much done to it," he said. "Might take me hours to figure it out."

Ryan turned to Eleander. "Can you help?"

"They keep keys in that office over there," she said, indicating an outdoor kiosk that had been brought inside and set up in one corner of the barn.

"Find them."

Eleander ran off toward the kiosk.

"Want to consider another wag?" Ryan asked.

J.B. was still in the truck's cab. "This is the one that will get us out of here. Besides, the others are probably rebuilt just like this one. Same problems."

Ryan turned to see Eleander return with a ring full of jangling keys.

"Which one?" he asked.

Eleander shrugged.

Ryan passed the key ring to J.B., who began to try the most likely keys in the wag's ignition.

Several keys slid into the slot, but none of them turned.

Just then, there were voices shouting outside the barn.

"Keep trying," Ryan told J.B. "Don't stop for anything."

He headed toward the door with Eleander in tow.

"Stay with J.B.," he said, then went to see what was going on outside.

THE SEC MEN were getting closer.

Krysty and Mildred checked their weapons and that of the sec men usually stationed outside the wag pool. He had a hunting longblaster that had been remade several times and didn't look all that accurate or reliable anymore. They'd use the weapon if they had to, but only after they'd used up their own ammo and only in close when they were sure they could hit something with it.

Two sec men had run up to the fence and were inspecting the lock and chain hanging broken from the gate.

Krysty kept low behind the sandbags, making sure that only the sec man's western-style hat was visible from the gate.

"You guys all right?" a sec men called.

Krysty waved, keeping her hand tightly clenched in a fist so as to not betray her feminine features, and to give the sec men a good look at the dead man's jacket.

Over in the other position, Doc waved the ball cap.

Seeing that the area was secure, the sec men began moving on.

Krysty and Mildred brought their blasters to the ready.

But before they'd taken a dozen steps toward the

wag pool, Doc rose and shouted, "They went that way!" He pointed to the left, toward the ville wall. "We wounded two of the rat bastards. If you hurry, you can catch the fucking assholes before they reach the wall."

And then Doc was gone from view, hidden behind the sandbags.

The sec men looked uncertainly in the direction Doc had pointed.

A moment later Doc was up again. "Hurry," he shouted. "Don't let the rad-blasted outland scum get away!"

That seemed to do the trick.

The sec men turned and began to run toward the wall several hundred yards away.

When they were gone Doc looked over at Krysty and raised his head just high enough to let her see his smile.

Krysty was only sorry that Jak hadn't been there to see it. He would have appreciated the way Doc's mouth had come in handy.

She gave Doc a nod and a thumb's-up, and resumed watching for sec men.

JAK LEANED against the sandbags that surrounded him on all sides and tried to catch his breath. The wound in his shoulder had settled down into a constant dull ache. The pain was nothing he couldn't handle, but there was something else wrong with his body. His skin was wet and clammy, and his heart seemed to be beating triple fast.

The world was spinning slowly to the left.

Jak squeezed his eyes closed and shook his head, hoping to shake away the demons that were haunting his body.

He could barely stand up straight, and all he wanted to do was lay on the ground and fold himself up into a ball, like a child.

But he couldn't do that, he had a job to do.

So Jak planted his boots in the dirt, steadied himself against the sandbags and resumed his watch.

SATISFIED DOC HAD SENT the sec men off on a goose chase, Ryan returned to the wag where J.B. was still trying out keys.

"Any luck?" Ryan asked.

"Some fit," J.B. answered, "but they don't turn."

As if on cue, the latest key he tried slid easily into the ignition. J.B. looked hopeful a moment, but then the key wouldn't turn.

"Keep trying," Ryan said, then turned to Eleander. "Are there any weapons stored here? Anything we can use?"

"Uh, there are some fuel tanks stored at that end of the barn. Some tools…"

"Show me."

She led him to the far corner of the barn where red metal and plastic cans were lined up against the wall next to a workbench covered with tools, some handmade, others pre-Dark. Ryan marveled at the selection of screwdrivers, wrenches, pliers and other tools he didn't even know the names of, or what they could be used for. If they had the time, Ryan would have had J.B. look over the tools to see if there was anything he could use and that was light enough to carry, but there was no time.

He moved to the fuel cans and opened up a few of

them. They all contained some sort of alcohol-based fuel that was nothing like what was in the tanks of the large wag.

They couldn't use any of it to extend the vehicle's range, but it would still come in handy.

"Help me carry these to the wag," he told Eleander.

Ryan grabbed the two heaviest cans he could find and carried them back to the wag. Eleander followed, with a pair of slightly smaller plastic cans.

When they reached the wag, Ryan looked for a way to open the large steel door at the back of the wag's box, but the big flap wouldn't budge.

Without looking up from the job he was doing with the keys, J.B. said, "Won't open unless the box is raised, and I can't raise it unless the engine's running."

Ryan nodded, pleased to know that no one would be able to open the rear door to get at them, but unsure how he was going to get them up into the big steel box.

A moment later he climbed up into the box and reached down, gesturing to Eleander to lift the cans up to him as best she could. She struggled with the heaviest cans, but managed to get them high enough for Ryan to grab hold and haul into the box. When he had all four cans inside with him, he turned his attention to J.B. "How many more keys are there?"

"Three more," J.B. answered.

A moment of silence was followed by the faint sound of a key being unsuccessfully tried in the ignition slot.

"Two more."

Another moment of silence and then the same faint sound again.

"Last one."

Ryan took a breath.

"Fits!" J.B. said.

Ryan leaned out over the box and looked down into the cab.

"Turns, too!"

But the wag's engine didn't rumble to life.

Ryan climbed down from the box. "Know what's wrong?"

J.B. scratched his head. "Could be anything. Dead battery. Fuel starvation. Fuel flooding. Bad wiring… Anything."

"You've got five minutes. If you can't get it going, we walk out of this ville on foot."

J.B. shook his head as if he didn't like the alternative, and then began scanning the instruments and switches without a word.

Ryan climbed down off the wag and kept watch on the door to the barn.

Suddenly, the wag's engine turned over, then rattled to life. A black plume of smoke erupted from the exhaust behind the cab, and the inside of the barn suddenly grew a bit darker.

"Needed to flick one of these switches," J.B. said with a smile, obviously appreciative of the ingenuity of the baron's mechanics. "Turns it on."

"All right, then. Let's move."

# Chapter Eighteen

Baron Robards led a group of sec men into the baron's residence. In pre-Dark days it had been an apartment building with twenty-eight units spread over three floors. Over the years, the baron had spent a small fortune converting the top two floors of the building into a single residence, leaving the rest of the units for his staff, friends, sec men and supplies.

"We'll do it floor by floor," Robards told them. "I want every exit on the ground covered by two men. A team of four will go up each stairwell, with two on each team searching the floor and then teaming up with the two at the other end of the building. I don't want the stairs left unattended for a moment. The only way out for these bastards is going to be to jump off the roof, or to fall off it dead. Understand?"

There were mumbles and mutters from the assembled sec men and none of them seemed too excited about running into the building after a group of deadly outlanders.

Robards had known that giving members of the sec force access to the ville's drugs had been a dangerous step. But it had been a calculated risk on his part and so far it seemed as if it had paid off. The sec force had been compromised, but their allegiance to Robards was already secured and Baron DeMann had quickly been forgotten. However, the sec force had become undisciplined and unmotivated in the past months, and judging by the looks on the men's faces, they really didn't care if the outlanders were caught or not.

"A week off for anyone who chills an outlander, and a month's worth of dreem to the one who chills the most of the scum."

That seemed to bring them back to life. Even the sec men who weren't hooked on dreem knew the value of what was being offered.

"I'll lead the north stairwell. Grice, you take the south stairs. We'll start in the basement."

The man named Grice nodded.

"The rest of you watch the ground floor, and the roof, in case they show up on top of the building."

The sec men broke up into three groups.

"I'm coming with you," Baron Schini told Robards.

"I don't need you," Robards said.

Baron Schini smiled as she shook her head. "I wouldn't be so sure of that, but I'm not coming with you to find the outlanders. With the deal we made, I'm coming along to protect my interests, keep you from getting chilled."

Baron Robards turned away and headed into the building without another word.

RYAN LEANED toward J.B. so his ear was near the Armorer's mouth. The wag's engine was so loud, especially inside the wag-pool barn, that it was the only way they could communicate.

"Doesn't run too bad," J.B. said, gunning the accelerator and listening to the engine rev. "But I can't be sure how much power the fuel mixture will give it."

"Faster than walking speed?" Ryan asked.

"That shouldn't be a problem, but we're not going to outrun anything, especially another wag. Mebbe not even a man on foot."

Ryan considered the problem.

"Keep it running. I'll be right back," he said.

Ryan hurried over to the corner of the barn where the rest of the fuel cans remained. He picked up two of the heaviest and ran toward the school bus. Once there he uncapped one of the cans and splashed the fuel all over the bus's tires, as well as the engine compartment. He did the same to the rest of the wags in the barn, using less and less fuel on each one so he would have some fuel left over for the barn itself.

"Open the barn door!" he told Eleander.

The woman ran to the large sliding door that measured twenty by ten feet and slid back and forth on a rusty cast-iron rail. She unlocked the latch that kept the heavy wooden door closed, then pushed against it using the handle on the latch.

The door barely budged at first, but after a few moments it began to slide to the right, allowing a blade of sunlight to cut into the interior of the barn, lighting it up as bright as day.

When the door was open wide enough for J.B. to

drive the wag through, Ryan tossed the fuel can aside and searched his pockets for a piece of flint.

He had a shard of the stone in one of his pants pockets and rubbed it clean of lint with his fingers. Then he found a patch of dry stonework foundation at the base of the barn and began drawing the flint across it. He rubbed the stone slowly at first to see if it would spark the flint, and when it did, he repositioned himself and began striking the concrete more deliberately, trying to aim a spark at the soaked wood that sided the barn.

It took five tries before a trio of sparks landed against the wet wood, glowing red for a moment, then erupting into a bright orange flame that wasted no time in climbing up the side of the barn and fanning out in all directions.

"That's it," Ryan shouted. "We're out of here!"

J.B. tried the wag's horn and to his surprise it gave a decent blast, hopefully warning the friends outside that they were on the move.

Ryan caught up to J.B. just before he exited the barn and climbed up inside the heavy steel box where he found Eleander trying to hold the four fuel cans in place with her body.

The wag rumbled out of the barn where all of the friends were waiting.

J.B. brought the wag to a stop.

Ryan reached down and pulled Krysty into the box. Next came Mildred, still wearing the clothes of the dead sec men.

"This is rather impressive," Doc said, sizing up the wag. "This should get us out of here rather nicely."

"Shut it, Doc, and climb aboard!" Ryan said.

"I must insist you take young Jak next," Doc replied. "I fear he's looking a little more pale than usual."

Mildred glanced at Eleander, then leaned over the edge of the box. "You all right, Jak?"

The albino teen nodded, then clenched his teeth and said, "Doc first. Age before beauty."

Without another word, Ryan, Mildred and Krysty pulled Doc into the box. Then the four of them reached down and helped Jak up and over the steel sides.

Mildred held on to Jak's hand until he was seated in the box and leaning comfortably against one of its sides. Jak's skin felt clammy and a little bit hot.

"He's burning up!" Mildred said.

Eleander put a hand on Jak's forehead.

"Well, I daresay he has every right to," Doc muttered. "That barn is rapidly turning into Dante's *Inferno* and the last man out would certainly feel the heat. I know I am feeling rather tepid myself."

"No, he's running a fever."

"From his wound?" Ryan asked. "Is he infected?"

Eleander looked at Mildred and shook her head.

Mildred sighed, then turned to Ryan.

"He's not infected, and he's not sick."

"What then?"

"He needs a fix."

# Chapter Nineteen

J.B. pulled the wag onto the streets of the ville. The flames had reached the top of the building, and black smoke began to billow out of the seams in the steel roof. A few people were running inside the barn carrying buckets of water.

"Which way to the gate?" J.B. shouted.

Ryan turned to Eleander. "Give him directions!"

Eleander nodded and climbed to the front of the box, then lifted herself over the left side of it so she could give J.B. instructions. "Turn left here!" she said.

J.B. nodded, released the wag's clutch and the huge vehicle lurched forward.

In the back of the steel box, Ryan watched over Jak, who looked to be in even worse shape than he'd been a few minutes earlier.

"What's going to happen to him?" Ryan asked.

Mildred shrugged. "Can't be sure, since I don't know what sort of drug they gave him, but if it's any kind of narcotic, he'll be screaming like a madman in no time. And if he's like any of those addict muties we came across before, he'll want to slash our throats first chance he gets."

"Will it pass?"

Mildred just looked at Ryan. "I don't know."

Ryan turned to Eleander. "Do you know?"

"He couldn't have had much of the drug, so if he makes it through the need for a fix, he'll probably be back to normal in a day or so."

"What do you mean, *if* he makes it?"

"If they gave him a pure dose, then going without another fix might kill him. But if it was diluted, he should make it, although it won't be pretty to watch."

The wag slowed.

Eleander and the others peered over the sides of the box and saw that they'd come to a crossroad.

"Turn right," she told J.B.

Slowly the wag started to move again.

"What do we need to do?" Ryan asked.

"Tie him up and make sure he can't get a hand on anyone. He's going to be strong, and determined, so don't take any chances on the way you secure him."

Ryan nodded.

"Mildred, Doc," he said. "Give me the sec men's clothes."

The pair slipped out of the vest and jacket that had once belonged to the sec men guarding the wag-pool barn. Holstering his SIG-Sauer, Ryan took his panga from its sheath and began cutting the clothing in strips.

When he was done, Ryan looked at Jak.

The albino teen's eyes were glassy and half-rolled up to the sky. His breathing was coming in short bursts, and his skin was damp with sweat.

"You understand what's going on, Jak?" Ryan asked.

The youth barely moved his head in a nod.

Doc put a hand on Jak's arm. "If anyone has the strength and resolve to make it through such an ordeal, I know you are the one, Master Lauren."

Jak reached out, put a hand over Doc's mouth, then grabbed a strip of cloth from Ryan's hand and draped it over his own wrist.

"Right," Ryan said. "Cut the chatter, Doc, and let's get him tied up."

The friends set to work.

THE SEARCH HAD REACHED the third floor, but there were no signs of the outlanders anywhere.

After letting his sec men cover the basement and first floor, Baron Robards decided to check the second and third floors himself, thinking that his men had to have missed something in their search.

But there was no evidence anywhere that the outlanders had gone through the building. Not a footprint, not a broken door or window, not even a body.

And the farther they went up the building, the more danger there was of the sec men looting the baron's quarters. There were all kinds of valuables laying about in there, from music boxes to weapons, books to new boots. There were piles of jack, gold and silver, even stockpiles of jolt and dreem. If he let the sec men wander through there on their own, none of them would be able to resist the temptation of pocketing a few items for themselves. Normally Robards wouldn't mind—he himself had stolen from Baron DeMann in the past—but now they wouldn't be stealing from DeMann, they'd be stealing from him.

But how could he call off the search, without his sec force questioning his motives?

The answer came from the outlanders themselves.

"Wag pool's on fire!" someone shouted from the other end of the building.

Robards ran down the hall to the north stairwell and looked through one of the smashed-out windows.

The wag pool was on fire, and couldn't be saved, but he could see that several people had managed to move out a few wags from inside the burning building. The wags were smoldering now, but hopefully a couple of them had been gotten out early enough to be saved.

"Let's get over there," Baron Robards said. "That's where the outlanders are."

The sec men headed down the stairs.

BARON SCHINI lingered at the window, watching the big barn go up in flames.

She'd been wondering how she might send a proper signal to her sec force, lying in wait outside of the ville. They'd brought a flare gun with them, but that might not be enough depending on how far her force was from the ville. Now she didn't have to do a thing.

The plume of black smoke rose a hundred feet or more over the ville and would be visible for miles around, catching the attention of her sec force, and anyone else who might be in the area.

The baron smiled.

It was all unfolding for her much more easily than she had a right to expect.

But she wasn't complaining.

She was quite happy to let the outlanders take care of the ville's sec force for her. And if they got away, well, the life of her son would be a small price to pay for a ville that made more jack in a year than she'd done in the last ten.

And all she had to do was watch it unfold.

J.B. SLOWED for instructions. They had been close to the wall several times and a few spots looked weak enough to break through with the giant wag, but there was no telling how far they'd get once they'd smashed down a wall of hulking steel wrecks.

"Straight down this road," Eleander instructed. "Once you pass the baron's residence, the gate is at the end of the road that forks to the left."

J.B. nodded and got the wag moving again.

"I want everyone to keep low," Ryan ordered. "The baron's residence is three stories tall, and there may be sec men on the roof with a clear shot into the box."

Mildred nodded in Jak's direction.

Ryan shook his head. "We've got to leave him there. Too risky to move him now."

The friends looked at Jak, his chest heaving as he struggled against the demons the drug had unleashed inside his body. "Not worry…for me," he said. "Get out ville…be fine."

Ryan turned away from the youth without another word. Then he picked up the scattergun that had belonged to the sec man.

"Going somewhere, lover?" Krysty asked, scooping up shells for the gun that were rolling around the bottom of the box and handing them to Ryan.

"J.B. needs some cover."

"I believe the term is 'riding shotgun,' is it not?" Doc asked.

"Something like that."

Ryan peeked over the top of the box. The baron's mansion was still a block away, and the streets still looked fairly clear. If Ryan was going to get by J.B.'s side, now was the time to do it.

Shouldering the scattergun and the rest of his weapons, Ryan climbed onto the heavy metal plate that extended forward from the box to protect the driver inside the cab. He moved to the right edge of the plate, then lay on his stomach so that his feet hung over the edge, and then down next to the passenger-side door.

J.B. kept the wag running steadily, allowing Ryan the chance to find the open window with his boots, then grab hold of the bars holding the rearview mirror in place, and then finally slip into the cab through the window.

"Just dropping in?" the Armorer asked.

J.B. had his Uzi on the seat next to him, but Ryan knew he was running short on ammo.

"Thought you'd need some help."

"Thought right."

"Any sign of sec men on the roofs?"

J.B. shook his head. "Not on the roof, on the road."

Ryan looked down the road and saw a dozen or more sec men spilling out of the baron's residence and onto the street.

"You think you can turn around?" Ryan asked.

"Nope. Street's too narrow. Wag's too big."

"Got to go through, then."

J.B. said nothing. Instead he pushed harder on the wag's accelerator. The giant vehicle slowly picked up speed.

"I REMEMBER this gaudy slut in a place called Marksville." Sec man Sherman shook his head. "She was something else."

"Good at what she did, eh?"

"Good's not the word. My sec squad fended off this mutie attack and saved the ville from being overrun, and the baron, Markus Shields, he says the whole squad could have an afternoon in the gaudy house on him."

"No shit."

"Yeah, but see, this gaudy house was nothing special and on the day we went there was just a single slut working."

"And how many in the squad?"

"Twelve of us, but two of them didn't like women so they drank all afternoon and went off to a room together. That left ten of us and just this one slut."

"What'd she do?"

"What do you think? She took us all on."

"One at a time?"

"Hell no. She set herself up in the middle of the big

room and we all had at her, one after another, two at a time, you name it."

"Bet she was sore after that."

"Mebbe, but if she was she wasn't lettin' on. To tell the truth, she looked like she was enjoying it. At least that was the impression I got each time I stepped up for a poke."

"Both times?"

"It was six..."

The two men laughed, until Roy glanced in the direction of the ville and saw the plume of black smoke beginning to rise up over the center of it.

Roy tapped Sherman in the arm. "You think that's the signal?"

Sherman gave him a sarcastic look. "You think?"

"I don't know, that's why I'm asking."

"Yeah, it's the signal."

"So what now?"

"We let the sec chief know that it's time to move in."

BARON ROBARDS RAN out into the street, only to stop in his tracks.

Just up the road the ville's best construction wag was rumbling down on him, smoke billowing out of the exhaust stack and two men inside the cab.

Outlanders.

Not only had they torched the wag pool, they'd stolen one of the ville's most valuable vehicles.

Any thought of letting the bastards go vanished from Robards's mind. If he let them, they would destroy the ville and leave it a smoldering wreck.

He'd become baron, but it would mean nothing if he had to lord over a ruin and contend with angry ville residents who would look to him to lead them back onto the path of prosperity. The outlanders had to be stopped.

Wiped out.

"Take cover," Robards shouted. "And take aim. Chill the outlanders, but save the wag."

Finding parts for the vehicle would be tough enough, but if any of the wag's tires were blown out in the fight, they would be almost impossible to replace.

The sec men scattered, taking up positions behind buildings, and the scattered chunks of concrete and steel that littered the sides of the street.

"Hold your fire until you can see the bastards behind the wheel!" Robards shouted.

The giant wag picked up speed.

# Chapter Twenty

By the time sec men Sherman and Roy found Sec chief Viviani and the rest of Baron Schini's sec force, they were already packed up and in their wags, waiting for the two men to return from their forward-area recon.

"Baron sent the signal," Sherman said, reporting in to the sec chief.

"You mean that huge column of black smoke rising up from inside the ville?"

Sherman turned around. Although this position was several miles away, the smoke could still clearly be seen.

"That's the one."

The sec chief looked disgusted. "Take your position. We're rolling in five minutes."

RYAN LEANED OUT the open window as far as he dared and shouted to the rest of the friends up in the box.

"They're all out on the street," he said. "We're going to need cover fire to get through this."

"Copy that," Krysty replied.

J.B. had taken his Uzi from the seat and now had it in his right hand. It was resting against the door as he pointed it out the open window on his left. When the shooting started he would have to slide down in the seat, shooting and driving almost blindly, just to keep the sec men back and behind cover. At long range the wag's big engine and front end provided J.B. and Ryan with some protection, but they'd both be vulnerable to fire for a few seconds as they passed the sec men, and for that they just had to hope that their ticket for the last train west had yet to be punched. Once they were through the line of sec men the wag's huge rear end and steel box would provide them with more than adequate protection for the rest of the run to the gate.

Ryan pointed the scattergun out the broken front windshield of the wag so that the spray of lead from the blaster could clear the road of any obstacles. He put his SIG-Sauer out the open side window and took a quick look at several potential targets.

There was a sec man taking cover behind a rusted-out garbage bin who looked to be carrying a badly remade longblaster. It was taped together in two places, and the butt and barrel had been fastened together at odd angles making the thing look broken. The sec man clearly wasn't a threat, but he was in a position that was clearly visible to all the other nearby sec men. If Ryan could chill that one first, the others would think twice about sticking their necks out to get a clear shot at the wag.

"You ready?" J.B. asked.

"As ready as I'll ever be. You?"

"Not really, but how can you prepare for something like this?"

"Exactly."

In moments the firefight would begin.

"PICK YOUR TARGETS carefully," Krysty told the others.

She had taken a look over the top of the box and saw that more than a dozen sec men lined the street, and driving through their ranks would be running a gauntlet of blasterfire.

The best course of action would seem to be holding their fire until the sec men made themselves visible in the attempt to take a shot at the wag. If they could keep them behind cover, their aim would be compromised and they'd have a better chance at getting through.

Krysty climbed up on the steel plate over the cab, which would give her good protection from below and a great view of all targets in front of the wag. Mildred climbed up next to her, but remained slightly behind, covering the left side of the wag.

Inside the box, Doc had to forego his LeMat for lack of ammunition and was forced to use Jak's Colt Python. Compared to the LeMat, the Colt felt almost light in the time traveler's hands. And while Jak was in no condition to care, Doc knew that the young man wouldn't appreciate him using his weapon. "Forgive me Master Lauren, but circumstances have rendered my own blaster useless, so I am pressed into using your beloved Colt. I assure you I will treat it with the utmost care and once we are through this predicament I will return it to your person in better condition than in which I took it."

"Use it," Jak struggled to say. "Chill bastards did this..."

A shot rang out somewhere in front of the wag, immediately followed by another.

And another.

The friends held their fire for several more seconds.

Jak suddenly screamed in agony as the demons writhing through his body took control.

J.B.'s Uzi crackled from inside the wag's cab.

And then all hell broke loose.

# Chapter Twenty-One

Ryan crouched in his seat. The first shot from the sec men had hit the steel step just below the door and deflected off the big steel box behind him. A second shot hit the door, but it had to have been a small-caliber bullet from a poorly maintained remade blaster, because the round failed to punch through the sheet metal.

Ryan squeezed off a round of his own in the general direction of the sec man he'd targeted earlier. He heard a scream, but couldn't be sure if he'd hit his target or not. Blasterfire erupted from all over now, including the back of the wag.

And people were screaming.

J.B. squeezed off a few rounds from his Uzi, trying to keep the left side of the road clear.

Ryan glanced out the front window over the engine cowl and saw a sec man standing in the middle of the road. He had his blaster aimed directly at J.B. and was waving his other arm as if he were trying to flag them down.

He was obviously on jolt or dreem, or some other drug, because what he was doing was the same as committing suicide.

"Stupe sec man!" J.B. muttered, never once lifting his

foot off the accelerator. He kept the wag going in a straight line, headed straight for their drug-crazed enemy.

As they neared the sec man, he squeezed off a few rounds.

Ryan could hear the bullets zip through the cab, shattering the small window at the back of the cab and hitting the heavy gauge steel of the box behind them.

Just before the wag impacted with the sec man, a shot came from above their heads, most likely Mildred's ZKR target pistol. The bullet struck the sec man in the forehead just above the right eye. His head snapped back as a large chunk of his skull came away from his head. The corpse wavered a moment on two dead legs, then was plowed into the ground by the oncoming wag.

The wag bumped and jostled as the right-side wheels bounced over the body.

Heavy fire came from all sides, and from all manner of weapons, small arms, longblasters and scatterguns. The friends in the box were safe from most of it, but Ryan and J.B. were still quite vulnerable.

Ryan decided to use the last of his ammo as cover fire. If they could keep the sec men down for just a few seconds more, they'd be through the fire zone.

He peered over the bottom of the open window, picked out the locations of several sec men and began to fire.

KRYSTY AND MILDRED were doing their best to lay down cover fire, but there were too many sec men for them to handle all at once.

They'd chilled four of them when the firefight started, but the rest were too well covered to pick off and were managing to get shots off at the wag's cab.

And they were running low on ammo.

"Bomb!" Doc shouted.

Krysty turned to see Doc moving quickly to the center of the box where a glass jar was rolling from side to side across the floor with its oil-soaked rag burning brightly from the top end.

J.B. had called such things Molotov cocktails and had explained that they had been devised by rebel fighters during a pre-Dark war in a place called Spain. It was basically a glass bottle containing gas or some sort of fuel with an oil-soaked rag or something similar around the neck. The rag is lit before the weapon is thrown at a target and when the bottle breaks on impact, the liquid inside the bottle ignites, starting a fire.

That was the way it was supposed to work, but this bottle had hit Jak at the back of the box and had failed to break when it landed on the floor. Now it was rolling around inside the box with its wick burning. That shouldn't have been a problem, but there were four cans of fuel inside the box, and if the flame reached the outsides of the cans the whole box could go up in a fireball.

Doc was struggling to keep the rolling bottle away from the fuel cans and every once in a while he'd attempt to pick it up, only to be thwarted by the burning rag.

Krysty jumped down off the top of the cab and came to Doc's aid.

Seeing the titian-haired beauty with him inside the

box, Doc stopped the rolling bottle by putting his boot on it. That gave Krysty a chance to pick up the bottle—which at some point in its history had contained an amount of Watkins Liniment—at the thick end farthest from the burning rag.

But even though the flame was at the other end of the bomb, the whole thing was very hot and she wouldn't be able to hold on to it for more than a few seconds.

"Get down!" she said.

Doc and Eleander crouched low in the box.

Jak didn't move. He stared blankly at Krysty with a pair of wild red eyes.

She threw the bottle as hard as she could at the side of the baron's residence and hit some brickwork over a window on the second floor.

The bottle shattered and the fuel inside ignited, raining sparks and flame onto the sec men on the street below.

There were screams of pain and shouts of confusion, and suddenly all blasterfire coming from that side of the street stopped.

"That's giving them a taste of their own foul medicine," Doc quipped.

A few more seconds and they'd be through the gauntlet.

BARON ROBARDS TURNED his head and put up an arm to shield his eyes from the flames.

To his left, one of his sec men was on fire and screaming in agony as the flames lapped at his twisting body.

There were sec men and a couple of residents of the

ville who looked as if they wanted to put the fire out, but the man was moving too wildly for them, crying out in pain as the flames ate away at his hair and flesh.

There was some activity on the road as a few of the sec men continued the fight against the outlanders in the wag, but most of the men were entranced by the sight of their fellow sec man burning, oblivious to the sounds of his screams. But then one of the sec men finally stepped forward and pushed the burning man to the ground, rolling him around in the dirt to smother the flames.

The sec man was no longer on fire, but his flesh continued to smolder and the pain would go on forever, if he managed to survive.

Robards went to the man's side and stood over him for a moment.

"Please," he cried. "Please help me."

Robards lifted his blaster and put a round into the man's head.

"Well, are you going to let this man's death go unavenged? Let's get those bastards."

The sec men started down the road after the wag.

"WE'RE THROUGH," Mildred called down to J.B. and Ryan in the cab.

Eleander came forward. "The gate is over to the left."

"She says look to your left for the gate."

J.B. nodded and the wag began to ease to the left side of the roadway.

"I hate to spoil the well-deserved moment of self-congratulation, but I'm afraid we still have a few persistent sec men to deal with."

Krysty lifted herself up to peer over the back of the steel box and saw that three sec men were running after the wag with their blasters held waist-high.

The one in the middle got a shot off and Krysty instinctively ducked, only to hear the round tink against the heavy gauge steel of the box's back door.

She rose up again and saw the sec man on the left lighting another Molotov cocktail.

The chances of another of the homemade bombs falling unbroken into the steel box were slim at best.

"Mildred!" Krysty called out.

The doctor turned her focus from the front of the wag to the rear.

"There's another bomb on the way. Try to take it out before it joins us."

Mildred nodded and scanned the roadway behind the wag and the three sec men following it.

At that moment the sec man launched the bomb at the wag.

It flew in a flaming arc that was sure to land in the middle of the box and shatter against one of the heavy steel sides.

Mildred steadied her ZKR 551 target pistol on the flaming bottle and squeezed off three shots. The first two narrowly missed the target, but the third caught it fully, shattering the glass and creating a giant fireball that fell well short of the wag.

Inside the box, Doc grabbed one of the lighter fuel

cans and began swinging it on the end of his right arm, back and forth, back and forth until he had enough momentum to toss the can over the back end of the box.

After the can was over the side, they all listened for the sound of it hitting the ground.

*Whumpf!*

They could feel the heat coming from the ignited fuel, and when they looked over the end of the box they could see a line of flame burning across the road, cutting off the friends from the rest of the pursuing sec men.

"That should keep them off our back for a while," Krysty said.

"One hopes a long while," Doc interjected. "It would seem we have another problem in front of us."

The wag came to a stop. The gate was just past the building in front of them.

The gate was closed, and the sec men guarding it didn't look as if they were about to open it without a fight.

# Chapter Twenty-Two

Ryan got out of the cab and climbed up the side of the wag into the box.

"How many sec men are on the gate?" he asked Eleander.

"Just two."

"And probably well-armed," Ryan said.

"I can open the gate," Eleander told him. "I know how to operate it, and I've done it before."

Ryan nodded. "All right. Krysty and I will take you to the gate."

Doc took a step forward. "I am going with you."

Ryan looked at Doc and Eleander in turn and knew the old man wouldn't be dissuaded.

"All right, the four of us, then. Let's move!"

SEC CHIEF VIVIANI brought his force to within several hundred yards of the ville's front gate. He wanted to advance through the gate and into the ville, but it was impossible to do with the gate closed off and scores of muties living just outside the ville's walls.

If his men got hung up trying to fight their way through the gate or over the wall of wrecked vehicles, they would likely be torn apart by the muties, who he had heard would tear a man's body apart in the search for something he could trade or barter for a small dose of bang.

Baron Schini had called her sec force to be ready with the smoke signal, but there was no way in at the moment, or at least no way in that wouldn't cost the sec chief half of his force. He was left with no other choice but to wait for the gate to be opened by someone on the inside.

ROBARDS STOOD helplessly in front of the line of flame, unable to see where the outlanders had gone with what was now one of the ville's prize wags.

Several sec men were trying to put out the fire across the roadway by kicking dirt over the flames, but it was hardly enough to douse the gallons of slow-burning fuel.

Men were arriving on the scene with shovels and buckets, but even with such firefighting tools, by the time the fire was finally put out the outlanders would be long gone and Robards would have already failed in his first test as baron. His hold on the ville would be tenuous at best in the early days of his reign, and he needed a show of strength to secure his position.

"You," he called, catching a young man on his way to fight the fire. If he remembered right, the man's name was Grayson, the younger brother of one of his more experienced sec men. "Go to the wag pool and tell them to bring me any of the wags that are running."

"Yes, sir," Grayson said, running off toward the wag pool.

The fire in the street had spread, and now flames were traveling up a set of wires that brought electricity to the upper floors of the baron's residence. The flames seemed harmless enough, but if they passed an open window and a gust of wind brought the fire in contact with some curtains or some other window dressing, the entire mansion might go up in flames.

Robards singled out three of his sec men fighting the fire on the street. "You men go back into the baron's residence and watch that the fire doesn't get into the building from the street."

"Yes, sir," they answered and headed back inside.

As he watched the men leave, Robards saw Baron Schini coming out of the mansion. She'd missed the excitement and was now just standing around watching the ville burn.

There was a hint of a smile on her face.

"Don't just stand there," Robards shouted. "Help us put this fire out!"

Reluctantly, the baron picked up a shovel and began moving dirt.

JAK WAS SCREAMING.

Every muscle in his body was tensed, and he strained against his bindings as if one more hard pull might break him free.

J.B. had left the wag's cab and joined Mildred inside the steel box. He was better protected up here and could lay down a better perimeter of defensive fire than he could from inside the cab.

"Is there anything you can do to keep him quiet?" J.B. asked.

He'd left the wag's engine running, fearing that if he shut it off he might never get it started again. But while the wag's engine made a lot of noise, it was a constant rumble. Jak's screams on the other hand were high pitched and erratic, and would give away their position inside the building cloud of smoke far more easily than any other noise they could make.

Besides all that, he was making it hard for the rest of the friends to concentrate on the task of keeping themselves alive.

"He's going through withdrawal," Mildred answered. "He's just going to have to ride it out."

"Can't scream if he's unconscious," J.B. suggested, gesturing with the butt of his Uzi.

"No, there might be another way."

Mildred picked up a spare bit of clothing left over from the sec men's uniforms and wadded it up in a ball.

"Hold his mouth open for me."

J.B. holstered his weapons and approached Jak. The teenager was snarling and snapping at anything that moved, including J.B.'s hands. He had to be careful not to get bit, almost as if he were trying to catch a snake.

J.B. hesitated. None of the friends had ever hurt one another, and it was strange to be forcing Jak to do something against his will, but it couldn't be helped.

If Jak was going to live, if they were all going to live, he would have to be silenced.

J.B. grabbed Jak's face with his right hand and his lower jaw with his left and pressed his head firmly against the steel door Jak was lashed to.

Jak's mouth opened up.

Then J.B. lost his grip on the albino teen's jaw, but a second attempt caught the jawbone solidly, and he was able to keep Jak's mouth open wide enough.

Mildred quickly stuffed the balled cloth into Jak's mouth, careful not to push it too far or to pack the mouth too tightly. When she was done, a torn remnant of the blue cloth hung out of Jak's mouth like a fabric tongue. He would be uncomfortable for a while, but he wouldn't be seriously hurt. And, most important of all, he was quiet now.

Mildred and J.B. returned to scanning their surroundings for the enemy.

RYAN AND KRYSTY crouched behind the corner of a building across the street from the gate.

One of the sec men was still in the crow's nest high above the wall and had his longblaster trained on the approach to the gate. The second sec man was at the gate itself, making sure the heavy wooden timber keeping the door locked from the inside remained in place.

Doc had left Jak's Colt Python behind, deciding he would be far more successful approaching the sec men accompanying Eleander unarmed.

Ryan trusted the old man's instincts enough to allow him to give his plan a try. But if it didn't appear to be working, he and Krysty would be taking the sec men out with good old-fashioned blasterfire.

"The outlanders," Eleander shouted as she and Doc ran toward the gate.

The sec man in the crow's nest moved his longblaster so that he had the two of them square in his sights.

Ryan aimed the SIG-Sauer on the crow's nest and readied his finger on the trigger.

"Did the outlanders come by here?" she asked the sec man at the gate.

"Are they on their way?" the sec man asked. "What's going on over there?"

Eleander turned to look at the smoke rising up from the fire coming from around the corner. "Oh, that. One of the baron's stills blew up. Took out two windows and spread fire all over the street."

Doc looked up and saw the man in the crow's nest and instinctively moved Eleander away from the gate and out of his field of fire.

The sec man followed them.

"You didn't see the outlanders come by this way, eh?" Doc said. "I could have sworn I saw one of them scum bastards go down that alley there."

"Couldn't have been," the sec man said, moving toward the alley for a look. "I've been standing here the whole time. I would have seen anyone trying to come by this way."

"Better have a look," Doc said, gesturing toward the alley with a flick of his head.

The sec man went to take a look.

Doc unsheathed his sword and ran it through the sec man's heart.

The man let out a slight cry, then slumped forward, almost pulling the blade out of Doc's hands.

When he was sure the sec man was dead, Doc signaled to Ryan to let him know the job was done.

Ryan acknowledged the signal by squeezing off a round and catching the sec man in the crow's nest in the right shoulder. The round didn't chill the man, but it was enough to knock him out of the crow's nest and down into the crowd of muties on the other side of the wall.

If the fall didn't kill him, the muties would surely tear him apart.

"Right," Doc said. "Let us get this gate open so we can get out of here."

Eleander moved to the sec man's station and looked at the ropes that were neatly tacked into place. One of the ropes operated the pulley system that would slide the timber to one side, allowing the gates to be opened.

But which one was it?

"I think this is it," Eleander said.

With Doc's help she began to pull on the rope. There was terrific resistance at first, but the more rope they moved the easier it was to pull.

In seconds the timber began to move, and five pulls later, it was far enough out of the way to let the door crack open.

"Keep pulling," Doc shouted.

"No, leave it like this for now."

"But we can't drive the wag through it."

"You get back to the wag," Eleander commanded. "I'll open it the rest of the way."

"What?"

"Go!"

"But if I leave you here, you will never make it to the wag in time. The muties outside the wall will ravage you the moment they break in."

Eleander shook her head.

"But surely you are coming with us. You do want to escape this cursed ville, do you not?"

Eleander said nothing, and didn't move. There was a sadness on her face, and a tear was just beginning to leak from the corner of her left eye.

"What is it my dear?" Doc asked. "What is wrong?"

"I'm not going with you."

"What?"

"Believe me, I want to, but I can't."

# Chapter Twenty-Three

Robards led his men in the battle against the fire. There were other ways to get to the main gate, but if they let the fire burn freely, it would take out the baron's residence and a half dozen other buildings on the block, several of them stocked with barrels of alcohol, oils and other flammable materials.

He had organized a few of his men and other ville residents into a line that was now passing buckets of dirty rainwater that had been collected from the roofs of the buildings inside the ville. The trough of every building in the ville was channeled to a gross of oil cans placed in a twelve-by-twelve square near the center of the ville.

As the fire raged, buckets were dipped into the barrels and passed along to the end of the line, where the last person threw the water on the fire, then rushed back to the barrels carrying the bucket and took their place at the end of the line. It was a crude fire brigade, but Baron DeMann had practiced it many times because of the volatile nature of his operation. There were dozens of open flames in buildings throughout the ville, and a careless worker could easily end up turning the entire place into a mound of ash.

And now, DeMann's thinking was paying big dividends for the new baron. The brigade had succeeded in stopping the fire in front of the baron's residence from spreading, and was slowly bringing it under control. However, the wag-pool fire was still going strong, and it might be some time before the fire was put out and who knew how far the outlanders might be by then.

"Where's the damn bus?" Robards shouted. "Or any other blasted wag."

"Would you like me to go find out, sir?" a young sec man in the fire line asked.

Robards hesitated, then said, "No, I need every man working on the fire now."

"But the outlanders?"

"Fuck the outlanders. We have to save the ville first!"

And then out of the smoke the bus appeared.

Its right half was charred black and one of the rear wheels on that side was still smoldering, but it seemed to be running under its own power, and it was no longer on fire. Even the horn still worked, as evidenced by the incessant honking being done by Sec man Grayson behind the wheel.

"Stop that noise," Robards snapped. "Why don't you just shout out, 'I'm over here, shoot me now!'"

"Sorry, sir."

"How well is it running?"

"Doesn't have a top gear and we couldn't refuel it, but it's running well."

"Well enough to get through that wall of fire?" Robards said, gesturing to the flames that still danced across the road.

"You're going to drive through that?" Grayson asked.

Robards drew his blaster and pointed it at the young man's head. "No, you are."

Grayson swallowed once, nodded and put the vehicle in gear.

"Not yet, you idiot. Wait till I get some men on board."

"Yes, sir."

"Stay here." Robards went back to the fire. "All of you on this side of the street, get in the bus. We're going after the outlanders."

The sec men on the right of the street dropped their buckets and shovels, then picked up their blasters and ran toward the bus.

"Hey, what about us?" someone asked from behind him.

"You stay here and put out this damn fire. If I get back and find the mansion burned down, you'll all hang for it."

Robards started toward the bus when he saw Baron Schini still helping with the fire. "Aren't you coming with us?"

"You go. I'll stay here and help with the fire."

Robards didn't like the setup, but he had no time to argue with the woman. Instead he called over the nearest sec man. "I want you to keep an eye on Baron Schini. If she takes anything, harms anyone or does anything even remotely strange I want you to chill her on the spot."

The sec man looked at the visiting baron and smiled. "My pleasure, sir."

"All right, then, let's chill us some outlanders."

"THE FIRE'S DYING DOWN," J.B. said, looking back at the burning roadway behind them. "We need more flame."

Much of the fire had gone out and with each second that passed another bucket of water, or shovelful of dirt was dousing the flames and making the road passable again.

Mildred took the lighter of the two remaining fuel cans and lifted it over the edge of the steel box. J.B. was waiting for the can and took hold of it as soon as he was able.

"Be careful," Mildred warned. "They might be able to see you through the flames."

J.B. nodded. He ran down the road, staying close to the buildings to the right. When he reached the line of fire, he uncapped the can he was carrying and began spilling fuel across the road.

The flames immediately doubled in height and intensity.

A scream could be heard coming from the other side of the wall of fire, probably from a sec man who had been standing too close to the flames.

When the can was empty, J.B. tossed it into the middle of the road where it would burn and provide an obstacle for whoever would be coming through the flames first.

The fire restored, J.B. ran back to the wag and waited for Ryan, Krysty, Doc and Eleander to return.

Hopefully they wouldn't be too much longer.

The flames would protect them, but they wouldn't last forever.

"BUT YOU MUST come with us," Doc pleaded. "After they have learned that you helped us escape, the baron's men will chill you, or even worse."

"I can handle myself in this ville."

Doc shook his head. "I do not understand. When we first came upon you and Moira, I got the impression you were trying to escape. Now you have the opportunity to leave this ville behind forever, and you are refusing."

"I can't leave my daughter behind."

"We shall come back and get her."

Eleander shook her head.

It was obvious to Doc that no matter what he said, Eleander was going to say no for one excuse or another.

"I can't leave," she said. "It was foolish of me to think I could leave this place behind."

Doc felt it was hopeless, but he had to keep trying.

"All right then, if you cannot leave this place, do not think of it in that way. Think of it as coming with me. I have seen many excellent pieces of land in my travels. We could pick one, grow our own food. We could start up a business, anything you like, as long as we are together."

Eleander smiled at that. "You're so sweet."

Doc returned the smile. "Then you will come with me, with us?"

"No, I can't. There might have been a way, but I haven't prepared for it."

"I don't understand."

She raised her hand and gently placed the back of it against Doc's cheek. Then she reached over with her other hand and pulled back the sleeve covering her right arm.

Doc glanced at her arm. "Oh, Eleander, no."

Eleander simply nodded.

Doc looked more closely at her arm, which was pitted and scarred with dozens of needle marks and sores.

"I can't leave this place because it has what I need. If I left, I would go mad within a week, and then the memory you'd have of me would be a painful one. It's better that you leave now, and remember me as a love you will cherish forever."

Doc's eyes darted quickly about as if he were searching for a solution to this tangled situation. "I could get you through this. Mildred Wyeth's a doctor, a real pre-Dark doctor, and she could get you off that junk so you would never need it again."

Eleander just shook her head. "I've been on it so long the withdrawal would probably kill me. Just go, before you put your life and the lives of your friends in danger."

Eleander leaned forward and gave Doc a kiss. "Goodbye Theophilus Algernon Tanner."

Doc struggled to say the word. "Goodbye."

And then he was gone, running toward the wag.

THE BUS WAS about to drive through the line of flame when the vehicle suddenly came to a jarring halt.

"What the fuck's wrong?" Robards shouted.

"The fire's started up again...burning hotter."

Robards ran to the front of the bus and slammed his fist on the dashboard. "Damn outlanders!"

"What do you want me to do?" Grayson, the driver, asked.

"Go through it!"

Grayson hesitated.

"I said go through it!" The baron's left hand shot out and struck the driver in the side of the head.

Grayson recovered, rubbed his head and put the bus into gear.

"WHERE'S THE WOMAN?" Ryan asked when Doc reached the wag.

"She elected to remain behind to open the gate for us."

"Not joining us?" Krysty asked, helping Doc up into the box.

"No, she must stay for reasons—" he shook his head "—that I do not quite understand."

Krysty put a hand on Doc's shoulder. "I'm sorry, Doc."

"As am I," Doc said with a sigh. "As am I."

"Talk about this later," Ryan said. "We got a busload of sec men on our tail."

The friends turned and saw the yellow bus approaching, its engine racing as it plowed through the wall of fire. When it burst through the fire, licks of flame clung to the sides of the vehicle and the rear tires ignited, sending plumes of black smoke trailing behind it like it were some ancient pre-Dark locomotive.

"Hang on!" J.B. warned.

The big wag the friends were riding in started to move.

# Chapter Twenty-Four

Sherman and Roy moved as close to the ville's main gate as they dared. Any farther and they would have a crowd of muties to contend with before they even got inside the ville.

There was a mob attacking a man to the left of the gate. He'd fallen from the crow's nest overlooking the ville and within seconds of his hitting the ground, more than a dozen muties were tearing into his flesh.

"Think the baron will be able to get the gate open for us?" Sherman asked as the sec force waited.

"You doubt the baron?" Sec chief Viviani answered.

Sherman realized his mistake. "No, not at all, it's just that she only went in with two men. The gate's guarded and—"

"Do you see the smoke rising up from the ville?"

"Yes."

"Do you think everything is calm inside, that it's business as usual in there?"

"No, but, uh—"

"The gate will be opened for us, either by the baron or someone under her control."

And then as if on cue, a sliver of light appeared between the two doors.

"Hey, it's opening."

Viviani sneered at Sherman in a show of disgust over his doubting the baron. "Get ready to move!"

RYAN CLIMBED UP into the box.

"Mildred," he commanded, "take the forward position and keep the muties away from J.B."

"Right."

"Doc, take the left side, Krysty the right."

Ryan then looked at Jak. He was breathing heavily through his nose and his head moved from side to side as if he were trying to shake off some demon. His face looked as if he were racked with pain. His body strained to get free of his restraints, but the effort just caused him more pain and frustration.

Ryan picked up the scattergun that had belonged to one of the dead sec men guarding the armory and rested it against the top of the back wall of the box. Then he looked over the lid so he could take aim.

The wag hit a bump in the road as he squeezed the trigger, and the big blaster's load of lead was off the mark. Instead of hitting the driver and everyone else at the front of the bus, he sprayed the engine compartment with buckshot.

Steam poured out of the front of the bus. The vehicle slowed slightly, but it didn't stop.

Ryan checked the blaster to see if there was a shell in the second chamber and was happy to see there was.

If he could lift the blaster off the steel box, he could have a better shot, no matter the condition of the road. He moved the last gas can so he could use it as a step, but his plan was called off by J.B.

"Brace yourself!" he shouted up from the cab. "Gate's not opening fast enough."

Ryan turned and looked forward. The gate was opening, but too slowly to be out of the way by the time the big wag passed through it. They were going to have to partially ram the gate and hope that the wag's frame was solid enough to withstand the force of the impact.

Ryan jumped down onto the floor of the box. "Everyone get down!" he ordered.

All of the friends, except for Jak, got into a crouch and waited for the moment of impact.

THE BUS DRIVER CHOKED on the steam that rose up from the front of the bus. The temperature gauge, one of the only things that still worked on the big wag, was quickly rising. A few more minutes at this rate and the whole engine would blow, or seize up.

"I've got to stop," he said.

"What?" Robards asked. "You're not stopping for anything. I want those bastards for what they did to my ville."

"Your ville?" Grayson asked. "What do you mean, your ville?"

"Baron DeMann's dead. He was murdered by those outlanders, and I want them to pay for what they did."

"Didn't the baron ever name a successor?"

"He never said a word to me," Robards said. "I'm in charge now, and I say keep driving."

"But the engine is going to overheat, and after it seizes up you'll never be able to use it again."

Robards had had enough with Grayson. His job was to follow orders, not to question them. And it would do Robards no good to have sec men questioning his authority, not now in a time of crisis, or later when everything had been sorted out.

He raised his blaster and put a round into Grayson's head.

Then he grabbed him by the jacket and pulled him from the driver's seat, throwing him down the steps and out the open doorway.

The bus swerved slightly to the left without a pair of hands keeping the wheel steady, but Robards took the driver's seat and managed to bring the bus under control.

While he'd been arguing with Grayson the bus had slowed to a crawl and the big wag had pulled away. Robards stomped on the accelerator and the bus jumped forward.

More steam began to billow out of the front of the bus, but the engine was still running.

Hopefully it would run long enough for them to catch and kill the escaping outlanders.

THE HUGE WAG'S front end struck the heavy wooden gates and seemed to stop dead in its tracks, but then the doors burst apart into thousands of splinters and the wag was through.

But instead of the way being clear, the road was covered with muties. They all had their hands stretched out toward the wag and their teeth bared and ready to rip into flesh.

Ryan and Krysty climbed up onto the steel sheet over the cab. Ryan switched the SIG-Sauer to single shot, and Krysty unleathered her .38-caliber Smith & Wesson. Together they began to clear the way of muties, shooting at anything standing in the wag's way.

Ryan took out a pair of muties with rounds to the chest, as they stood in the middle of the road reaching out to the wag as if they could stop it with their hands. They fell to the ground in a heap, and the wag easily drove over them, spraying blood and gore in every direction.

After a few moments it became obvious that the muties in front of the wag were no more than ants in its way. The real problem was with the muties trying to climb into the cab.

Ryan let his right arm hang over the side and began to take out muties as they tried to crawl up into the cab to get at J.B. Head shots were easy at this range, and Ryan took his time with each mutie, making sure he chilled the muties with a single round.

On the other side of the wag, Krysty was also keeping the cab clear. Ryan counted four shots from the Smith & Wesson and hoped Krysty had a few extra rounds in her vest pocket.

But after the first rush toward the wag, the muties backed off, or rather were content to tear apart the bodies of their fallen comrades, instead of being made mutant meat by the friends' blasters.

"I think we're clear," Krysty said.

Ryan took a look and the road was indeed clear in front of them, but there was a need to remain on alert. "Stay ready," he cautioned. "We've still got a bus full of sec men on our tail."

Ryan and Krysty climbed off the metal sheet and into the steel box. There was blasterfire coming from the bus behind them, but the rounds bounced harmlessly off the rear steel door in a series of staccato *tinks*.

"Need armor-piercing rounds to cut through that steel," Ryan said. "Let's just hope we keep moving and they don't have anything more powerful than what they're using."

The metal-on-metal sound stopped for a moment, and then a loud pop sounded.

"They're going for the wheels," Mildred said.

"Considering that there are eight rather large wheels at the back of this monstrous wag, probably belted with steel," Doc said, "I can only assume that they are in rather dire straits."

Ryan peeked over the top of the box and noticed the bus was falling behind them. More importantly, there were great plumes of steam gushing out of the bus's front end, signifying that the radiator had finally broken open. There was also more black smoke coming from the tires at the back of the bus. Presumably all four wheels back there were on fire.

"Their bus broke down," Ryan reported.

"That's it?" Mildred asked. "We're out?"

Ryan nodded. "Looks that way."

"Good, at least now I can attend to Jak."

Ryan turned to Krysty. "Tell J.B. he can take it easy now."

"Right." Krysty went to the front of the box, but stopped to steady herself when the wag took a sharp turn to the left.

Ryan was about to ask what was going on when he heard them.

Engines.

Gas-burning, diesel-burning, alcohol-burning engines. He looked over the right side of the box and saw a dozen vehicles heading toward the ville. The lead vehicle was a war wag, followed by a Hummer, and a ragtag bunch of old cars and trucks, each of them adapted or modified to carry weapons and men.

"If I didn't know better, I'd say that the ville is about to be invaded."

"By who?" Mildred wondered.

"Another baron, most likely," Ryan answered. "The visiting baron who was watching us in the arena would be my guess. Probably been waiting for a chance like this for years."

"And we gave it to her," Krysty said.

Ryan shrugged. "I don't care who runs the ville. I get the feeling one baron's as bad as the next around here. Important thing is we're out...and safe."

They all turned to look at Jak.

His eyes were turned up and his skin was covered in

sweat. Mildred put a hand to his forehead, then shook her head. "Cut him down, quickly."

Ryan's panga was in his fist a moment later, cutting at the ties binding Jak to the back door of the steel box.

The friends eased the albino teen onto the floor.

Ryan knelt by Jak's side and turned to Mildred. "Is it withdrawal?"

"It shouldn't be."

"Then what?"

"I'm not sure. All I know is that it's bad."

# Chapter Twenty-Five

Baron Robards pumped the accelerator several times, but the engine wasn't responding. The steam pouring out of the bus's engine was creating a fog so thick he couldn't see more than a few yards in front of it.

Finally the engine stopped running, expiring with a rough clanking, followed by a sound that was very much like a very tight spring being unsprung. With the engine seized, the bus came to an abrupt halt and several of the sec men standing in the aisle between the seats fell forward onto the floor.

"Outland scum!" the baron exclaimed.

The outlanders had managed to slip away, but that was the least of his worries now.

There were muties all around the bus, every one of them eager to ravage their bodies for something they could trade for bang. They would have to move quickly if they wanted to get back into the ville alive, and even then with the main gate shattered, it would be difficult just keeping the muties out of the ville.

Robards was out the driver's window, unseen by the muties on the other side of the wag.

His wag.

But that bit of luck allowed him to move away unnoticed and head back to the ville.

When he was halfway to the gate he heard blasterfire behind him. He looked back and saw several sec men trying to fight off the muties, but failing miserably. There were too many of them to hold back, and the mob had already gotten their hands on blasters and ammo....

The sec men wouldn't stand a chance.

That might just give Robards the chance he'd need to rebuild the gate and secure the ville.

Just then he heard the sounds of several powerful wags approaching. There was a war wag at the front of the line, followed by a number of other wags that had been modified for fighting.

"That bitch!" Robards swore, realizing what was going on.

He recognized the eagle insignia on the lead wag as the Schini family seal. Obviously she had been planning an attempt to take over the ville for some time, and the appearance of the outlanders was just the catalyst she needed to put her plan into action.

The ville was in ruins, its wags had all been torched save for the one that had been stolen and his sec force was in shambles with countless dead, and the living left without a will to fight.

He'd been baron of the ville for all of half an hour.

Robards fell to his knees. Tears began to well up in his eyes as he began to laugh and laugh...

The wags roared past him and raced into the ville. He

could feel the power of their engines, and smell the well-oiled mechanisms of their blasters.

Robards had never felt so small in his life.

One of the wags stopped beside where he knelt in the roadway.

"Hey, isn't this guy the sec chief of the ville?" someone said.

Another wag came to a halt beside the first. Robards recognized the man in the passenger seat of the wag as Sec chief Viviani.

"I've seen you before," Viviani said. "You're Sec chief Robards right?"

Robards shook his head "no," and then raised his blaster to the side of his head, pushing the barrel tight against his temple.

An alert sec man in the first wag jumped onto the road and pulled the blaster from Robards's hand.

"Take him," Viviani said. "He might be of some use to us."

Two men grabbed Robards under the arms and tossed him in the back of their wag.

And then the procession continued on into the ville.

Schiniville.

"WHICH WAY do you think we should go?" Ryan asked J.B. as the Armorer sat in the driver's seat of the wag, his wrists resting lazily on the steering wheel.

"I wanted to take a reading with the sextant but couldn't get to the roof of the baron's mansion to do it. And there was too much ground light to get a reading from the street. But from what I could tell from overhearing the sec men, my guess is that we're somewhere in the middle of what used to be Indiana."

"Best to head east, then."

"Yeah, that was my thought, too. East or south."

"Head east for a while," Ryan said. "At least until we reach that river we found the two women swimming in."

J.B. nodded. "How's Jak?"

"Pretty bad. Mildred's not sure what's wrong. Seems worse than just a simple withdrawal from drugs."

"Bastards!" J.B. spit. "Wouldn't mind going back there and blowing up the whole ville."

"The thought crossed my mind," Ryan replied. "But we don't have any grens to do it with, we're also way low on ammo, and... First thing we've got to do is take care of Jak, and he'll need plenty of water, some food, too."

J.B. put the wag in gear and pointed it east.

Ryan climbed up into the steel box to check on Jak. "Any change?"

"No," Mildred answered. "And he's becoming catatonic."

"What's that mean?"

"Well, he goes through alternating periods of muscular rigidity and mental stupor, and great excitement and confusion."

"So he could go wild again at any moment."

"It's possible."

"Tie his hands and feet together," Ryan ordered.

Doc, Krysty and Mildred set to work lashing Jak's

hands together behind his back, and his feet together at the ankles.

"His mouth, too," Ryan said. "But just a gag this time, in case he wants to bite somebody."

Doc took a long strip of clean cloth and pulled it tight against Jak's lips and tied it securely behind his head so he couldn't bite anybody in one of his wilder moments.

Ryan sat down with his back against the left side of the box. "Isn't there anything else you can do for him?"

Mildred shrugged and shook her head at the same time. "If I knew exactly what they put into his system I might be able to give him something to counter it, but I don't know what they used, so there isn't a whole lot I can do. I can't even give him something to keep him calm because whatever I give him might interact with the drugs that are already in his system."

Ryan nodded, understanding.

"We're heading for the river."

"Hopefully the water will be good enough to drink."

"Should be, especially since we'll be upriver from the ville."

"Good, if nothing else, Jak needs to be drinking a lot of water so he can flush out his system."

Just then the wag hit a bump in the road and Jak opened his eyes.

"Hi, Jak," Krysty greeted.

Jak suddenly began twisting furiously against the bindings around his hands and feet. He screamed, too, but his cries were muffled by the gag.

Ryan jumped on top of Jak and did his best to hold

him down so he wouldn't hurt himself against the sides of the steel box. But Ryan's weight alone wasn't enough to keep Jak still, and moments later, Doc and Krysty were also holding down the surprisingly strong albino teen.

Mildred heard his muffled cries for help, then looked into Jak's burning red eyes and saw that he was in great pain, agony. She could only hope that somehow she could provide him with some relief.

And soon.

THE FIRE on the street in front of the baron's residence had finally been put out. The street was black and charred, and the pre-Dark asphalt had buckled under the heat of the fire. The sides of the baron's mansion were also scarred by the flames, with windows on the first three floors melted from the heat.

But while the street fire was out, the wag-pool barn was still blazing fiercely. A great pall of smoke hung over the entire ville, making it look as if the place had just been through a war.

Baron Schini stood in the middle of the street in front of the baron's mansion with fisted hands resting on her hips. There was a cheroot jammed into the corner of her mouth, and a tight smile holding it in place.

It had all been so easy.

She had expected a firefight for the place with dozens of dead and twice as many injured. But the outlanders had taken care of most of the opposition just escaping from the ville. The ville's sec force had been cut by half, and the half that remained were exhausted from fighting the fires.

On the other hand her sec force hadn't fired a single round and were able to just ride into the ville in their wags and take over control. There were still a few sec men about and a few of them would undoubtedly remain loyal to Robards, or even to DeMann, and there might even be a movement afoot to get rid of her from within. But all of that would be addressed in the next few days.

For now, she was the only baron in the ville, and in fact, she was now baron of two villes, and she had never had a sweeter moment of triumph in her life.

Just then, the first of her sec men were approaching in their wags. The first two wags drove right by her, setting a perimeter around the baron's residence building, which would do very well as her command center.

The third wag came to a halt just in front of her. When the smoke cleared she saw that Robards was sitting in the passenger seat with the blasters of the two sec men behind him pushing hard against his skull.

"Ah, Sec chief Robards…or should I say, Sec *man* Robards." She gave him a little smile. "How did you enjoy being baron?"

Robards didn't answer.

"I bet you savored every one of those twenty minutes." She plucked the cheroot from the corner of her mouth and laughed.

"Tell these men to pull back their blasters, or I swear I'll—"

"You'll do sweet fuck-all, asshole." Baron Schini spit the words in a show of contempt. "You're nothing in this ville now. Especially since it was you who chilled Baron DeMann in cold blood."

A crowd of ville residents began to gather around them.

"I did not," Robards said. "It was you, you were the one who shot him in cold blood."

"So you're a liar, too, I see."

"No, you chilled him." Robards began moving his head in all directions as if he were talking to everyone at once. "Check the round, it's from a snub-nosed .38. I use 9 mm ammo. Check it and you'll see, it's a perfect match to her blaster."

"Thought of everything I see," the baron said. "You used my blaster, or one just like it in an attempt to frame me." She shook her head. "You're more despicable than I thought."

The crowd of people looked at Robards with disgust.

"Take him into the basement and hold him there until I decide on a suitable punishment for him."

"Yes, ma'am," the sec men said.

They restarted the wag and drove Robards away.

"Now, let's get that front gate blocked off," the baron ordered. "Last thing we need is muties wandering around while we're trying to get this ville back on its feet."

At that moment a man stepped out of the crowd. "Who decided that you'd be the new baron?" the man asked.

Baron Schini didn't answer. Instead, the sec man on her right raised his blaster and fired off a single round that punched a hole through the man's neck and spattered blood on all of the citizens standing behind him.

"Any other questions?" the baron asked.

The crowd was silent.

The baron smiled. "Good, then let's get to work."

THEY REACHED a quiet bend in the river just as the sun was beginning to fall out of the western sky, tinting the clouds strange hues of orange, red and yellow.

If the friends hadn't been so tired and hungry, and if Jak hadn't been fighting for his life, it could have been a very pleasant evening for them. But the moment J.B. brought the wag to a halt and cut the engine, Ryan was on his feet and barking orders.

"Doc, you and Krysty find out if there are any fish in the river worth eating."

"As you wish," Doc said with forced humor. "I shall fish."

"Mildred, you and I'll get Jak onto the ground. This box gives good protection, but the steel will get awfully cold at night."

"How are we going to get Jak out of here?" she wondered aloud. "I don't think he's going to be helping us any."

"We'll see if this box can tilt. If it does, the job's easy, and if it doesn't, we'll try to make Jak as comfortable as we can inside the box."

Ryan peeked over the top of the box. "You think this box still goes up and down?"

"Don't know," J.B. replied. "There's a control here that reads Up and Down. I suppose that one's worth a try.

"Give me a minute," Ryan said, as he climbed down

from the box. He got Mildred to pass him the last can of fuel, and anything else that needed to be removed from the box before it was raised.

When Ryan was done, J.B. started up the wag.

Ryan positioned himself behind and to the side of the wag and gave J.B. the signal to raise the box.

J.B. revved the wag's engine and after a few moments, he flipped the control in the cab to the Up position.

The wag's engine started to falter, but continued to run roughly as the steel box slowly began to rise.

Ryan moved directly behind the steel box and watched as the large rectangular door lifted up off its restraints and began to hang freely open.

"Far enough!" Ryan shouted.

Even though raising the box farther would make the opening wider, Ryan didn't want Jak and Mildred to come sliding out of the box since the rocky ground near the river's edge would make for a hard landing.

J.B. moved the control to the middle position, causing the box to stop rising and the engine to run much smoother.

Ryan grabbed a few nearby tree branches to prop the door open and then reached inside the box for Jak.

He was in a dormant stage, and Ryan easily picked him up and carried him around to the side of the wag. Then he put him onto the ground as quickly as he could, not wanting to be holding the teen if and when he suddenly turned wild on him.

With Jak on the ground and Mildred attending to

him, Ryan removed the branches holding the box open and told J.B. to lower it.

A few moments later the box was down and the wag's engine was once again shut down.

"I'll get some water for Jak," Ryan said. Then he turned to face J.B. "You see if you can use the wag to set up some sort of shelter for us."

J.B. nodded silently and went off searching for materials to make a shelter for the friends.

Night was coming.

And judging by the condition Jak was in, it was going to be a long, hard one.

# Chapter Twenty-Six

Shortly after dark, Baron Schini's sec force had closed off the main gate and were working toward controlling the key functions of the ville.

Her men had taken over the armory, which was full of remades and ammo, even a few pre-Dark grens, and they'd set up guards around the smoldering ruins of the wag pool. They had cut off the supply of fresh water from the ville's main well and diverted the flow to just a single pump so they could control the consumption of water. Whoever recognized her as the new baron of the ville got as much water as they needed.

Those who opposed her would die of thirst.

Any sec men who openly defied her were either shot or imprisoned. And if they refused to give themselves up, then their entire families were wiped out.

A funeral pyre of bodies burned in the open roadway between the baron's mansion and the front gate.

A small triage area was set up next to the fire, where pancreases, livers and other chemical-producing and -storing organs could be harvested before the bodies were placed on the fire.

The smell of burning flesh was putrid and traveled

throughout the ville, reminding those who chose to hide that no one and no place was safe for those who opposed the new baron.

But once you got past the sec men and the ville leaders, and stepped down a few rungs on the social ladder, few citizens really cared who ran the ville. In the gaudy houses and taverns, there was no change in the supply of drugs and people continued to use dreem and jolt to escape their reality. For them, a new baron meant that one form of tyranny had been exchanged for another, and they were still stuck inside the ville's walls. When morning came they would still be making bang and smash for easterners whose lives were just as hopeless as their own.

For people on the ville's bottom rung it was a case of the old saying that the more things changed, the more they stayed the same. However, even though things had changed, few thought that the changes would be permanent.

"Raise a glass to the new baron," one of Baron Schini's sec men said, trying to rally support for the ville's new leader.

About half the customers lifted their mugs in reply.

"What's the matter, ain't you going to toast the bitch in charge?" a gaudy-house slut said to one of the old-timers playing blackjack in the corner.

The old-timer lifted his mug quickly, then set it down again. "I'll toast the new baron when there is a new baron. The battle's over for today, but I got a feelin' the war ain't over yet."

"What do you mean? The new baron's got a sec force of over thirty men."

"And DeMann had a force of over forty that was pretty much wiped out by a handful of outlanders."

"So who's going to be the new baron when all this is over with?"

"Don't know that. But I do know it won't be Schini..."

"*How* do you know?"

The old-timer shrugged. "Just do."

The dealer dealt another card to the old-timer, who turned his cards over showing a total of twenty-one.

BY THE TIME darkness fell on their camp, J.B. had constructed a lean-to against the side of the wag that provided Jak a modest amount of protection from the elements. Ryan had given up his coat and the other friends had done the same, hoping to keep Jak warm through the night.

Doc had managed to net a few catfish from the river and along with the few dried provisions they could muster, the evening meal provided an acceptable amount of nourishment, if not flavor. The fresh water and a few bites of food had seemed to help Jak, stretching out the time he was dormant so that his wild outbursts came roughly every hour. However, his fever was still running dangerously high, and his wild times were becoming increasingly more savage. During the last one he had bitten cleanly through his gag and let out a loud blood-curdling cry that had surely been heard for miles around.

And so, expecting company, Ryan and J.B. took the

first watch, but Krysty and Doc didn't feel much like sleeping so the four of them kept an eye, and ear, on the darkness while Mildred tended to Jak.

Using the wag as a home base, Ryan scouted a perimeter of fifty yards starting from the river's edge and making a broad circle around the wag, crossing with J.B. roughly in the middle, before continuing on until he hit the river's edge once more.

Ryan and J.B. were about to cross paths for the sixth time when they stopped for a few minutes to talk.

"Think Jak will pull through?" J.B. asked.

Ryan shook his head. "If Mildred doesn't know, how should I? I do know that if anyone can make it through this, Jak's a good bet to be the one."

"Can't argue with—"

J.B. stopped in midsentence to listen to the dark, dark night.

"I heard it, too," Ryan whispered.

The two men dropped to a crouch.

"Direction?"

"I make it to the left, ten o'clock."

"Yeah, that's sounds about right."

Ryan looked behind him and saw that Krysty and Doc were aware of the danger and had also taken up defensive positions.

"You circle right," Ryan said, "I'll circle left. Let's see if we can get behind them."

J.B. and Ryan started to move when a voice boomed out of the darkness.

"Hold it right there, One-eye!"

Ryan froze.

J.B. kept moving.

"You, too, thin man."

J.B. reluctantly stopped in his tracks.

"We don't want any more trouble from you, Baron," Ryan said, trying to find someone in the darkness, but without any luck. "You let us go now, and we'll cause you no more trouble. But if you want more of a fight, we'll only chill more of your sec force and bust up your ville."

"Of that I have no doubt," the voice in the darkness said.

Ryan didn't recognize the voice. It didn't sound like either of the barons he'd heard speak in the ville. This one sounded, well…earthier, maybe even older. It was the voice of someone who lived off the land, and had done so for a very long time.

"But before you decide on fighting us, let me warn you that there are fifteen members of my family surrounding your little encampment. We've got automatic weapons with plenty of ammo, so it won't bother us in the least firing a dozen rounds into the darkness for just a single hit.

"And before you consider sneaking down to the river and away in the current, I should tell you that I've got two of my sons on the other side of the river waiting for you, just in case."

This was no baron, Ryan was sure of it.

But if not a baron, then who?

"My name is Ryan…Ryan Cawdor, and not One-eye. Who are you?"

The voice, somewhat softer this time, said, "A friend."

# Chapter Twenty-Seven

As darkness fell over the ville, Baron Schini's sec men cleared the muties from the entrance to the ville and began working on rebuilding the gate, using their wags to push and drag derelict vehicles from different parts of the wall to plug up the gaping hole that had replaced the large wooden gate. The makeshift patch would do for this night, as long as there were guards posted, but in the morning they would need to repair or rebuild the wooden gate and rerun it on its hinges.

Meanwhile, the baron had ordered Robards chained inside the steel box with the doors left open so that the rest of the citizens of the ville could see what had happened to their former sec chief…and baron.

The prisoner who had been hanging from the walls of the box, a former sec man named Desmond, was let down and set free. When first told of his good luck, Des had a hard time believing it.

"Go on," Sec chief Viviani told him. "Get out of here!"

"But the baron will kill me the moment I step out of the box," Des said, crouched in a corner and cowering in fear.

The sec men laughed.

"What...what is it?" Des asked.

"The baron don't give a fuck about your scabby little ass!"

"But he'll kill me—make me an example for skimming jack off the top of the operation."

"That's history now, asshole," Viviani said. "There's a new baron in town now."

The others brought Robards into the box.

"And she's got someone else to use as an example to the rest of the ville."

Robards was shoved up against the wall, striking his head hard against the steel.

"Sec chief Robards?" Des said in amazement.

"He ain't even a sec man anymore," Viviani said as the others began to chain Robards to the wall. "Think of him now as Sack of Shit Robards."

The sec men laughed.

Des, beginning to realize what was going on, began to laugh, too, leaving Robards as the only one in the steel box who wasn't wearing a smile.

And then the laughter suddenly stopped as the sec men slapped and punched Robards about the head and body, drawing blood and causing him to vomit a string of pale yellow bile onto his chest.

Des stared at the former sec chief in wide-eyed amazement, wondering how so much could have changed in just a couple of days.

"Now get lost," Viviani said. "And tell everybody you meet what you saw in here. And tell them to come by and take a look if they don't believe you. I'm sure there are a few in this ville who wouldn't mind taking a free shot at the former sec chief."

"Yeah, all right, I'll do that." Des walked awkwardly out of the box, his legs and arms not working very well after being chained to the wall for days.

"Why don't you just kill me?" Robards said through cracked and bloodied lips.

"That would be too easy. You're more valuable to us alive, so we're going to keep your heart beating as long as we can...to remind people that the old way of doing things is gone, and now it's our way or the hard way."

Robards spit at Viviani, but his mouth was too dry to do much damage.

The sec man replied with a punch that cracked Robards's jaw and knocked loose three of his teeth.

"See you around," Viviani said, spitting a gob of phlegm into Robards's eye.

"WHAT KIND of friend?" Ryan asked the darkness. "Do I know you?"

"No, I never met you," the voice said, "but I owe you a debt of gratitude."

Ryan tried to recall the voice, but he couldn't place it in his travels. "Step forward so I can see you, so we can talk face-to-face."

"You tell your friends to put their weapons down, and I'll tell my family to do the same."

Ryan thought about it. If the man had wanted to harm them, he could have done it easily by now. He called himself a friend and he was willing to talk, and that was enough for Ryan to listen to what he had to say.

"Put your weapons down," Ryan ordered.

The friends lowered their weapons, then a shrill whistle sounded in the darkness, followed by the sound of blasters being holstered.

"Will I have to speak to the dark all night," Ryan said, "or are you going to show your face?"

Footsteps sounded in the darkness and a moment later an elderly man, bald on top with white hair banding his head around the back from ear to ear, stepped into the clearing in front of Ryan.

"Name's Bennett Johnson," the man said. He carried a nicely preserved Winchester Model 12 scattergun, a dangerous weapon at close range.

Ryan could see his face clearly in the dim light, but didn't recognize him. "Do I know you?" he asked again.

"No reason you should."

"Then why do you call me friend?"

"You saved my wife from getting chilled in Spearpoint. Mebbe you remember *her.* She was dancing in a gaudy house there, going by the name Big Dumpling."

"I think I remember her," J.B. said. "We were with Hun and Poet back then."

Ryan nodded, remembering it as well.

"She was about to be done in by members of Levi Shabazz's crew and you people stopped them. When the whole place was blown to hell, me and Dumpling left Spearpoint with a bunch of others to start a sort of family together, so I'm sorta grateful to you. In your debt, you might say."

Ryan breathed a sigh of relief.

"Incredible," Krysty said. "We were almost chilled by a couple of barons because two of their family members were on the wrong side of a firefight years ago, and now we're going to be helped by a man who says you saved his wife's life."

"Not so incredible, my young red flame," Doc said, stepping forward to join Ryan, J.B. and Krysty. "I have been traveling with Ryan, J.B. and various others for some time, and I have seen them chill many people. But as a wise man once said, for every action there is also a reaction, so for every detestable, abhorrent and despicable sec man that Ryan chills during the course of a battle, there is also someone whose life is saved, either directly or through some trickle-down effect. It is simple mathematics, actually."

Ryan listened to what Doc had to say, but he was more interested in the old man and specifically why he happened to be here, outside of the ville and by the river in the middle of a hell-dark night.

"I'm happy to meet you, Bennett Johnson," Ryan said, "but I'm curious why our paths happen to cross here and now."

"No mystery," Johnson answered. "The word came out of the ville that they'd caught the one-eyed man who chilled the baron's brother at Spearpoint. Well, when I heard that I had a feeling that you were also the one-eyed man who saved my Big Dumpling's life, so I was actually on my way to helping you get out of the ville." He paused a minute looking over the wag. "But I can see you people did fine all by yourselves."

Slowly the rest of the man's family began coming forward and out of the darkness. There had to be a dozen or more of them, all sporting blasters.

Ryan looked back at the wag to check on Jak. "We managed to get out of the ville, but not all of us made it out all right."

"What is it?"

"The baron got a member of our group addicted to some drug."

The old man shook his head. "Probably bang. That's a real bad one. Doesn't take much to get hooked, and it eats away at your brain in no time."

"You've had experience with it, then?"

"Got me eight who I call my children, fourteen who are grandchildren. A couple of them ventured into the ville over the years, tried all sorts of things before coming back with their tails between their legs."

"Do you know how to get someone through the withdrawal?" Mildred had come to join them.

"How many hits did they give him?" Johnson asked.

Mildred shrugged. "I don't know. It can't be more than one or two."

"He's lucky then. Any more and it might take months to get him back to normal. If what you say is true, it won't take him more than a few days to get over it, but of course there's a good chance he could end up mad."

"Mad!" Mildred exclaimed. "Eleander never told me he could go insane."

Johnson shook his head. "People in the ville have never seen anyone quit bang cold turkey. Inside the ville they either keep taking the drug, get some help getting off it, or get killed trying to get more of it. But any way you do it, it's not a pretty sight."

Ryan stepped forward. "You said people in the ville can get help getting off it. What kind of help?"

"Best way is to slowly reduce the amount of the drug taken, but I don't think you're the type that want to give your friend any more drugs than he's already had."

Ryan nodded in agreement.

"You got that right," Mildred said.

"Then antibodies would be your best bet."

Ryan looked to Mildred for an explanation.

"Antibodies either bind foreign agents that invade the body by tagging them for destruction by the body's own white blood cells, or they activate chemical systems in the body that render the foreign agents harmless."

"All right," Ryan said. "Where do we get these antibodies?"

Johnson flicked his head in the direction of DeMannville. "Inside the ville."

Doc opened his mouth in disbelief. "But, if there are such things, why didn't Eleander provide us with some, or at least tells us that they existed?"

The friends all looked at Johnson.

"This Eleander, she work for the baron?"

Doc nodded. "She showed me where they make insulin and penicillin, but she told me she made other kinds of drugs as well."

"Like bang or smash, most likely. She probably don't know about the antibodies being made by a small cell inside the ville working to overthrow the baron. They've been trying the antibodies on addicts for months now, working toward creating a small army of people who want to overthrow the baron, get rid of the sec chief and stop the production of the junk drugs coming out of the ville."

"Well, as far as we can tell, Baron DeMann is dead and most likely Sec chief Robards is too."

"Then who's running the ville?"

"Another baron. A woman named Schini."

"Oh, I know her. She's a bad one, but I imagine with all the confusion going on inside right about now, there might be a revolt coming any day."

"Not our problem," J.B. said.

"He's right," Ryan agreed. "We don't care who controls the ville. We just want the antibodies for our friend Jak. Do you know where they're kept?"

"Yes."

"Will you take us inside to get some?"

"I was on my way to the ville anyway." Johnson nodded, then looked around at the group surrounding him. "Besides, one way or another, all these people owe their lives to you, Ryan Cawdor. Of course I'll help you. It's the least I can do."

Ryan nodded. "Right, when do you want to move?"

"Darkness has just settled in, so we have many hours

before morning. Let's get your friend to a comfortable place and put some food inside your bellies. Then we'll talk about getting inside the ville."

"A wise preparation," Doc said, rubbing his empty, growling stomach.

"And you might be needing ammunition for your blasters. If so, we have some to share."

It was J.B.'s turn to nod. "We're all runnin' pretty low."

"Good," Johnson said. "Replenish yourselves, stock up on ammunition and we'll be inside the ville within two hours. If all goes well, your friend will wake up with the sun and not even be aware that any of this ever happened."

Behind them, Jak screamed in agony and thrashed against his bindings.

"Let's move," Ryan said.

# Chapter Twenty-Eight

The knock on the door consisted of two sharp taps followed by three more, spaced further apart.

The sec man on the inside of the door turned the handle and slowly opened it. "Anyone with you?"

The man in the doorway shook his head.

"Anyone follow you?"

Again he shook his head.

The man inside stepped back to let the other pass. Then he stuck his head out the door and looked up and down the alley to make sure the man hadn't been followed. There were no signs of anyone lurking in the darkness. He closed the door, locked it and put up a chain.

"All right then, we're all here," said a sec man in the middle of the room named Lowachee, who had been a squad leader under Sec chief Robards. He passed around hits of jolt to the men in the room. Some took them and immediately cracked open the vials, some pocketed the drug for later use, or sale, and some refused the offer outright.

"Baron Schini is in control at the moment, and she's got a good part of her sec force with her," Lowachee said. "That'll make it bastard tough to take her down, but not impossible."

"But we're all that's left," said a voice in the corner. "There can't be more than ten of us still alive. What are we going to do against Baron Schini's force?"

"Yeah," said another voice that was quickly joined by others. "We'll get chilled before we raise a blaster."

"That's right."

"Too many of them."

"Suicide to take them on."

Lowachee let the men's rumblings run their course. "Too many of them, eh?" He shook his head. "And it only took six outlanders to turn this whole ville upside down. We got nearly twice that number, and we know this ville like the backs of our hands. We can take out Schini's forces, one at a time if we have to. What we can't do is *nothing*."

"Why not?"

Lowachee looked around the room in search of the one who had said that, but no one would admit to it.

"I'll tell you why. Because there's no guarantee Schini is going to let us stay sec men. Come morning, she might have us all give up our blasters, our ranks, everything. Then it'll be working in the labs or factories, and there'll be plenty of citizens who'll remember us as sec men, and won't be afraid of taking us on now that we're all on equal footing."

Lowachee let that last bit of wisdom sink in. He knew every sec man in the room had roughed up more than his fair share of citizens over the years, for no other reason than because they'd been sec men and they could get away with it. Without the title, and without the blaster that went with it, some of them wouldn't last a day among the general population.

"I'm with you," the voice in the corner said.

"Me, too," another said.

And soon they all joined in, preferring to fight the new baron than risk the wrath of the citizens of the ville.

"What about Sec chief Robards?" someone asked.

"What about him?" Lowachee replied.

"I heard that the baron chained him up in the box. We could bust him out, so he could lead us in the fight."

Lowachee said nothing for several long seconds. "Fuck Robards! He's the rat bastard that got us into this rad-blasted pile of shit. The last thing we need is to give him a chance to make it any worse for us than it already is."

The men seemed unconvinced.

"We'll all fight together as equals. And when we win..." A pause. "And when we win, we'll elect a baron from among ourselves in this room."

"What about the rest of us?"

Lowachee sighed. They already wanted to know how the ville would be split up even before they began the fight. It wasn't a good sign, but he had to give them an answer. "We'll all be members of a security council and we'll each have control over a certain aspect of the ville, with the baron overseeing the entire operation like the chairman of the board."

That seemed to do the trick, judging by the smiles on most of the men.

Lowachee knew that ten or more members of a security council would be unwieldy, but he wasn't counting on more than six or eight of them to live through their little revolt. And even if it didn't work, he could always switch his allegiance to Baron Schini before it was over, and then direct her men in executing the traitors.

"All right," Lowachee said. "This is what we need to do."

BARON SCHINI walked slowly through the rooms on the top floor of the baron's residence. Baron DeMann had filled each room with beautiful pieces of furniture, black velvet artwork, picture books and all sorts of electronic equipment, even though he would never have wasted what little electricity the ville generated on such luxuries. Still, it was nice to have tape players, and record players and assorted games. They were a symbol of status, of success, and now they were Baron Schini's to do with what she pleased.

"The former baron lived well."

"Yes, he did, Baron," Viviani said.

She opened a humidor with not only a selection of cheroots, but two actual cigars. She sniffed one of the cigars and put it into the corner of her mouth.

Viviani offered a flame from his lighter a moment later.

"And now I will live well, with two villes under my command."

Viviani cringed slightly. "I think it's necessary to remind you that we don't have control of the ville yet. The citizens might cower under our thumb, but the surviving sec men might not be brought in line so easily."

"Then wipe them out."

"What?"

"Wipe them out. Chill them on sight. They're all stoned on jolt anyway. No good to us."

The sec chief paused to choose his words carefully. "We might get rid of a few that way, but stoned or not, once they know they'll be chilled the moment they're found out, I suspect the rest will either slip into the population and be a thorn in our side forever, or they might band together and fight us."

"Then handle it however you see fit. Just take care of the problem and quickly. I want to start enjoying my new acquisitions, and I want this ville back to normal operations and making jack within a couple of days." She puffed on her cigar, nearly choking on the high-quality tobacco. "Understood?"

"Yes, Baron. Understood."

BENNETT JOHNSON and his family lived in an underground enclave by the river. It was virtually invisible to the eye until they were less than twenty yards from its main entrance, and it was only visible to them because the front door was open and there was someone standing in the doorway waiting for them.

"Is that the famed Ms. Dumpling?" Doc asked as they neared.

"No, that's one of my grandchildren," Johnson said.

"Big Dumpling, bless her heart, died two years ago after giving birth to my youngest."

"I'm sorry to hear that," Doc said. "Please allow me to offer my condolences."

Johnson shook his head. "Don't need no charity. We got a good-sized family here, and we make do with what we can trade, find or borrow from the ville."

"Borrow? Don't you mean steal?"

"No, we borrow most stuff," he said. "We fully intend to give it all back someday, but we ain't done with it yet."

"I see."

"Bring him down into your momma's old room," he instructed two of his rather burly sons, who had carried Jak to their enclave on a makeshift stretcher.

"I'll go with him," Mildred said.

"And get Genevieve to bring a little syrup to calm the boy's nerves."

"Syrup?" Mildred asked.

"I call it syrup, you might know it as whisky. A good shot of it will keep him calm till we get back with the antibodies."

Ryan looked at Mildred. "Will that help Jak?"

Mildred shrugged. "Couldn't hurt him."

Ryan nodded and Mildred followed the two men carrying Jak through the doorway and down under the ground.

"The rest of you follow me," Johnson said.

He led them down a flight of stairs, and then to the right where a table was lit by candlelight and covered with an assortment of dried fruit and vegetables, nuts, bread and jugs of water.

"Dark night," J.B. said in appreciation.

Doc blinked. "By the Three Kennedys, it's a veritable cornucopia."

"What Doc said," Krysty muttered.

"Help yourselves," Johnson offered.

The friends needed no encouragement, not having eaten since early in the morning.

"We're all low on ammo, too," Ryan reminded the old man between bites of food.

Johnson smiled. "Not surprised. I don't think the baron would be providing you with ammo when all he intended was to chill you."

"Do you have any ammo you can spare?" J.B. pressed the point. "We need mostly 9 mm and .38-caliber—"

"And I am in need of somewhat more exotic caliber rounds and materials," Doc said.

"Not a problem," Johnson said. "Every one of my boys is a real blaster nut. Built up a real good workshop down a couple of levels. Got a few special weapons stored down there, too. Show it to you later."

"Ah, excellent." Doc smiled.

"Uh, not that I don't believe you, sir, Mr. Johnson, but where do you get your materials from?" J.B. asked. "I don't see anything around here but stone and sand."

"Why do you think we've dug down so far into the ground here? Got us a vein of potassium nitrate and another of sulfur that provide us with all we'll ever need."

J.B. was impressed.

"As for the rest of it, well, I scavenged Spearpoint for weeks after it was all blown to hell. Picked up as many spent cartridges as I could carry. That's how I got started in the business."

The Armorer nodded. "Smart."

"There are plenty other places like that, too. We make trips every few months, combing the ruins of villes all over the east looking for empty brass."

Ryan looked at Johnson curiously. His setup sounded a little too good to be true. "I'm surprised the baron never tried to take over your operation here."

Johnson laughed again. "There's only one way in they know about, and I got that covered with a blaster that fires enough rounds per minute to cut down as many people they want to send through the door. And even if they did take it over, I'd wager that within a week they'd be making odd-sized rounds that would blow the ends clean off their blasters."

"Point taken," Ryan said.

"'Sides, who do you think makes the ammo for all the blaster and ammo dealers within a hundred miles of here?"

Ryan stared at Johnson. "I have a feeling I'm looking at him."

"If you deal so much ammo, why not just trade for the antibodies?" Krysty asked.

"No shortage of ammo around here, thanks to me. Antibodies, well, they're pretty rare, especially since they're all made in secret. Couldn't *trade* for any if my life depended on it—especially on short notice—but I suspect I can *borrow* as much as I need." He gave Krysty a little wink. "If you know what I mean."

Ryan and the friends knew what Johnson meant. They had been in countless situations where they would have gladly bartered for their freedom, only to wind up having to blast their way out of trouble, chilling countless people along the way.

It didn't make sense to fight when negotiations could be more productive to all concerned, but such was life in the Deathlands.

Johnson flashed a smile. "Enough small talk. Your bellies are all full now, so let's get you loaded, so we can get some help for your friend."

Johnson got up from his chair and headed down a flight of stairs, deeper into the ground.

Ryan, J.B., Doc and Krysty followed.

# Chapter Twenty-Nine

The sec detail inside the front gate was pretty easy. They'd chilled or scared off most of the muties hours ago, and now it was just a matter of staying awake long enough to be relieved by the next watch.

But it wasn't as if there was nothing to do.

With so many sec men on the gate, a few of them had left their posts and searched the ville for some jolt and dreem. Seeing as how that's about all DeMannville was good for, it wasn't long until they came back with more than enough hits to go around.

Jaydee had taken a half-hit of jolt an hour into his watch and that would probably last until he was finished. That would leave him the other half to take along with a few tankards of ale in the gaudy house the baron's sec force had taken over on the eastern edge of the ville. Word was that there were eight sluts working there full-time and they didn't seem to be tiring.

Some jolt, a few drinks and a big-titted gaudy slut to keep him warm added up to one of the best days he'd had since joining Baron Schini's sec force two months ago. If things kept on like this, then joining the sec force would be the best decision Jaydee McDougall had made in his eighteen years on the planet.

"Hey, pal!" a voice called.

Jaydee turned around to see who it was…just in time to get a pointed kitchen knife thrust deep into his chest.

He reached out to grab his attacker, but the person had turned and fled before Jaydee even knew what was going on.

Next he tried to stop the blood from leaking out of the hole in his chest, but it was flowing too strongly to be stopped by a pair of hands.

Finally, he screamed, as loud as he could, which wasn't very loud at all.

BENNETT JOHNSON was as good as his word.

A few levels down below the surface, he had built up an arms workshop that could produce just about any type of round or caliber size, from shotgun shells to .44 Magnum. He was even able to provide Doc with enough rounds for three reloads of his ancient, yet massive, LeMat blaster.

Ryan had originally wanted to leave Doc behind with Mildred and Jak, but he'd said that if there was such a thing as antibodies that could ease someone off the drugs they were making inside the ville, then there was a chance he could convince Eleander to come with him.

"That's not why we're going back," Ryan told Doc.

"I know."

"And we won't be spending any extra time looking for her."

"I understand."

And now they were on the outside of the ville with three more hours before the dawn.

Johnson had led them to the south end of the ville where he said there was a path leading over the wall of cars and into the ville. Arriving at that section of the wall, Ryan recognized it as being the section of the ville that had been overrun by muties several nights earlier, although it seemed much closer to the baron's residence than he remembered.

When Ryan told Johnson about the muties, the old man wasn't surprised.

"Probably planning a raid for days," he said. "And they would have made it, too, the ville's sec force being as drug-soaked and corrupt as it is. You and your friends probably saved the baron's ass on that one."

"We don't always get to pick sides in a firefight," Ryan responded. "Usually the side picks us."

Johnson shrugged. "No way you could have known, 'specially when the muties would have killed you just as easily as the baron's sec men."

"Are you expecting any mutie trouble tonight?" Krysty asked.

"From what I heard, your little action yesterday chilled a whole lot of muties and sec men. Everyone's regrouping right now, so if we're lucky we'll catch 'em all napping and be in and out before they know it."

J.B. turned to look at Johnson. "If we're unlucky?"

Johnson slapped a hand to his scattergun. "Then we'll be spreadin' a lot of the bad luck around."

J.B. smiled, approving of the old man's way of thinking.

Johnson glanced at his wrist chron. "It ain't gettin' any darker, so it's time we climbed the wall."

BARON SCHINI swirled a bit of the amber liquid in her glass, and then sniffed it sharply with her nose. It was a little stale, but the scent of the brandy still came through. She swirled it around once more, then brought the glass to her lips. The last taste of alcohol she'd had was a bottle of newly made red wine. It had been cloudy with a thick track of mud on the bottom of the bottle. It had tasted awful, but it had given her a pleasant little drunk. This brandy would do the same thing, only it would taste delicious going down.

As she was about to upend the glass, there was a knock at the door.

"What?"

Viviani stepped into the room. "Sorry to disturb you, Baron, but one of our sec men is dead."

"And?"

"Well, he was murdered by someone from the ville."

The baron nodded, then put the glass of brandy back to her lips and drank from it. She took a long moment to savor the taste, then put down the glass. "You sure it wasn't one of Robards's sec men that did the killing?"

"No, the man was stabbed in the chest with a small knife, the kind someone might use to prepare food."

"Spread the word about what happened to the men and make sure they're all on full alert." She poured another glass of brandy. "Then when the sun comes up pick a family at random, one with a couple of children, and bring them to the middle of the ville. When there's a crowd of people gathered to see what's going on, chill the family and tell everyone that when the next sec man is murdered by someone from this ville, two families will be chilled…and so on. I'm sure they'll get the idea."

Viviani hesitated several seconds, then said, "Yes, Baron."

"If you're not comfortable carrying out my orders, I can find someone else to do your duty for you."

The sec chief snapped to attention. "That won't be necessary, Baron."

"I didn't think so."

Viviani bowed slightly, then turned to leave the room.

"I'm going to nap for an hour, but I'll be down on the street before sunrise. I'm sure you can look after things until then."

"Yes, baron."

JOHNSON WAS FIRST to go over the wall, showing the ones that followed where the solid footing was in order to avoid the groan of metal or the clang of steel.

The breach in the wall wasn't far from the baron's residence. Luckily for them the front of the building had just a few guards posted, the rest of the ville staying clear of what had been a hot spot just a few hours before.

Inside of the ville and clear of the baron's residence, Johnson hid behind a rusting oil drum where he could provide blasterfire if needed while the rest of the friends came over the wall. Ryan went first, followed by Krysty, J.B. and Doc.

Once the friends were in safely, six members of Johnson's family took up positions to make sure that that section of the wall would be secure for the friends when they returned.

The antibodies were stored in a secret underground cairn below the bell tower that stood in front of the remains of what used to be this ville's pre-Dark city hall. They were stored under the ground because it made it easier to regulate temperature and other conditions that helped give the drugs a longer lifespan. They would have to leapfrog through town with Johnson leading the way, and the pairs of Ryan and Krysty, and J.B. and Doc, overlapping each other's path while covering the progress of the other pair.

"We have to go three streets west and two streets north," Johnson instructed them. "I'll travel from street to street, and you'll follow taking a half a block each time. We'll be there in ten, and back here in thirty."

And without another word, Johnson was off, running in the shadows until he reached cover at the corner of the next street west.

"Go!" Ryan said.

J.B. and Doc traveled half the distance to Johnson, and found cover. Then Ryan and Krysty covered the length of the block, joining Johnson, who headed off for the next street, with J.B. and Doc leapfrogging past Ryan and Krysty until they were in position in the middle of the next block.

The system seemed to be working well.

But just as Ryan and Krysty headed out once more, someone screamed somewhere to the north of their position.

The sound was followed by desperate shouts for help.

And then…

Blasterfire.

Ryan and Krysty didn't stop until they reached Johnson's position.

"Sounds like a firefight," Ryan said.

"Yeah, and it's going on right between where we are and the place we've got to get to."

"Can we go around it?" Krysty asked.

Johnson shook his head. "Nope. There's only one way to get there from here and that's through that blasterfire."

Ryan glared at Johnson. "You saying you want to turn back."

"No, but if *you* want to we can."

"Stop wasting time," Ryan said.

Without another word, Johnson was off, headed for the heart of the firefight.

# Chapter Thirty

Two sec men stood guard over Jaydee's body. The kid had been chilled by some citizen of the ville who'd been looking to strike a blow at the new baron. Well, people in this ville had another think coming if they thought they could get away with something like that with Baron Schini's sec force on the job. Come morning there would be a whole family of them pissing in their pants awaiting their fate while the sec force let the ville know that a mother, father and two children would be paying for the sec man's life with their own.

That would bring them in line, and if it didn't there were plenty of other ways that they could chill people in this ville, until they'd be scared to look at a sec man the wrong way.

"That him?" A pair of sec men coming on shift approached the two guards.

They stepped back to reveal a body covered by a blanket and a heavy winter jacket.

"Yeah, go ahead," one of the guards said. "Take a look if you want."

The sec man stepped forward and was about to pull

back the blanket when something heavy struck him in the back of the head. "Hey!" he exclaimed.

"What?"

"Shit!" the sec man said, holding the back of his head. Blood trickled between his fingers. "I got hit. I think it was a rock."

The guards looked around, but could see no one, or any movement in the shadows.

"You sure?"

"Course I am— Ah!"

Another one of the guards looked up just in time to see the fist-sized rock that would knock him out cold.

Rocks were beginning to thud against the sec men's bodies and onto the ground. They raised their blasters against the stony shower, but their enemy was unseen.

The muties had taken cover behind ruins and the rusting hulks of cars and were lobbing the stones and rocks all together, sending up a barrage against which the sec men had no defense.

"Fucking mutie bastards!" a sec man cried out, firing his blaster into the shadows.

But the rocks continued to fall, hitting the man in the head and chest, staggering him, then knocking him out, then pummeling his body to death, turning it into a bloody mess.

When the sec men were all dead, the muties rushed the wall, grabbing blasters and knives, and then heading into the ville.

Looking for more sec men to kill.

JOHNSON WAS the first to reach the firefight.

When Ryan and Krysty joined him, they saw that they were behind a position held by Robards's sec men, who were fighting it out with members of Baron Schini's sec force.

There were no candles burning in any of the windows of the surrounding buildings, but there was a good chance that many of the ville's residents were watching the firefight.

Ryan wondered how long it would be until they entered into the equation. An angry mob, backed by a few men with blasters, could overrun just about any position, as long as people in the mob knew that a lot of them would be chilled before the fight was over. Ryan didn't think that was going to happen here, since citizens had never had much say in how the ville was run and probably didn't care who was at the top of the ladder. Still, there would be a few who did care, and they would be the ones who shifted the balance of power.

J.B. and Doc finally caught up to Ryan, Krysty and Johnson.

"No way getting by there without getting caught up in the fight," Johnson said with a shake of his head.

Ryan took another look at the situation. All they wanted to do was to get by and down the road, which gave them an advantage, since their objective wasn't being defended by anyone in this fight. He made a quick assessment of the intersection and took inventory of what he had to work with. It was an average city street corner with old traffic lights, overhead lights on lampposts and a few billboards and store signs whose messages had gone unnoticed and unread for more than a hundred years.

"Follow me," he said.

Ryan hurried down the block until he was directly behind four of Robards's sec men.

Making sure they were all busy returning fire against Baron Schini's men across the street, Ryan switched his SIG-Sauer to single fire, and began putting a round in each of the men's heads.

The first two just slumped away, their heads vanishing in a spray of blood and gray matter.

By the time Ryan was taking aim at the third sec man, the fourth had turned around and seen them.

There was an expression of confusion about his fate for a split second, and then his face was gone as a round from Krysty's Smith & Wesson wiped it away in a wash of red.

"J.B., Krysty and Johnson, keep them busy for a minute!" Ryan ordered. "Doc, dust off your blaster. I've got a job for it."

Without a word of response, J.B., Krysty and Johnson began firing back at the sec men across the street, having no better luck at eliminating them than the sec men Ryan had just chilled.

The one-eyed man pointed to a billboard that was bolted to the building on the northeast corner of the intersection. "See that sign hanging across the street?"

"The one that says, 'There's a whole new world coming'?"

Ryan nodded. "Yeah. Take it down with the LeMat."

Doc rested the barrel of the giant blaster on a pre-Dark newspaper box that was chained to the corner lamppost and took aim at the sign.

"Be ready to cross the street on my order," Ryan warned.

Doc continued to adjust the blaster.

"Any time you're ready, Doc."

"Patience, my dear Ryan. The LeMat is not a Czech-built target pistol, it needs to be aimed thoughtfully and with, I must admit, a bit of imagination in terms of wind and climate and so forth. If I were to miss, or otherwise not achieve the desired results, your plan will have been foiled and we will be forced to come up with another... And, considering this is your first plan, I don't hold out great confidence for the successful outcome of the ones that will follow it."

"He always like this?" Johnson asked.

"Just fire the damn blaster, Doc!"

"As you wish."

Doc pulled the trigger and the Civil War blaster's .63-caliber scattergun boomed.

An instant later the sign across the street twisted savagely as if it had been struck by hurricane-force winds, and then it came apart from the wall it was secured to, tearing several bricks out of the wall along with it.

The sign fluttered down on the sec men. It had looked small hanging over the street and secured to the wall, but by the time it was on street level, it had covered three of the sec men, while the fourth had his head sheared off by one of the twisted, jagged edges created by the force of Doc's round.

There were screams and shouts coming from the other side of the street.

"That's it, let's move!" Ryan said, his SIG-Sauer covering the rest of the friends as they scrambled across the intersection and down the street.

In moments the firefight was behind them, and judging by the sounds of things, it was over as well.

"That was quite the plan," Johnson said, obviously impressed. "No wonder Spearpoint was toast after you were through with it."

Ryan wasn't interested.

"Is that the tower?"

Johnson turned around and like the others, saw the bell tower, still pretty much intact, rising up in the center of a large open square.

"That's it, all right."

"Where's the stuff buried?"

"Underneath it, but you have to access the vault through the building over there, or a stairway at the edge of the square."

"Take us to the stairway."

Johnson shook his head. "I don't have a key for that door." Then he looked at Doc's smoking blaster. "But then again, mebbe we won't be needing a key."

JAK'S SCREAM was painful for Mildred to listen to.

The albino teen had been brought into a sort of large shower room that Bennett Johnson and his family used not only to keep themselves clean, but as an infirmary as well.

There were a few rudimentary medical tools on shelves on the walls and a few basic supplies stored in jars, but the best aspect of the room was the homemade wooden table in the center of it. The table was basically a workbench that had been converted into a sort of bed. It was covered with a rag-filled mattress, and a series of leather belts was positioned periodically at its edges starting at the head, and going down the body. Obviously Johnson's family had had to deal with dangerous patients before, maybe even on a regular basis.

Mildred had done her best to make Jak comfortable, keeping him hydrated as she toweled the sweat from his body. She also used damp towels to keep his body temperature down to acceptable levels.

A few of the Johnson family members had offered her some rudimentary sedatives that were something like pre-Dark Valium, but Mildred was hesitant to give Jak anything she really didn't have to, since she didn't know when the others would be returning and couldn't be sure how whatever she gave him to rest would react with the antibodies they would be bringing her later on.

Jak let out another bone-jarring, blood-curdling scream.

But while Mildred was affected by her friend's pain, the rest of the Johnson family seemed unbothered by the sound of the albino teen's suffering.

"We've heard much worse," one of the older children said. Mildred remembered his name being Lars. "When my brother came back from the ville, he'd been on bang for three months. He screamed for seven days before he was finally off the drug. For him—" he gestured to Jak "—it hasn't even been seven hours."

Mildred wondered how long it *had* been and glanced at her wrist chron.

Not even two hours since the friends had left.

# Chapter Thirty-One

Sec chief Viviani was the first to crawl out from under the sign.

"Are you all right?" he asked, looking left and right. "Is everyone all—" He stopped in midsentence when he saw the head of one of his sec men several yards away from the man's body.

"I'm all right," one of the other sec men said.

"Cut my arm, but I'll live."

Viviani looked away from the dead man.

"How is he?" another sec man asked.

"Dead."

A moment of silence.

"Where did they go?" the sec chief asked.

"Who?"

"Robards's sec men."

"Gone."

"Mebbe they're trying to get around us and knocked down the sign as a distraction."

A sliver of fear crept up Viviani's spine. Mebbe taking control of the ville wasn't going to be as easy as Baron Schini thought. "Back to the baron's residence. We'll set up a position there. If we can't take over the rest of the ville, at least we'll control the main gate and the ville's control center."

"IT'S DOWN THERE," Johnson said.

There were the remains of a pre-Dark fence on the edge of the square, and the entrance to the cairn itself was a three-sided rectangular box that had one end open to a stairway that led down into the ground.

"There's a door at the bottom of the stairs that leads under the bell tower. It was a room they kept electronic and public-address equipment in for the square—you know, so they could make announcements at special events and such."

"Why store medicine there?"

"Why not?" Johnson answered. "Few people know where it leads, the room is dry and cool in both winter and summer, and it's easy to get to…if you have a key."

Johnson led them to the stairs.

When they stopped there, they all looked at Johnson, whose own eyes were wide in surprise.

The door at the bottom of the stairs was unlocked, and open.

THE MUTIES had stormed through the main gate, stoning the sec men there, then taking their weapons before charging into the heart of the ville.

They were tempted to head for the baron's residence first, but it was the most heavily defended part of the ville and attacking it now was akin to suicide. They were better off taking over the back alleys and side streets, and rolling the dealers for both their drugs and their jack. Some of them even carried blasters, which would give their inevitable assault on the baron's residence an even better chance at success.

The muties stayed close to the shadows, although their rambling gait betrayed their presence, as looping hands and feet often strayed into the light as they walked.

But they made no sound.

The leader, an older man with a body covered in open sores, led them to a part of the ville known for its gaudy houses and jolt dealers—Jarvis Street.

As they neared the street, it seemed as if no one in the neighborhood was aware that the ville was under siege. The lights were on in each of the gaudy houses, and there were jolt dealers on every street corner.

But once they reached Jarvis Street itself, it was obvious that the gaudy houses had been affected by the change in power and were busy doing business with the new sec force. And while the dealers out on the street were still there, now they had a sec man watching over them, ready to take the baron's cut of the dealer's gross…or what the new baron would take as a cut once she figured out the intricacies of the ville's finances.

They took out the first sec man with a handblaster to the head at short range. That convinced the dealer to give up his money, jolt and bang, as well as his blaster, a single-shot homemade weapon strapped to his right wrist.

When a sec man came out of the gaudy house to see what was going on, the muties chilled him with a blaster round to the back of the head.

And then they took his blaster.

When another sec man came out to see what had happened to the first, they used the first sec man's blaster to chill him as well. And then they took his weapon.

Eventually, sec men stopped coming out into the street.

That's when the muties moved on to the next gaudy house, dividing the appropriated jolt and bang between themselves. As a result, they were an army that was becoming increasingly well armed by the hour.

And thanks to the jolt and bang, they were also becoming more fearless, not to mention reckless, the deeper they moved into the ville.

"WHAT'S PAST the door?" Ryan asked Johnson, the friends' guide through the ville.

"There's a short hallway just inside and then another door, without a lock on it, that leads into the storage room."

"How big's the storage room?"

"Ten by twenty feet."

"If we go in blasting, will we damage the antibodies?"

"Hard to say. If they're still in storage, no. But, if there's someone in there and they've got the antibodies in their hands or in a pocket..." His voice trailed off.

"We'll take our chances. Me and J.B. will lead."

And then without another word, Ryan slipped down the stairs, followed by J.B. Krysty, Doc and Johnson stayed above ground, making sure the others would have an escape route and wouldn't get holed up in the stairway.

At the bottom of the stairs, Ryan pushed the door fully open with the point of his index finger. It swung open silently at first, but then creaked on its hinges. Ryan couldn't stop the door from moving and hoped that whoever was inside would think it was just the wind.

Ryan and J.B. remained alert, their blasters pointed through the doorway and ready to fill the darkness with lead the moment someone appeared.

No one did.

They pressed on, through the door and into the darkness. Surely, whoever was inside had a light with them, an open flame or lantern. Then, as they got closer to the second doorway, a sliver of light materialized on the floor beneath the bottom of the door.

They watched the light for several moments.

Ryan turned to J.B. and first put up an index finger, then added his middle finger, asking the Armorer if he thought there were one or two people inside.

J.B. held up a single finger.

Ryan nodded, then glanced to J.B. to see if he was ready.

J.B. nodded.

Ryan moved his SIG-Sauer in a side-to-side motion, suggesting that J.B. spray the room with fire from his Uzi.

The Armorer nodded.

Ryan moved closer to the door. It was a steel door and would probably stop their 9 mm fire from causing any damage inside the room. They needed an unobstructed line of fire and they would have it in seconds.

J.B. took a position about a yard from the door, planted his feet, then raised his Uzi to waist height.

Ryan reached for the doorknob and put his hand on it. He took a breath, then turned the knob and pulled the door open in a single swift motion.

J.B. opened fire, the Uzi spraying lead into the room at a rate of six hundred rounds per minute.

The light that had been filling the room went out and in the flash of the Uzi's muzzle, they could see a single figure in the room, caught in a hail of blasterfire and being thrown back against the wall opposite the doorway.

After less than two seconds of explosive blaster chatter, followed by a single short scream, everything went eerily silent.

"Let them know we're all right," Ryan said. "And call Johnson down here so we know what we're looking for."

J.B. went back to the bottom of the stairs.

Ryan moved forward into the room. There was a small amount of light from above streaming down the stairs, but he would need a smaller, more intense light to find what they needed.

Ryan found the body in the middle of the room and stood next to it so the others wouldn't stumble over it.

In moments, Johnson was with them.

"You have a match, lighter?"

A tiny flame suddenly erupted in Johnson's hand. He handed the lighter to Ryan.

"Is it here?" Ryan asked. The room was filled with a couple of banks of pre-Dark electronic equipment, and other parts of the room had been used for storage of all sorts of things, from ropes and chains to shovels and swords. There were plenty of boxes, too, but they didn't have time to go through them to discover their contents.

Johnson went to one corner of the room where a heavy steel cabinet was already open. "It's usually in here," he said. "Whoever that is, they were probably after the same thing. I imagine the antibodies will be pretty valuable now that the flow of drugs might be disrupted for a while."

At Johnson's mention of the body, Ryan brought the lighter to its face to see if they recognized who it was.

"Fireblast!" Ryan said.

"What is it?" J.B. asked.

"Take a look."

J.B. knelt to take a look and his face was masked in surprise. "Dark night."

"What's wrong?" Johnson asked, scooping up the antibodies from inside the cabinet.

It was the woman Doc had fallen for, Eleander.

"What's she doing in here? If she knew about the antibodies, why didn't she come with us?"

Ryan brought the flame down closer to the woman's face.

And then her eyes gently fluttered open. She looked over at Ryan. "I know you," she whispered.

Ryan said nothing, but his face had to have relayed the question that was on his mind.

"Didn't want to leave," she managed to say. "Like drugs..."

Ryan reached down to hold her hand.

"But when Doc left..." She coughed up some blood, and it trickled out of the corner of her mouth. "Thought about it...wanted to change...my life—"

Her body was racked by another cough. She took a breath, but was choked off by blood inside her lungs.

Eleander was still.

Johnson stood over them. "Someone you knew?"

Ryan looked at J.B. The Armorer's lips pressed together in a thin line and he adjusted his fedora.

"No," Ryan said.

Johnson nodded. "Right, then. All done here."

They left the room and headed for the stairs.

# Chapter Thirty-Two

There were more and more people gathering in front of the baron's residence, but only a fraction of them could be seen.

Most of the people were members of Baron Schini's sec force, standing guard over the building and waiting for daylight so they could move through the ville and get rid of what was left of the previous baron's sec force.

There were muties moving into the area as well. They had had their fill of bang and were far less tenacious than they'd been no more than an hour before, but they were still interested in taking whatever they could get, control of the ville if possible, or if not that, then jack and as much drugs as they could carry.

A few people hidden in the shadows were former sec men of Baron DeMann, who had served under Sec chief Robards. The sec men had split into two groups, the ones who had hated Robards's guts and would have run him through with a steak knife if they thought they could get away with it, and the ones who liked Robards enough to wonder where he'd gone and what he might be planning to take back the ville.

And finally, there were citizens, many of whom had

helped put out the fire in front of the baron's residence earlier in the evening and were now hanging around to see who was in charge of the ville, and to see if they should bother showing up for work in the morning.

Viviani arrived in front of the baron's residence, out of breath after a firefight with the former baron's sec force a few blocks away.

"Where's Baron Schini?" he asked.

"She hasn't come down yet."

"Why didn't you go up and get her?"

The sec man looked at the chief. "Sorry, sir, but I'd rather not be the one to wake up that woman."

The sec chief nodded, understanding. He was about to enter the building to wake her up and bring her down when blasterfire erupted on the other side of the street.

Instead of waking up the baron, Sec chief Viviani dived for cover.

"HAVE YOU GOT the medicine for Jak?" Doc asked.

Johnson smiled. "Got it right here."

"Excellent!"

"Trouble down there?" Krysty asked.

"Lone person," Ryan said. "Looking to loot the place."

"Wrong place, wrong time," J.B. added.

For a moment the two men looked at each other, then Ryan turned away. "Let's get out of here."

Then to Johnson he said, "Think we can go the same way we came?"

"Best way there is," Johnson answered. "But we'll

need to be careful. I expect more sec men to be out on the streets."

"Keep an eye out," Ryan said. "Triple alert until we're out of the ville."

They began to move, double-time, Johnson leading the way.

"You need not worry about me," Doc said. "I have been scanning the darkness for a sign of Eleander, but so far the gods have not seen it fit to give her up to me."

"Doc," Ryan whispered.

"Yes, Ryan?"

Ryan hesitated, then said, "Don't let your search slow you down."

"Ha, mine eyes are as sharp as if they were coupled to the wings of an eagle, and that may give you some insight into how swiftly I will move when the need arises."

"That's great, Doc."

INSIDE THE STEEL BOX, Robards felt the chill of the night against his skin.

His wrists ached as the steel dug into his flesh.

His muscles burned as they had flexed and contracted long past the point of exhaustion so that he could no longer use them to try and make himself comfortable.

His joints cracked and popped, moving slightly an inch to the left or right, after hours in the same awkward position.

His bladder filled and emptied, the contents of it dribbling down his leg.

His stomach panged with hunger.

And his heart burned with thoughts of revenge and of taking back the ville, the one he'd worked so hard to prepare for the day that he would make it his own.

But for now, he was stuck, chained in a steel box, waiting for someone to remember where he was, who he had been, and then come to rescue him from this hell.

No one was coming.

It was as if he'd been forgotten.

There was a storm brewing just outside the box. He could hear it and feel it in the air.

Something big was going to be happening very soon.

Real big.

His only consolation was that it would all be going on *out there* and he'd be safe inside the box.

PER JOHNSON, the eldest son of Bennett Johnson, arrived an hour behind the rest of his six other brothers and sisters, an M-1 rocket launcher on his shoulder and a second M-9 in two pieces tucked into the small of his back.

"Are they back yet?" Per asked his younger sister, Dari.

"Not yet," she answered, taking the two pieces of the M-9 and locking them together so that they formed a second firing tube similar to the single-piece M-1. "What took you so long?"

"I had to make a new fin for the second rocket. I got the shape of it right, but the weight is probably off so this one should only be used at close range, or at a really big target."

"Are you going to let me fire it?" Dari asked, smiling.

"You can fire it, just get Mats to set it up for you and help you aim it, all right?"

"All right!"

He gave her the two pieces of the M-9 and a rocket, and sent her off to find her older brother.

Then he climbed to the top of the metal wall at the point where his father and their guests had entered the ville and begin getting the M-1 ready to be fired if the need arose.

Personally, Per was hoping that there would be a need. He had lived inside DeMannville for two years and had barely made it out with his life. After just six months he'd been hooked on jolt and was experimenting with nightmare, an especially potent form of dreem. He was about a week or two away from buying a ticket for the last train west when his father found him in a gaudy house and dragged him out of the ville and home again.

His stepmother, Little Dumpling, his father's third wife and mother to six of his half brothers and sisters, had cared for him day and night for six weeks until he was able to sleep through the night without screaming for drugs.

When he came out of the drug-induced haze, he'd thought a week, mebbe a month had passed him by, and had been shocked to hear that he'd been away for more than a year.

And all because of the ville and the drugs that made it run.

Well, he wouldn't mind settling a score with the ville, and a rocket into the baron's residence seemed as good a way as any.

He just hoped such action would be necessary.

BARON SCHINI appeared in the doorway of the baron's mansion, standing behind the large glass pane that was slightly clouded by the fire from the night before.

The sky was tinted with a light, reddish orange hue and she was reminded of an old saying her father used to tell her some nights before she went to sleep. He'd say, "Red sky at night, sailor's delight. Red sky at morning, sailor take warning."

Her father hadn't been a sailor, but he had been on a boat in the ocean once. And the saying never meant much to her since the sky was always one shade of red or another. But now, looking out over the deep, almost purplish red, she had an uneasy feeling about her. As if the shit was going to hit the turbine.

The pane of glass in front of her suddenly shattered.

Shards of glass rained down around her as the glass fell away from its frame.

The baron jumped aside as six more rounds zipped through the empty space the window had been occupying.

"Viviani!" the baron shouted, taking her snub-nosed .38 Browning from its holster.

There was no answer over the shots that were coming from across the street.

The baron crawled over the glass covering the floor, tearing her clothes and cutting her skin. She needed to get outside, behind the barricades set up by her sec men.

Suddenly a roar of fire erupted from somewhere just in front of her and then there were hands on her arms, lifting her up and guiding her down to the street in front of the residence.

"What the fuck is going on here?" she said.

"There's been resistance to our taking over of the ville."

"I told you to wipe out Robards's sec force."

Viviani ducked as a blaster round zinged over their heads. "We must have chilled more than a dozen of the old sec men and another six have joined us."

"Then who's left?"

"Can't be more than another five or six sec men."

"That's all."

"And people living in the ville…and muties and addicts looking for drugs. A bunch of them swept through the ville last night, took four of our men with them and stole a month's worth of jolt and dreem from dealers on the east side."

"So which are the ones shooting at us?"

"All of them. Baron's residence is the only thing worth having right now, so they all want a piece of it."

"Well, fuck them all," the baron said. "It's mine now." She rose and began firing her Browning fearlessly at the shapes and shadows across the street.

When her fire was returned, she ducked back down, a lot of her strength and resolve suddenly gone.

"Give Sherman and Roy as much extra ammo as they can carry and send them up to the roof of this building. Tell them to take out everyone without a family seal on their arm. If there's anyone friendly you'd like to see live, give them an armband."

Viviani nodded to one of his lieutenants, who would pass the word along to Sherman and Roy.

"And you head down that street and double back and get ready to take down anyone who runs from Sherman's and Roy's fire."

Viviani nodded. "Yes, Baron."

"This afternoon, I want to drive around this ville in a show of strength. And when that's over with we'll chill that family we were talking about. That should quiet things down."

Or incite more people to violence, Viviani thought. You had to have strength and control before you could demonstrate it, and an iron fist wasn't always the best tactic.

"You hear me?"

"Yes, Baron," he said, then headed off to carry out her order.

BY THE TIME they reached the baron's residence there was a firefight going on in the street in front of the building. The crossfire looked as if it were being weaved by three different parties, none of them able to get the upper hand.

"Looks like some sort of standoff," J.B. muttered.

"Everyone's dug in," Ryan commented. "No one's moving."

J.B. removed his fedora and wiped his brow. "What do you say we do?"

"We either try to slip by or we join the fight," Ryan said.

Krysty checked the ammo in her Smith & Wesson, and without looking up from her blaster said. "Not our fight."

Johnson shook his head. "Mine, neither. I'm just as happy if they blow themselves all to hell. Easier for me to pick up the brass what's left over."

A blaster round whistled over their heads and slammed into the building behind them, sending bits of rock and brick into the air.

J.B. shook the dust from his hat. "Which still leaves us with the question of how best to get by them."

"I think we hide in plain sight. Join the fight, blend in and slip right on through."

"Sounds like a plan," Johnson said.

"All right then, let's move."

At that moment, the sound of automatic blasterfire opened up from two positions at the top of the baron's residence.

"Get down!" Ryan shouted.

The friends all got close to the ground, as hot lead rained down on them like hailstones.

When the blasterfire stopped, J.B. asked Ryan, "Got a new plan?"

"You want to take out those positions?"

"Not really."

"Then the plan's the same. Only it's going to take us longer to make it work."

"I just hope dear Jak has the time to spare," Doc said under his breath.

J.B. looked to Doc as if he were going to tell the old man to shut up, but he just swallowed once and said, "We all do, Doc. We all do."

# Chapter Thirty-Three

Bennett Johnson unbuttoned his jacket and began taking the tiny containers of antibodies out of his pockets and distributing them among the rest of the friends.

"Case I board the last train west instead of going back home," he said.

Ryan nodded, stuffing a couple of the containers into the inside pockets of his coat.

"We'll be moving in a few minutes. Bennett, you still have most of the medicine, right?"

Johnson nodded. "I can hand out more—"

"No," Ryan cut him off. "You go first. You'll have the best chance of making it. We owe you that much. You've done us a big favor."

Johnson nodded in reluctant agreement.

"J.B. next. Then Doc and Krysty."

None of the friends argued the order, knowing Ryan had his reasons, even if they couldn't figure out what they were.

The blasterfire had come from the top of the building. Everyone on their side of the street dived for cover, and the shooters on the rooftop had free reign on the entire street below.

If anything moved, it would be chilled.

It was amazing how the situation had changed in such a short time. When they'd arrived at the firefight, the danger had been from the crossfire coming from across the street. Now that blasterfire had become negligible in light of the new threat from above. But while the threat was different, the difficulty was basically the same, perhaps now even worse.

There was a short empty space between their current position and the base of the wall. If they could move through the emptiness in the middle there were plenty of places to find cover at the wall, and the entire climb over the top could be done under some sort of cover. Further to that, any shooter would be wasting ammo on anyone trying to get *out* over the wall, so just reaching the wall was the big obstacle.

"Bennett, you ready?" Ryan asked.

Johnson nodded. "No, but what the hell."

"On the count of three, Krysty, J.B. and me—"

"And *I*," Doc corrected.

"Krysty, J.B. and I will put up cover fire against the positions on the roof. Doc will lay down a bit of cover on the street, just in case they figure out we're not shooting at them."

Johnson took a deep breath.

"When you get to the other side, you give the medicine to the fastest runner in your family."

There was silence among them for several moments.

"One," Ryan said. "Two…"

Johnson started for the wall.

"Three."

Three of the friends unleashed a volley of blasterfire against the rooftop shooters. But instead of having their fire fly harmlessly over the building, they did their best to catch the concrete and metal flashing capping the roof. At least that would suggest to whoever was up there that putting their head over the edge of the rooftop was a bad idea.

A few of the citizens who'd gotten caught up in the firefight took advantage of the cover fire and began running south.

One was caught by a round from Doc's LeMat and knocked off his feet. The other two kept running, making it out of the immediate danger zone alive.

Their escape prompted Ryan to check on Johnson's progress.

He'd reached the wall in one piece. There were two of his family there to receive him. Together they helped him climb the wall.

Ryan felt a bit of relief wash over him. Jak would be receiving the medicine he needed in short order.

That part of their mission had been a success.

Now they had to save their own hides.

VIVIANI SET UP his forces just inside a pair of storefronts about a block down the street from the baron's residence.

The storefronts were on opposite sides of the street, and the broken front windows of each provided perfect cover from anyone running from the fight at the baron's residence.

"Be on the lookout," Viviani warned. "Everybody coming down the street is to be terminated. We'll wait for them, and if they don't show we'll move up toward the baron's residence."

Just then, as if on cue, two people came running in their direction. They were covered in dust and one of them had been hit by blasterfire in the shoulder. They didn't seem to be sec men, in fact one of them looked to be an old woman.

Viviani hadn't expected refugees from the fight, only sec men and rebels.

"Let them go!" he said.

"But you just told us to chill anyone—"

"I know what I said. Let them go!"

"But—"

"They're just running for their lives," Viviani shouted. "What will we have in this ville if there's no one left to make it work?"

The sec man lowered his weapon, considering the sec chief's wisdom.

And then two shots burst from the storefront across the street, cutting down the two citizens as they ran.

Viviani sighed, realizing it was futile to try to spare the innocent.

"All right, then," he said. "Chill them all."

"YOU READY, J.B."

"Gimme the count."

"Everyone loaded?"

In less than a second, Doc and Krysty replied in the affirmative.

"One... Two..."

J.B. was gone.

The friends fired again, but this time with only two blasters on the rooftop positions.

The rest of the firefight continued unabated, the other forces using the cover fire to try and hit their enemies across the street.

The crackle of blasterfire was deafening.

Ryan checked on J.B. and was happy to see that his wiry frame was covering the distance to the wall in even less time than Johnson.

"That's good," Ryan shouted, silencing the friends' blasters. "Two down, three to go."

"But with each one we send over the wall, there's one less blaster to provide cover fire. I'm afraid your plan will leave you in a rather difficult position, Ryan."

"Been in worse," Ryan replied, replacing the clip on his SIG-Sauer.

"Yes, but not many."

Ryan had heard enough from the old man. "You're next, Doc."

"It has been several hundred years since I ran sprints for Oxford, but I shall run as best as I am able."

"You'll run like the wind, Doc."

"Thank you Miss Wroth, but I imagine like a schoolboy will be a more apt description."

"Just get ready, Doc."

THE MASS EXODUS of sec men and rebels never materialized.

After chilling two civilians, Viviani and his men had done nothing but wait.

After a while Viviani began to fear that there was some sort of escape route through a building or down some alley between his position and the baron's residence.

"Let's move out," he ordered. "We'll head toward the baron's residence and box the bastards in."

The sec men left the storefront and began moving up the block.

DOC WAS PREPARING for his dash to the wall, when blasterfire erupted behind them. Several rounds zipped past Doc's head, forcing him to jump back and crouch for cover.

All at once, several of the sec men who had been pinned down by the fire coming from atop the baron's residence turned and began firing at the new threat behind them.

And then the shooters on the roof began to pick off these sec men like fish in a barrel.

"Fireblast!" Ryan muttered under his breath. He had his back pressed hard against an old garbage can and his knees bent to keep his body close to the ground. Hot lead was chipping away at the concrete pole to his left, and every once in a while a round would hit the trash can he was positioned behind.

"What now?" Krysty asked. She was a few yards away, tucked inside the entrance to a building.

Ryan didn't have a plan. They were pinned down on two sides, and any attempt to fire in one direction would leave them exposed to fire from the other. "I'm open to suggestions."

"I suggest," Doc said, "that it is rather ironic that out of all of our group, Jak currently has the best chance of seeing the dawning of the morning sun."

"Suggestions that might help us get out of here, Doc."

Doc was silent.

The bullets continued to zip and zing all around them.

MILDRED PACED back and forth in the small room, listening to Jak's labored breathing and wondering what sort of difficulties the friends had encountered that would make them take so long.

Jak had been strong, and even now she could sense that he was fighting the urge to scream and thrash about. The drug had given his mind and body the equivalent of several hard kicks from a steel-toed boot, but Jak refused to allow it to push him down. But even he had his limits and if the medicine didn't arrive soon, Mildred was worried that Jak might suffer serious harm.

Just then, sound began coming from the upper floors. There was obviously some great commotion going on up there, and Mildred responded by raising her target pistol and aiming it at the room's lone doorway.

If the baron's men were storming Bennett Johnson's home, they wouldn't be taking Mildred or her patient without a fight.

Boots on the stairs, shouts.

A figure appeared in the doorway.

"Don't shoot!" It was one of Johnson's children, out of breath and struggling to speak. "I have the medicine for your friend."

Mildred breathed a sigh and holstered her blaster. "Are the others here?" she asked.

The young woman stepped into the room, shaking her head. "No. My father got out of the ville first, and he gave the medicine to me. I ran all the way here."

Mildred took the antibodies from her and opened up the containers. She was glad to see they were in liquid form and would be absorbed into Jak's system more quickly through his bloodstream than internally through his stomach.

She had a sterile syringe in her med kit, so injecting the antibodies wouldn't be a problem, but how much should she give him? Too little and Jak might not recover, or suffer more than he had to. Too much and she might kill him. And how could she even be sure these antibodies were safe? After all, the nearest analytical laboratory was a hundred years and a nukecaust away.

The truth was she couldn't be sure.

She would have to trust that Bennett Johnson was a man of his word, that Baron DeMann made antibodies as well as he made jolt and dreem, and above all she had to trust her instincts.

But even if her instincts told her it was too risky to give Jak the antibodies, in the end she'd probably have to give them to him anyway because Jak didn't really have a choice.

If he didn't take them he'd likely go mad.

But taking the antibodies would at least give him a chance.

Mildred took the syringe from her bag and decided to start slowly, drawing just ten units into the syringe. Then she found a vein in the pale white skin of his left arm and injected the antibodies.

She would monitor his vital signs closely over the next hour, and if he was showing any signs of improving, or less intense fits of terror, even longer stretches between each one, then she'd give him another dose.

But for now, she watched, and waited.

J.B. LOOKED BEHIND HIM, expecting to see Doc climbing up the wall at any moment.

But he wasn't there.

There was more blasterfire coming from the baron's residence and surrounding area, but J.B. couldn't pinpoint where it was coming from.

"Where are the others?" Per Johnson asked him.

"They must be pinned down by more blasterfire."

J.B.'s attention was now focused on the rocket launcher the man had over his shoulder.

"I didn't see this before. What make bazooka is it?"

Per Johnson lifted the long tube up in front of him and looked at it with pride. "M-1. My brother and sister have an M-9 over there."

J.B. turned and saw the two young people holding the rocket launcher together on their shoulders.

"These would help get my friends out of there."

"I was thinking of using one of them on the two men at the top of the building, but I had to make a third fin for this rocket and I can't be sure it's going to go where I want it to."

J.B. took at look at the building and the men on the roof and agreed with the man's assessment. Hitting the top floor and knocking those men out of their position would be next to impossible with a single shot.

The repaired rocket needed to hit something bigger.

Much bigger, that would cause all sorts of damage.

And J.B. knew just the target.

SEC MEN and civilians were dying all over the street. The combination of fire from overhead and behind was too much to combat.

"Might have to make a run for it!" Ryan shouted over the roar of blasterfire.

"Too risky," Krysty responded.

"Might be our only chance."

Just then a loud boom emanated from the wall.

Ryan and the others turned to see some sort of rocket slicing through the air headed toward the baron's residence.

A moment later the rocket slammed into the side of the building about two floors up, exploding in a brief fireball and then sending up a huge cloud of bricks, shattered glass, dirt, dust and mortar.

A few seconds later the dust cleared enough for them to see the damage.

There was an entire corner of the building missing as a bite about ten feet across was taken out of the wall and the third floor. A fire had started deeper in the building and was gaining strength as it burned.

But for all the noise and commotion, the blasterfire from the rooftop hadn't abated.

"Great shot!" Krysty said, sarcasm in her voice.

"Give it time," Ryan answered. "I think I know what J.B.'s doing with those rockets."

And then, as if on cue, a second rocket shrieked over their heads and smashed into the building about a dozen yards from the point of impact of the first rocket.

An explosion every bit as powerful as the first ripped into the building, sending a second cloud of smoke into the air and making the air around them acrid and full of dust.

"Cover up!" Ryan said, as he pulled a kerchief around his neck and over his nose.

Krysty and Doc did likewise, although Doc took the extra time to fold his kerchief neatly before tying it tightly behind his head.

The blasterfire from the rooftop suddenly stopped.

Ryan looked up and saw the two men trying to gain their footing.

The building was trembling beneath them.

The blasterfire elsewhere on the street stopped, too. Everyone's attention was focused on the baron's residence as they all wondered if it was going to fall.

All except for Ryan and the friends.

Ryan stood straight, leveled his blaster on the sec men behind them and fired into the group.

Bodies jerked and spasmed, sec men fell to the street.

Dead.

Soon, Krysty and Doc had joined in on the slaughter, and the few sec men who had survived the opening barrage of fire had turned and ran.

Some were able to get away.

Most died before they could take a step.

"Let's move!" Ryan ordered.

The three friends turned and ran for the wall.

Behind them, and then all around them, the ground began to rumble.

And a moment later, a great sound of breaking concrete, twisting steel and shattering glass boomed out from the baron's residence.

Ryan glanced just once over his shoulder and saw the face of the building falling away, slipping onto the street.

Screams mixed in with the sound of the crashing building as people on the street and in the building were crushed beneath tons of rubble.

The friends kept running, and then climbed the wall.

J.B. was there to meet them at the top.

"Nice shooting," Ryan said.

"Never mind." J.B. grinned. "I almost missed that first time."

Ryan turned back again and saw that the rest of the building had fallen as well, taking the new baron, her sec force and just about everyone else in the ville who lusted after power with it.

"Come on," Ryan said. "Let's see how Jak's doing."

# Chapter Thirty-Four

The sun was up by the time they reached Bennett Johnson's place.

Behind them in the distance, a cloud of dust floated up over the ville in a column of gray and black. Small fires burned, too, lending a reddish cast to the gray haze that shaded the sky over the ville.

They were greeted by one of Johnson's daughters, who led them to the dining area and served them a hot meal of sausage, egg and plain cornmeal bread.

Upon hearing of their arrival, Mildred left Jak and went to meet with the friends.

"How is Jak feeling at this hour?" Doc asked.

"He's going to be fine," Mildred responded. "I wasn't sure about the antibodies, so I started him on them slowly. Turns out their quality is pretty good, and I've been increasing his dosage. He's pretty sleepy at the moment, but he's ready for visitors."

"That's great news," Ryan said, stuffing his mouth with sausage and bread.

Mildred took a chair. "How did it go inside the ville?"

"Been on worse missions," Krysty said.

"Baron's looking for a new place to live," J.B. stated.

"Ville might even be looking for a new baron," Ryan added.

Mildred turned to Doc. "Did you run into your lady friend while you were in the ville?"

Doc swallowed a mouthful of egg, then gently wiped the corners of his mouth with a clean bit of an old shirt that had been made into a napkin. "Alas, I did not. But as more time passes I suspect that while our paths crossed for a brief moment in time, I believe we were never destined for more than that."

Doc scooped up another forkful of egg.

"She was a lovely woman and she might have been just what I needed at the time, but I cannot help feeling now that there was something about her that was not right. I do not think she would have fit in very well with our group..." He shrugged. "And now that our ordeal inside the ville is over I feel that it is probably for the best that I did not find her."

The room was silent a moment.

Then Doc said, "Besides, no woman can ever replace the deep and abiding love I bear for my dear Emily. Our time together was as close as any man can come to heaven on Earth."

Doc looked up at the ceiling, his eyes glazing over in a blank and vacant stare.

"I am a fool to have loved and forgotten, and I vow never to commit such transgression again."

Doc's voice trailed off and he began to weep.

"What wrong with him?" Bennett Johnson asked.

Mildred came to Doc's side. "Nothing. He needs some rest."

Johnson signaled to two of his sons. "Take him to my room and make sure he's comfortable."

The two men helped Doc from his chair and escorted him out of the room.

"Let's go see Jak," Ryan said.

THE FRIENDS GATHERED around Jak's bed in the bowels of Bennett Johnson's underground home and waited for the albino teen to notice they were in the room with him.

They didn't need to wait long.

The young man's left eyelid began to flutter, then opened fully. The other eyelid followed, fluttering like the wings of some butterfly for a moment, then opening wide like that of an eagle.

Jak was alive and aware of his surroundings.

"Hi, Jak," Krysty said.

Ryan put a hand on Jak's shoulder. "Welcome back to the land of the living."

"Had us worried there for a while," J.B. chimed in, flashing an uncharacteristic smile.

Doc, recovered from his spell of confusion, had joined them in the infirmary. "Worried? I should say so," he commented. "Why, without the help of our gracious host, Mr. Bennett Johnson, we might never have been able to gaze into those pale red eyes of yours."

The rest of the friends made themselves comfortable, knowing that Doc would be talking for a while.

"And all the while you were no doubt oblivious to the

battle being fought on your behalf." Doc shook his head. "Each one of us nearly boarded the last train west several times during our ordeal, and all for the sake of one life."

Doc was smiling now.

"But we've all been close to death, have we not? I am reminded of a quote by Frederick Scott that goes, 'So often have I met death face to face, his eyes now wear the welcome of a friend's—'"

"Doc," Jak said, struggling to get the word out. "Doc!"

Doc prattled on for a moment, then realized Jak was trying to say something.

"Not think I say this," Jak said. "Glad hear your voice."

The friends laughed.

Even Doc cracked a smile.

HOURS LATER, with Jak resting soundly, Bennett Johnson asked Ryan what the friends' planned to do next.

"Depends on what Mildred says about Jak."

Mildred, sipping a hot cup of tea, said, "He'll need a day, two at the most, before he's strong enough to travel."

Ryan shrugged. There was Johnson's answer.

"Then you'll all stay here as my guests. I'm sure you have more than enough stories to pass the hours."

"Weapons could use stripping, oiling, repair," J.B. said.

Johnson beamed. "My workshop and all my resources are at your disposal."

J.B. nodded. "Appreciate that."

"Then you'll stay?"

Ryan thought about the possibility of having two days without having to look over his shoulder every minute for someone who wanted to chill him. He thought about two days with Krysty, reenergizing their relationship while getting some much-needed rest before they once again took up their journey through Deathlands.

"If you'll have us," Ryan said. "We'll stay."

"Deal."

# Epilogue

The roar inside the box had faded long ago.

All that remained was a faint echo, like the sound of the ocean inside a seashell or cupped hand.

Robards hung limply from the wall, the chains around his arms and ankles holding him upright and in place. His body ached, and blood dripped from the cuts the shackles had made on his skin.

Something big had happened outside. It has sounded like what he always thought a nukeblast would sound like—loud, powerful, destructive. The ground had shaken and dust had fallen from the ceiling of the box, covering his body in a fine layer of grit.

For all Robards knew there might be nothing left of the ville.

The thought made him laugh out loud.

The whole stinkin' ville wiped off the face of the planet, and the poor bastard chained inside the box makes it through alive.

He kept laughing. Serves the rat bastards right, locking him up. Him, Baron Robards…

The thought of revenge kept his mind busy making

plans for when he got out of the box. First there would be Baron Schini… He'd string her up by her ankles and do evil things to her with every power tool and cutting blade he could find in the ville. And any asshole who helped her would get the same.

Then it would be the backstabbing sec men who used to be under his command. He would chill them all personally. And if anyone had something to say about it, he'd chill them, too.

He'd chill them all.

Even the outlanders.

If he ever came across an outlander again, any outlander, he was going to rip them a new hole and fill it with grens…

The excitement of it all was too much for Robards to handle, and he found himself sliding in and out of consciousness.

And the new ville, Robardstown, would be his and it would be filled with people who were loyal to him. They would share the wealth with him…not all that much of it, but enough to keep them all happy.

He passed out again.

Only to wake up later with a young boy of about ten poking him in the leg. The boy was dirty, wearing torn clothes. His hair was long and wild, and his fingernails and teeth seemed as sharp as claws, deadly as fangs. He looked up at Robards with a pair of eyes that were crossed and dim. "Hey, mister."

Robards opened his eyes. "Huh!"

"What did you have to do to get locked in here?"

Robards hadn't eaten in more than a day, and his brain was having trouble processing his thoughts.

"Nothing," he said. "I was trying to save the ville from what happened, but the bad people put me in here."

The boy just looked at him, his eyes slowly glazing over.

"Do you have any food?" Robards asked.

"Huh-uh."

"If you get me out of here, I know where to get some."

The boy thought about it.

Then he grabbed a rock lying at the bottom of the steel box and climbed up on the step in front of Robards. He raised the hand holding the rock and readied it to strike against one of the chains.

"That's it," Robards said.

He couldn't believe his luck. The boy didn't know who he was, and was going to help him get out of the box on the promise of some food.

The boy held the rock in his hand, poised to bring it down against one of the chains.

He began to drool from a corner of his mouth.

"C'mon," Robards said. "What the fuck are you waiting for?"

"Want bang!" the boy said.

And then the boy brought the rock down hard…

Onto Robards's head.

DEATHLANDS · EXECUTIONER